THE DUCHESS DE NUIT

PART TWO:
A TALE OF REDEMPTION

C. DE MELO

DEDICATION

Thank you, D.

PROLOGUE
BUDA, HUNGARY
DECEMBER 1462

The Voivode of Wallachia, whose father had been inducted into the Order of the Dragon by the Holy Roman Emperor, hung his head in defeat. Vlad Tepes III, the fierce warlord who had been proving his military prowess to the Christian world since the fall of Constantinople in 1453, had been captured by the Hungarian king, Matthias Corvinus. Flanked by two soldiers, he descended into the bowels of Hell.

A foul odor emanated from the sulphuric springs running beneath the subterranean caves. Flickering torches revealed slimy stone walls, yet their feeble light did little to banish the blackest shadows teeming with crawling insects and rats. Located beneath the king's castle, the dreaded ancient labyrinth served as both dungeon and torture chamber. An agonizing cry pierced the darkness as the soldiers locked the Romanian prince in the small space before abandoning him to despair.

A torch burned against the wall of the outside corridor revealing another cell directly across from his own. Vlad approached the iron bars of his prison, gripping the rusty rods with the same calloused hands that wielded his trusted sword. To his astonishment, the other cell was fitted with bars that were twice as thick, twice as wide, and fashioned from the purest silver. Peering into the darkness, he noticed a pair of eyes glimmering brightly within a shadowy mass of muscle. The large figure stood unnaturally still, chuckling softly.

The sinister sound unsettled Vlad, making the skin of his nape prickle. "Who are you?"

A long moment passed before the reply came from a deep voice laden with unchallenged authority. "I am someone who knows the ways of men."

CHAPTER 1
BUDAPEST, HUNGARY
DECEMBER, PRESENT DAY

"Any truth is better than infinite doubt."
(Arthur Conan Doyle)

Pulsating strobe lights and wild dance music compelled people to gyrate beneath the glass ceiling of the iconic Géllert Bath. The medicinal waters of the establishment were derived from the same underground springs once used by the Knights of St John in the twelfth century. I rested my nape against the pool's smooth edge as my gaze roamed over the lovely patterned tiles and soaring ceilings. Opened in 1918, the bath complex stood as a crumbling testament to the *Belle Époque*, a long-gone era of thriving café culture, philosophers, and writers. Nowadays, these historic monuments served as mere selfie backdrops for vapid youths and tourists. Crazy weekend parties further aided in the desecration of their regal pasts.

Nothing lasts forever.

Beauty, fortune, fame, and even love eventually came to an end—for mortals, anyway.

I sighed with bored resignation as I studied the scene around me. High on drugs and alcohol, people recklessly threw themselves at one another in a futile attempt to fill the void. The rhythmic beat of the bass failed to mask the erratic pounding of their fragile hearts. My fangs itched to tear into their throats but I was too old to indulge in such an immature bloodbath.

Beside me, a silly girl giggled in the arms of a boy who was barely past puberty. They engaged in an intimate kiss, their mouthwatering pheromones permeating the steamy air. The adolescent couple eventually broke apart, faces flushed and filled with longing. I glimpsed actual affection in their eyes.

How sweet, how fresh.

How temporary.

Vampires were jaded, cynical beings. With the passing of time, words like "joy" and "excitement" eventually vanished from our vocabularies. I was one of the few who tenaciously held on to my residual humanity. I often wondered how ancients like Arsham and his half-brother, Rahim, managed to keep themselves relevant.

Three Asian teenagers, one with spiky green hair, paraded in front of me with cell phones attached to selfie-sticks. I watched with detached amusement as they attempted sexy poses to show off the puny muscles on their slick pale chests. Two voluptuous blondes in identical neon orange bikinis glided past the Asians, their nipples perked beneath the shiny spandex. Long and lithe, they cleaved through the thermal water like a pair of graceful nymphs.

Spiky hair finally noticed me sitting at arm's length from where he stood. "Excuse me, madam?"

I arched an eyebrow. *Madam?*

He held out his iPhone. "You take photo of me and my friends, yes?"

Selfie-sticks apparently had their limitations. I hesitated before grabbing the phone, then snapped a few photos of them, capturing the Nordic beauties in the background. Spiky hair offered me a thumbs up before he and his friends rejoined their Chinese tour group.

My gaze slid to Damien, whose eyes were locked on a pair of women pushing hardcore drugs on minors. One in particular held his interest—a brunette with dull eyes and mouth painted in a garish shade of pink. Having completed the illegal transaction, the woman entered the pool with her friend.

My lover left my side and moved with the predatory stealth that was second nature to our kind. I experienced a pang of disappointment as he headed for his prey. Damien had changed in a drastic way shortly after our departure from Grand Cayman. There were no more romantic walks along the beach or hunting in luxury resorts. His current preference for seedy bars, wild parties, and night clubs enabled him to feed on drug pushers, thieves, and killers. Gone were the days of preying upon delicious couples.

Two enormous men plopped down in Damien's vacated spot and began talking loudly in a heavy British accent. Sporting buzzed haircuts and bruises on their rough faces, I deduced that they were rugby players. Both heads eventually turned my way and they nudged each other.

Leering at me, one of them asked, "Want to join us?"

Ignoring him, I exited the main pool and headed to another area within the complex where I could at least enjoy the water in relative peace. Thankfully, the distance muffled a bit of the horrid music. To my relief, there was no one in the smaller pool. I sank into the hot water and liquid warmth enveloped my icy skin like a fleece blanket. I allowed my body to go limp while shutting my eyes to the world around me. I soon picked up the faint scent of classic after shave as a human male ventured near the pool. Inhaling deeper, I discerned that he was past the bloom of youth but not yet middle-aged.

Ugh. Not another sleaze ball trying to get laid.

The water moved slightly as the man's foot pierced the surface. I waited for him to settle before risking a peek. Surprise lit up my features for a split second before I rearranged my face into a stoic mask. Dr. Caleb Morgan—author, professor, and vampirologist extraordinaire—sat directly across from me.

My first instinct was to exit the pool but the lack of imminent danger combined with burning curiosity kept me rooted to the spot. Since his eyes were closed, I took the liberty of studying his face. Ginger hair clung to the fair skin of his damp forehead and a spattering of freckles hugged the bridge of his nose. A furrowed brow suggested that he was bothered by something. Opening his eyes, he caught me staring at him.

Vacating the pool would have been a good idea at that point. Instead, I did the unthinkable. "You're Dr. Caleb Morgan."

A pair of mottled green eyes regarded me coolly. "I am. Have we met?"

"I attended your lecture: *Vampire Legends of Europe.*"

"That was nearly a year ago at the University of Edinburgh."

"You work there, don't you?"

He frowned. "Yes. I currently head their parapsychology department. Are you a student?"

Sensing his mounting irritation, I replied, "No, only a fan of your work. I didn't mean to disturb you."

"No, no—it's fine." Rubbing his forehead, he added, "I sometimes get accosted by religious zealots who believe I'm evil incarnate and feel it's their duty to lecture me about God."

"You don't have to worry about that with me."

"A fan, huh? Have you read any of my books?"

"All of them. I've also had the pleasure of hearing several of your online presentations. I particularly enjoyed the one you uploaded to YouTube two months ago: *Incubus and Succubus*."

He chuckled in a deprecating manner. "I'm glad someone is listening to them. My TA, Rob, is a social media guru who handles that stuff. It was his idea to make lectures available online so I agreed to let him film me."

"If my memory serves me well, the video had over seventy thousand views."

Surprised, he exclaimed, "That many? Wow. I had no idea."

The clever TA probably raked in a tidy sum in profits from advertisements on his YouTube channel. I refrained from vocalizing that observation.

I ventured, "You propose quite a few daring theories…"

"Yes, well, it hasn't made me very popular with my peers."

A gaggle of inebriated college students stumbled into the room. I glared at them, staring down the alpha frat boy and compelling him to lead his friends to another pool.

As soon as they exited the area, Dr. Morgan shook his head disdainfully. "Not what I expected from a historic bath house."

"Is this your first time at the Géllert?"

"Yes."

"Were you unaware of the epic weekend parties?"

"The owner of the flat I'm renting informed me that the baths offered music on the weekends. Naturally, I imagined Bach or Chopin—not *this*."

I smiled wryly. "Have you been to the Rudas Bath?"

"No."

"Built in the sixteenth century during the Ottoman Empire, it's a historical gem. Be sure to go very early in the morning."

"Thanks for the tip. It's my first time in Budapest so I'm ignorant on many things." He paused. "Do you live here?"

"Just passing through."

"I almost didn't come...My girlfriend broke up with me after we had booked the trip." Rolling his eyes, he added, "I have no idea why I told you that."

"Relationships are complicated." My comment sounded pathetically trite even to my own ears.

"Very..." He searched my face. "What's your name?"

I threw one of my many aliases at him. "Nora."

"Nice to meet you, Nora."

"Likewise."

"Have you been to the National Gallery?"

"Yes, the last time I was in Budapest. It was a while back." Over fifty years to be precise.

"I'll be there tomorrow in the late afternoon doing some research. If you'd like to join me, I'll buy the coffee."

"Perhaps."

Catching myself, I stood, for I had now crossed the line from daring to foolish. Hanging out with a vampirologist could prove perilous for all parties involved.

"Leaving so soon?" he asked, barely masking the disappointment in his voice.

"The heat is making me dizzy," I improvised.

Dr. Morgan's eyes wandered over my body with obvious approval. My chic one-piece black swimsuit with plunging V-neck stood out in stark contrast to the many G-string bottoms and tiny triangle tops worn by the majority of women.

The peasants loved to flaunt their flesh.

I returned to the main pool where Damien's head was buried in a drug dealer's neck. Everyone was too busy partying to notice the handsome vampire feeding on a woman. I veered toward the showers. The hot water shot out of the stainless steel head with great force and I allowed the vicious drops to massage my spine. I dressed and went outside to wait for Damien. A group of young men dressed as American rappers sauntered past and I bummed a Marlboro off of one of them.

Inhaling deeply, I relished the soft crackling sound of paper being consumed by smoldering tobacco. A perfectly round smoke ring rushed from my lips into the cold December air. The ghostly circle floated into the darkness, dissipating into nothing.

Caleb Morgan. I shook my head, smiling in disbelief. What were the chances of me meeting one of the world's leading authorities on vampirism? The scholar possessed a brilliant mind and articulated his theories in a manner that intrigued me.

"Is that smile for me?" Damien inquired while exiting the establishment. "So, did you feed on that guy?"

"What guy?"

"Mr. Redhead."

I exhaled the smoke in my lungs. "No."

Taking the cigarette from me, he took a drag. "Why not?"

"We started talking—"

"Talking?"

"For your information, that was Dr. Caleb Morgan." The name obviously meant nothing to him. "He's a well-known—"

"I don't care who he is, Angelique."

"Will you hear me out?"

"I'm not interested in your excuses. I thought we had a deal."

"Come on, Damien. Isn't it enough that I'm here?"

"We agreed that when you hunt with me, you do it my way. Using humans for personal pleasure is wrong. It's bad enough we steal their blood."

"I didn't *use* him."

"The only time we need to go near humans is to feed, and we should select those deserving of punishment."

"Feeding on the dregs of society is *your* religion, not mine."

"You know I'm right."

"I'm sick of you treating me like a monster every time I interact with someone outside your accepted hunting category."

"That is exactly what we are, sweetheart. *Monsters.*"

Not wishing to argue, which was all we seemed to do these days, I bit my tongue and tracked his steps to the base of the hill. The moment we cleared the cars and people, we flew to historic Old Buda. The twinkling lights of Pest greeted us from across the wide expanse of the Danube River. The unification of the cities in 1873 gave birth to the name *Budapest.*

The historic townhouse we were currently renting stood amid many old homes on a quaint street. Suspended from the high ceilings were original nineteenth century chandeliers.

Damien threw the keys on the hallway table and pulled me into his arms. "Don't be angry with me."

I pushed him away. "You're always preaching to me like some crazed evangelical pastor. Why can't we hunt the way we used to? I miss targeting couples and having fun."

"I've already told you why I can't do that anymore. I foster a deep respect for life."

"You didn't have a problem slaying vampires before I met you. In fact, I don't recall any Sauvage fostering a deep respect for life—especially when one of them decapitated my sister."

"Vampires are unholy beings that God neither created nor ever intended to exist. Besides, we still go hunting together sometimes."

"Only when I'm willing to compromise, like tonight. I'm sick of feeding on crooks and thugs. Don't you get it?"

Ignoring my anger, he resorted to his sex appeal to end the argument. "You're hot when you're angry."

Kissing me roughly, he led me to the master bedroom where a king-sized canopied bed occupied most of the space. I finally gave in to his advances and returned his fervent kisses. Damien undressed quickly and then removed my clothing with deft fingers. Lifting me up, he set me on the bed then moved over me. The argument was forgotten the moment he entered my body. Lovemaking offered temporary closeness. Unfortunately, the illusion of intimacy ended much too soon.

CHAPTER 2

"Friends are the siblings God never gave us."
(Mencius)

Vlad studied the man occupying the cell across from his own—if such a creature could even be called a man. Refusing to reveal his name, the shadowy figure with the unholy eyes insisted on being called "Teacher."

Vlad eventually discovered that Teacher had been the prized secret weapon of his enemy, Sultan Mehmed. Possessing the strength of twenty men, the large warrior had fought with such ferocity in battle that he was rumored to have slain one hundred Christian soldiers in a single night. One of the survivors wielding a silver crucifix had noticed that the pure metal sapped the beast's strength. Some claimed this miracle a divine intervention. The Christians set a clever trap, binding the enemy with ropes punctuated with silver beads. While King Matthias mulled over what to do with the Ottoman's best warrior, one of the sultan's messenger's arrived with a ransom for his release. Shocked by the exorbitant amount Mehmed was willing to sacrifice, Matthias decided to preserve Teacher's life in the hope that he would eventually convert to Christianity and fight for Jesus Christ. To the king's irritation, the warrior refused to speak or listen to anyone.

Except Vlad.

The guards who prudently avoided Teacher's cell had warned the Romanian prince to pray fervently and frequently to God. Guards often died inexplicably during the night, their corpses little more than frighteningly pale husks. Their bodies were always found within the vicinity of the cell with the silver bars. Sometimes, there were dead rats strewn along the corridor and no one knew how they got there. No one dared to ask.

Teacher was cursed with a bizarre condition that evoked a deathlike sleep during the day yet kept him wide awake at night. His food trays were always left untouched, which meant that he neither ate nor drank. What's more, the warrior could stand perfectly still for several hours at a time.

Vlad noted these disturbing things, but that didn't stop him from listening intently to his companion's monotonous tone as he revealed the true nature of the world. The information Teacher offered was priceless, for he knew things that no mortal man could possibly know.

"I can get you out of that cell and into the castle," Teacher said to Vlad one night. "In time, you will find a mate and she will bear your sons."

"I have no desire to wed."

"But wed you will, and you will bide your time in Hungary until the moment is right for you to go and be the warrior you are destined to become."

"My lord, I have committed your words to memory without question, but this—"

"Silence!"

Vlad had never allowed anyone to speak to him in such an insolent manner—*until now*. Lowering his head in submission to Teacher's wisdom, he said nothing more.

"Vlad Tepes, you will soon free me from this wretched prison. In return, when the time is right, I will bestow upon you the power to destroy your enemies. One day, your name will be written in blood in the history books of men…Legends of you will span throughout the centuries."

***

I awoke to an empty bed the next night. Damien's current hunting preferences afforded me plenty of time to myself, so I wandered through the empty rooms of the flat with listless boredom. The kitchen table bore a note written in my lover's scratchy hand stating that he would be in the seventh district, Budapest's party neighborhood. Teeming with bars and clubs, he would have his pick of seedy humans to feed upon tonight.

Join me if you'd like—D.

I tossed the note into the trash, then went to the closet and surveyed my wardrobe. After selecting an outfit, I showered and got dressed. Adjusting the platinum post of my diamond stud earring, I studied my reflection. Tailored wool skirt, Italian leather boots, cashmere sweater—the elegant woman in the mirror stared back at me with a question in her eyes.

Unlike Damien and other young vampires, I didn't need to drink blood every night. Thanks to my late sister, Erika, I had learned how to go days without feeding. This was no easy task, even for a vampire of my advanced age and experience.

In any case, my hunger for intellectual stimulation and good company far outweighed my thirst for blood these days. Not having Micah, Valerio, and Omar in my life proved increasingly difficult for me with the passing of time. I missed my brothers so badly that it hurt.

You miss Arsham too.

I couldn't deny it. Despite everything that had transpired between us, my sire still haunted my thoughts.

Thunder rumbled in the distance as I slipped on my coat and stepped onto the pavement. The sound, too far away for human ears, signaled oncoming rain. The short stroll between the flat and the National Gallery afforded me plenty of time to reconsider the folly that I was about to commit.

Tourists with expensive cameras around their necks kept pace beside me as I crossed a large square. A few of them paused to photograph the stunning view of the city to my left. Countless lights twinkled across the river, casting a reflection upon the black surface of the Danube. I came to a halt outside of the museum—last chance to turn around.

I entered the classical building, purchased a ticket, and ascended the stairs. My favorite gallery, which housed an incredible collection of winged Gothic altarpieces, happened to be on the same floor as the huge head of King Matthias Corvinus. His coat of arms, a raven holding a ring in its beak, hung on the opposite wall. Beneath that stood an imposing equestrian statue of the king in full armor.

Sporting a pair of tasteful glasses, Dr. Morgan looked every bit the studious professor as he examined the statue. He jotted down some notes in a Moleskin journal, then glanced up at the sound of my heels clicking against the polished floor.

I came to a stop before the mighty war horse. "Matthias Corvinus must have been quite a man."

"Most definitely," Dr. Morgan agreed, closing his notebook. "It's getting late. I didn't think you'd come."

"You mentioned that you were doing research here today. May I ask what topic?"

"Vlad the Impaler."

Dracula. "Of course. The Buda Castle Labyrinth."

"You're familiar with the legend?"

I knew it quite well yet replied, "Somewhat, but feel free to elaborate."

"It would be my pleasure. Vlad Tepes held the role as *Voivode of Havasalföld*—or Warrior of Wallachia, also known as the land beyond the snowy mountains. His duty was to protect Christian Europe from Ottoman invasion, but he was accused of making a deal with the Turks. Matthias found out, abducted Vlad, and imprisoned him in the dungeons beneath his castle. He was eventually moved and placed under house arrest for many years. After his release from Hungarian captivity, Vlad became widely known as the most vicious crusader in Europe. I'm sure you're already aware that he impaled his enemies." He stopped and shook his head as though embarrassed. "I went into professor mode. Sorry."

"Don't apologize."

"Everything I've told you happened in the latter half of the fifteenth century. I took a private tour of the labyrinth this morning. What an unpleasant place—gloomy, dark, airless. Simply terrifying."

"Poor Vlad must have felt cold and alone down there."

"He was a pretty tough guy. I mean, the vicious manner in which he impaled men—I'm sorry. Perhaps I should stop."

"I'm not squeamish, if that's what you're worried about."

"A sharpened wooden rod would be inserted through the anus and shoved through the body, exiting through the shoulder or neck. Unfortunately for the victim, death was not instant if the procedure was done correctly. The pain must have been excruciating."

Despite being a creature of the night who had seen her fair share of human suffering, I shuddered at his words.

"I didn't mean to upset you, Nora," he offered.

"I'm not upset. History is drenched in blood."

"True…On a cheerier note, I was about to grab a coffee."

Dr. Morgan touched my arm through the wool of my coat and led me across the gallery to the stairwell. Once we were at ground level, he surveyed the crowded little café and found a spot for the two of us.

He inquired, "How do you take your coffee?"

"Espresso, black, no sugar."

I watched him order at the counter and he returned a moment later with two small cups.

Setting one down before me, he said, "I'm glad you came."

"Me too."

"I ah, I'm sorry about last night."

"Whatever for?"

He ran a nervous hand through his thinning hair. "I told you about my personal life. Nobody wants to hear that sort of stuff—at least not after the initial meeting."

"No harm done. I'm still one of your fans."

He chuckled. "If I may say, your accent is unusual."

"I've lived in many places."

"You must travel a lot." I nodded and he added, "Wish I could do the same. I'm lucky the university allowed me an extended leave to conduct research."

An announcement came on over the loudspeaker informing everyone that the museum was about to close.

"Do you want to get a proper drink somewhere else?" Dr. Morgan inquired.

Although I wanted to say yes, I stood. "Thank you but I really should go."

"Would you like me to accompany you home?"

"There's no need."

17

"I enjoyed our chat, Nora. I'm meeting with the curator tomorrow to see some of the items kept in storage. Another coffee?"

"I'd like that."

I'd like that? What was wrong with me? I shouldn't have met with the vampirologist tonight in the first place, let alone commit to seeing him tomorrow. I felt the heat of his eyes burning into my back as I exited the museum.

"Shit," I whispered aloud the moment I stepped outside. I had every intention of being at the National Gallery tomorrow to see Dr. Morgan.

I made my way across the square and onto the main street. A distinguished gentleman in a navy wool coat and tailored slacks strolled along the sidewalk ahead of me, then turned down a quiet alley. Although I had left the flat earlier with no intention of hunting, his fine garments and irresistible scent compelled me to track him. My heels barely touched the ground with each feather-light step. My approach was so silent that I deliberately cleared my throat to announce my presence. Startled, he turned around and faced me. Graying hair, blue eyes, prominent nose, late fifties. What was the trendy term for sexy mature men?

Ah yes. *Silver Fox.*

He peered at me. "May I help you?"

Posh British accent too. Jackpot.

"I'm lost," I said, feigning an American accent. "Would you please point me in the direction of the nearest bus stop?"

Curious eyes roamed over me before a smile touched his lips. "There's one nearby. I'm happy to take you there since I'm going in that direction anyway."

I kept pace, enjoying the aroma of his expensive cologne.

He inquired, "Are you here for the Christmas markets? The city is famous for them."

"I am, actually. No better place to shop for gifts."

We came to a halt at the bus stop and he inclined his head in farewell. I liked his manners. Old school. Gentlemen were rare these days. The gold wedding band on his left hand glimmered beneath the glow of the street light.

I asked, "Would you like to get a drink with me?"

"Thank you but my wife is waiting for me."

"Pity," I said flirtatiously with a pointed look.

His eyes bore into mine and, determining that I was serious, he emitted a deprecating laugh. "I'm old enough to be your grandfather."

Hardly. "At least let me thank you."

Before he could protest, I pulled him beneath the shadow of a wide eave and compelled him with my stare. I kissed him. My lips moved from his mouth to his neck where my fangs broke the skin. The man's head fell back and he sighed in pleasure as I drank his blood. I fled the scene afterward, leaving him on a public bench to recover from my bite.

I glanced over my shoulder at his silhouette before rounding the corner. When I first became a vampire, it didn't matter where I got the blood. I had greedily fed upon dirty peasants, gypsies, prisoners—easy targets, whatever came my way. Newborns need to develop their skills before attempting to feed upon challenging prey. For this reason, young vampires like Damien weren't choosy. The blood of a peasant and that of an aristocrat tasted virtually the same to them.

In time, I learned that vampire palates were much like human palates. There's a reason why children outgrow their fondness for Twinkies. Try serving the yellow chemical bomb to a middle-aged CEO who has traveled extensively and dined at the finest restaurants. Palates developed and evolved with experience and age.

Vampires can attest to the veracity of the statement: *you are what you eat.* The blood I had just consumed tasted wonderful because the man was clean and obviously in good health. In contrast, the blood of alcoholics, heroine junkies, or people with chronic illnesses tended to taste rancid.

Feeling invigorated by the blood, I flew into the night with reckless abandon. I landed on a rooftop and surveyed the city. Sundays were dedicated to church and family, so the Christmas markets were packed with people. Parents pushed strollers through stalls decorated with bright lights. Their older children frolicked alongside them. After a while I returned to the flat and settled in for my unholy sleep alone in the bed.

***

I awoke to an empty house again the next night. This time, there was no note. I got dressed and headed to the museum without hesitation. Dr. Morgan was on the second floor, exactly where he had been yesterday.

Pushing his glasses further up his nose, he smiled at the sight of me. "This is like a repeat performance. Coffee?"

"Sure."

When we got to the café downstairs, he made a face. "There are way too many people here today. Do you mind if we go somewhere less noisy?"

"Where?"

"I still haven't been to the New York Palace café. My rental car is parked nearby." When I hesitated, he teased, "I'm a safe driver, I promise."

A baby began screaming from within a stroller. The thin, high-pitched wail made a few people cringe, including me.

"Come on, let's go," I said.

What are you doing, Angelique?

We exited the museum and he led me to a parked car. I settled into the passenger seat of the Fiat 500 with the same excitement as a human girl about to go on her first date.

You're an Elder. This is so wrong.

"I'm impressed with Budapest," Dr. Morgan stated cheerfully while speeding down the hill toward the Margaret Bridge. "I had a chance to speak with the museum curator before you arrived and gleaned lots of useful information."

"Will you publish your findings in a book?"

"Yes," he replied, sparing me a glance as he merged onto traffic. "Vampire mythology. The last chapter will be dedicated to the life of Vlad Tepes. The university press is eagerly waiting to publish it but Rob wants me to upload it onto Amazon as well. Self-publishing has become surprisingly profitable these days."

"Rob?"

"My TA."

"Right. I've tried to imagine what would inspire someone to become a vampirologist and all I can think of is Bram Stoker."

"Actually it was *Dark Shadows*. My mum was a big fan so I got to watch plenty of reruns throughout my childhood. Bram Stoker came later." He dodged an oncoming car and cursed the careless driver under his breath. "I'm intrigued by the whole idea of immortality."

"Didn't you read Anne Rice's *Interview with a Vampire*?"

"I've read every vampire book in publication."

"Then you'll remember that Louis hated the fact that everyone he cared about died. According to him, immortality disguised itself as a blessing but in reality it's a curse."

"Yes, but I identify more with Lestat. I'm a researcher, an academic. Nothing brings me more joy than learning new things and exploring challenging ideas. An eternity isn't enough for an insatiably curious mind."

I felt the same way. "You make a valid point."

Glancing at my window, he pointed. "Wow, look at that."

I turned my head to the right. The Parliament building stood out on the riverbank like an illuminated beacon. "Let me rephrase what I said earlier. To the *average* human immortality is a curse."

He grinned. "Are you implying that I'm above average?"

Before long, we arrived at the stunning New York Palace Hotel. The historic edifice brimmed with whimsical architectural details like hooved demons holding round lamps. The icy air transformed Dr. Morgan's breath into white vapor as he led me toward the entrance. A cluster of tourists stood by the door waiting for vacant tables. The gilded café oozed with nineteenth century elegance. Pristine white tablecloths, gloved waiters, crystal chandeliers, and the gorgeous frescoed ceiling were reflected on the menu's price list. One of the hostesses materialized and we were shown to a table.

Dr. Morgan said, "Had you not come to the museum today, I'd be alone at the pub right now, so thank you." A smartly dressed waiter paused at our table and he added, "I heard that the hot chocolate here was incredible."

I looked at our server. "I would prefer an espresso." It was much easier to sip a bit of espresso than a hot chocolate topped with a big dollop of whipped cream. Consuming human food and drink didn't harm us, per se, but it proved extremely unpleasant.

When we were alone again, Dr. Morgan focused his full attention on me. "If I may make an observation, you seem quite sophisticated and independent for your age."

Was that suspicion or surprise in his tone? "My mother died when I was a child so I matured quickly."

"I'm sorry. How old are you, if you don't mind me asking?"

"Twenty."

I steered the conversation away from me and encouraged him to talk about himself, his job, and his theories on vampires. Pretending to sip my espresso, I listened while watching him indulge in the most decadent hot chocolate I had ever seen.

He eventually said, "You now know a lot about me but I still know nothing about you."

I sat back in my chair and crossed my legs. "What do you want to know?"

"Where were you born?"

"France."

"You have no trace of an accent."

"Good education, lots of travel."

A sultry young woman strutted past our table in a snug mini dress, thigh-high suede boots, and a bomber jacket. Heavy makeup enhanced her silver-gray eyes and full lips. She tossed her long black hair as she sat down at a table within my line of vision. I couldn't see the person sitting across from her, but I did glimpse a male hand. A tall blonde in a red wool coat eventually joined the raven-haired beauty at the table, but I couldn't see her face since she sat down with her back to me.

He inquired, "Where is home for you?"

"I don't know anymore," I replied distractedly.

"Do you travel *that* much?"

22

"I'm afraid so."

He continued asking me harmless questions and I replied to them with cautious half-truths. At length, we stood and headed for the exit. The girl in the bomber jacket stared at me with an odd expression, then averted her gaze before Dr. Morgan urged me outside into the cold drizzle. Quickly, he unbuttoned his wool coat and moved to cover me with it as we raced to his car. I found his chivalry endearing.

Once we were inside his Fiat, he removed his glasses and dried them with a cloth. "Where are you staying?"

"Near the National Gallery."

Replacing his glasses on his face, he grinned. "Me too."

Another coincidence?

He drove back to Old Buda and parked in front of my rented flat. We sat in the car while tiny frozen drops accumulated on the windshield.

"I'm taking another tour of the labyrinth tomorrow," he said.

"I thought you already went there."

"A local guide accompanied me last time. Unfortunately, there are some tacky displays catering to the masses. This time I'll be with a native from Budapest who is doing his doctoral dissertation on the caves. He's fluent in English too."

"Fascinating."

Dr. Morgan's eyes sparkled. "We're meeting for lunch first. Why not join me?"

"Thank you but I've already made plans," I lied.

"Maybe we can meet later? I need to run a few errands after the tour but I should be done by seven-thirty."

"That's better for me, actually."

"There's a pub over there," he said, pointing to a yellow pool of light reflecting upon the wet sidewalk. "I'll be waiting for you beneath the awning."

"See you then," I said, opening the car door. "Thank you for another pleasant evening."

"It is I who should be thanking you for your company. Goodnight Nora."

"Goodnight Dr. Morgan."

CHAPTER 3

*"A truth discovered always seems so plain and simple that
we wonder why the discovery was so long delayed."*
(Vash Young)

Vlad was transferred from his dank musty cell beneath the ground to the king's castle, thus restoring the dignity of the Romanian prince. Matthias Corvinus negotiated a deal with his noble prisoner, allowing him to lead a somewhat normal life within the confines of Hungary.

Vlad crept to the dungeon in secret, veering straight to Teacher's cell. Extracting from his cloak a set of pilfered tools, he said, "My lord, I have come to free you."

The dark figure pressed his back against the wall farthest from the silver bars. "You know what to do."

Using a hammer and chisel, the prince broke the lock and yanked open the door. To his astonishment, Teacher vanished before his eyes! Vlad's head swiveled left and right, then froze. The newly-freed warrior stood in a pool of torchlight several feet away, allowing Vlad to see his physical attributes for the first time. Towering over the average man in height, Teacher's body consisted of sinewy muscle. Eyes the color of onyx stones sparkled in a chiseled face that was incredibly handsome yet frighteningly cruel. A gold chain flaunting a large gold medallion hung from his neck. Stamped upon the metal was a *Faravahar*, an ancient Zoroastrian symbol depicting a winged priest.

"I can smell your fear," Teacher said, his piercing gaze reflecting the forbidden knowledge of the world.

Trembling, Vlad lowered his head in order to break eye contact with the intimidating creature. "What are you?"

"I am your savior."

***

I awoke the next evening after sunset, which in Budapest during winter hovered between four and four thirty in the afternoon. To my surprise, Damien greeted me with a grin.

"Hey," he said, leaning up on his elbow beside me, completely naked.

"Hey yourself, party boy."

"I know, I've been traveling farther out and seeking refuge in the countryside."

"Why?"

"Boredom." He ran his hand along the curve of my hip, then kissed me.

"You should come hunting with me, instead. I fed on a tasty gentleman last night."

Damien slid over me and pinned me with his weight. "Is that so? Was he handsome?"

"As a matter of fact, yes."

Prying my knees apart, he said, "I'd rather do *this*."

His lovemaking, although passionate, felt forced.

Holding him in my arms, I whispered, "What's going on?"

Refusing to look at me, he asked, "What do you mean?"

"Something is obviously bothering you."

"Are you *trying* to start a fight?"

"Don't be ridiculous."

Leaning up on his elbows, he met my eyes. "Fine. Come hunting with me tonight."

I shook my head. "I'm done with your way."

"Well, maybe that's what's pissing me off."

"That's not fair, Damien. Plenty of couples have differing feeding preferences."

"I doubt those couples survive the test of time." When I flinched, he amended, "Forgive me. I shouldn't have said that."

A tense silence followed.

"Ever since you—" I stopped myself. "Forget it."

He scowled at me. "Ever since I *what*? Became a vampire?"

"I'm not doing this again."

Damien got out of bed and began dressing. "It wasn't my choice, remember? That fucking asshole—"

"Stop!"

He glared at me with venom in his eyes. "Still defending *him*. Unbelievable."

"Whether you like it or not, Arsham is our sire. Hating him won't change a thing."

His eyes narrowed as he hastily buttoned his shirt. "I could have killed him but I refrained for *your* sake...Because *you're* still loyal to him."

"I know another side of him."

Pulling on his pants, he demanded, "Is that supposed to make me feel better?"

I sighed in irritation. "I've abandoned my sire, my brothers, and the London lair...What more do you want from me?"

His eyes softened, offering me a rare glimpse of the Damien I once knew—the mortal with whom I had fallen in love. "I'm afraid of losing you, Angelique. That's the honest truth."

"Yet you push me away."

Male vampires were always aggressive at first, but Damien still fostered resentment and anger toward Arsham, which only worsened matters. I held on to the hope that, in time, his mood and demeanor would improve.

Shrugging into his leather jacket, he said, "I need to feed. See you later."

I sat in bed for a while after he had gone. Part of me wanted to take off to London. Immediately. How would my brothers and the coven react if I simply showed up?

How would Arsham react?

Throwing off the covers, I got out of bed and padded to the bathroom. I showered and dressed, then made my way downstairs in order to meet Dr. Morgan at the pub. No sooner had I stepped outside than I smelled cat piss and incense. A feline shape shifter lurked nearby. My muscles tensed as I crept toward the back of the townhouse.

Menacing rain clouds scuttled across the night sky, prompting me to pull the fur-lined hood of my parka over my head. Cautiously, I made my way down the street and with each footstep the odor became more pungent.

I spotted the pub up ahead and saw Dr. Morgan chatting amicably with a young man beneath a green awning. I studied the latter. Tall, pale, black hair and amber eyes. Odd-looking fellow. I sniffed the air and realized the odor came from him. Instantly, I hid behind a parked van where I could spy on them and overhear their conversation.

"Feel free to contact me if you have any questions, Dr. Morgan."

"Thank you, Elek."

Elek. Of course. In Hungarian, the name meant "defender of men." He had most likely volunteered his services to the vampirologist. Given that shifters worked closely with slayers to destroy our kind, the vampirologist could provide useful information.

Dr. Morgan continued, "Are you sure you don't want to come inside and grab a beer? I'm meeting a friend of mine in a few minutes. She's lovely, you'd enjoy meeting her."

Shit.

Thunder exploded above my head and fat raindrops doused the city a moment later. What were the chances that I would befriend a vampirologist who is now hanging out with a shifter? My sire would be most displeased. Furious, in fact.

Elek said, "Maybe another time."

To my immense relief, he ran into the slick street to catch a bus. I waited for the vehicle to drive away before abandoning my hiding place and taking refuge beneath the pub's awning.

Dr. Morgan spun toward me. "Nora! Elek just boarded that bus. I wanted you to meet him."

Pushing back the hood of my coat and shaking out my hair, I added, "How was your tour?"

His eyes roamed over me. "Incredible."

"I'm glad to hear it."

Taking my elbow, he urged me into the pub. An old man sat at the bar quietly sipping a beer. Dr. Morgan greeted him, then ordered two pints of Guinness and some fries before selecting a table by the window.

He sat down and said, "Did you know those caves are over

three hundred fifty thousand years old? The passages stretch out over four thousand feet."

"I knew they were a UNESCO site but tell me more," I replied, taking a seat across from him.

He took a hearty sip of beer. "Reading about the caves is one thing, seeing them with your own eyes is something altogether different."

Dr. Morgan went on to describe many of the things he had seen. At one point, he extracted his cell phone and began flipping through a series of photographs. One image stood out in stark contrast from the others.

I reached for the device. "Wait! May I?"

"Sharp eyes, Nora. I found that image carved into one of the walls in the area where Vlad Tepes III was imprisoned. It's called a Faravahar, an ancient symbol representing Zoroastrianism, a religion founded in seventh century Persia. It has nothing to do with the legend of Dracula, of course…"

The first time I had ever seen a Faravahar was on the night that I became a vampire. It was stamped into the ancient gold medallion that my sire wore around his neck.

Could it be possible?

Dr. Morgan retrieved his cell phone and slipped it into his pocket. "Changing the subject, I thought about some obscure vampire books that you might enjoy. One even deals with those who were commissioned to kill the undead."

I feigned ignorance. "Oh?"

He removed the Moleskin journal from his jacket pocket and wrote down some titles. "Have you ever heard of the Sauvage family from France? Sanctioned by the pope, they were the most famous vampire slayers in Europe."

I eyed him warily. "Never heard of them."

He tore the page and handed it to me. "People once believed in the existence of vampires, thus the need for slayers."

"I'm aware of certain European traditions that were popular, like burying corpses with stakes through their hearts. Thank goodness no one believes in those fairy tales anymore."

"A few of us do."

"You're joking."

He drained the remains of his beer. "You may find what I'm about to tell you hard to take in so brace yourself."

I arranged my features into a mask of skepticism. "Okay."

"There are blood drinkers among us today."

The barmaid came to our table. She frowned in puzzlement at my full glass, then turned to Dr. Morgan. "Another pint, sir?"

He nodded in response to the question, then waited for the barmaid to leave before inquiring, "What do you say to *that*?"

"To you having another pint?"

"No, vampires."

I folded my hands on the sticky table top. "I'm assuming you mean those Goth kids who dress in black, line their eyes with kohl, and swap blood with their creepy friends."

The barmaid placed the Guinness on the table and he slurped the creamy head before taking a hearty sip. "Not Goth kids."

"You can't mean *real* vampires."

"That's precisely what I mean."

I forced myself to laugh.

He leaned in closer. "I *saw* a vampire."

I kept my expression deadpan.

He continued, "I saw him feed on a human before my eyes."

I looked at the pint in his hand. "Maybe you should go easy on those, Dr. Morgan."

"I'm serious!"

"I love your books and your lectures, and I'm sure many others find them entertaining, but—"

He held up his hand. "Look, the only reason I told you about it is because you seem like an educated young woman with an open mind. You're into my work, right?"

Get up and walk out the door, Angelique.

"I do have an open mind, but you're asking me to believe something that goes against natural law."

Lowering his voice, he continued, "I traveled to London for a conference last year. I was heading back to my hotel after a late dinner with colleagues when I noticed something zip over my head. Something *big*. Then I heard a gasp but the sound got cut short—you know, like in the movies when they abruptly slit someone's throat. I peeked down an alley and saw a vampire with its fangs in some poor woman's neck. He bled her dry then flew into the night."

In the ensuing silence, he grabbed his beer with trembling hands and consumed half of the contents in the glass. Shaken from merely recounting the story, I could only imagine his terror at having seen one of us in action. Only a newborn vampire would have behaved so carelessly.

Finally, he raised his eyes to meet mine. "Nora? Did you hear what I just said?"

"I'm a bit stunned."

He threw up his hands. "Imagine how I felt!"

"Shhh," I admonished, glancing around. "Have you told anyone about this?"

"Only Jennifer, my girlfriend, but she laughed at me." He studied my face. "Do you believe me?"

I hesitated. "I believe you saw *something*…"

"I haven't told my colleagues yet but I'm debating whether or not to add my eyewitness account into the book. I could dedicate an entire chapter to the undead lurking among us."

Duty demanded that I kill this mortal. He had seen too much and was now threatening to expose our kind to the world. Arsham would have snapped his neck without hesitation.

"Nora, say something," he prompted before draining the remains of his beer.

"You'll be a laughing stock."

"Excuse me?"

"If you publish your vampire sighting, no scholar will ever take you seriously. Neither will a publishing house. Vampire mythology is as valid a subject as Greek or Roman mythology. Stick to that, otherwise you'll come off sounding like those weirdos who get abducted by UFOs."

He stared at me with a hurt expression through the haze of inebriation. "Do you think I would make this up?"

"No, but a *vampire*?" I shook my head to further dissuade him. "Do as you wish but I wouldn't risk my reputation or my career over a crazy story."

Heaving a sigh, he cupped his empty glass with both hands and lowered his head. I sensed his remorse at having shared the story with me. It became awkward after that so I made to go.

Dr. Morgan's gaze shifted from me to the rain streaked glass. "It's still raining."

I reached in my coat for some money and placed it on the table. Dr. Morgan shook his head as he scooped up the bills and attempted to return them to me.

I put up my hand to stop him. "It's the least I can do after shortening your book by one chapter."

Smiling sadly, he lifted his drained glass to toast me. A half sip swished at the bottom. "To you, Nora. Thanks for being honest."

"Goodnight, Dr. Morgan," I said before exiting the pub.

Damien got in my face the instant I stepped outside. "What the hell are you doing, Angelique?"

"Speaking with Dr. Morgan. I met him at the Géllert, remember?"

Crossing his arms, Damien glared at my new friend through the window. "It's time for you to tell this guy to take a hike."

I stood in front of him to block the view. "And if I refuse?"

"I'll do it myself and I won't be as nice."

"I swear, if you lay a hand on that man—"

"Are you threatening me over some dude you just met?"

"He's not merely 'some dude.' He's a brilliant scholar."

"I don't give a flying fuck about *Dr. Morgan*."

"You're ridiculous."

Clenching his jaw in anger, he pointed to himself. "*I'm* ridiculous? Wow. Would you rather go back inside to continue your date?"

"At this point, yes."

He took off down the street without another word and I made no move to chase after him.

Dr. Morgan tapped on the window to get my attention before opening the door. He darted outside and guided me back into the warmth of the pub. "Was that your boyfriend?"

I nodded. "He saw me here with you and now he's upset."

"You don't deserve to be treated badly," he said, slightly slurring his words.

"Even after I've angered you?"

"You didn't anger me. You were only being honest and trying to help. Come, sit with me for a bit so I won't be alone."

I placed my hand on the door latch. "I can't."

"Wait." He scribbled something on a random bar napkin. "In case you want some company later, here's my address and my cell number."

"I don't have a phone."

"You're kidding, right?"

"No cell phone, no email."

"That's unheard of. How do you communicate with people? With your boyfriend, for example?"

"We speak face to face and leave notes for each other. It's old fashioned, I know." I pocketed the napkin.

"Actually, I like that idea."

"Thanks for a nice time, Dr. Morgan."

"I wish you would call me Caleb."

***

Damien was nowhere to be found the next night. I debated whether or not to seek out Caleb. His vast knowledge of history and folkloric legends impressed me. Not many humans dedicated themselves so thoroughly, *so passionately*, to one subject. I entered the shower and allowed it to steam up the bathroom. Body cream followed my hot shower and I chose an outfit appropriate with the icy climate to blend in with humans. Vampires were immune to the damage and discomfort caused by extreme temperatures, but strolling around in a sundress in December would draw unwanted attention.

The bus idled at the stop near the pub. On a whim, I boarded the vehicle and chose a seat at the back. The bus crossed the bridge and wove through the main city. I watched the outside world through foggy windows. At the last stop, I got off and headed in the direction of the river. The Danube's icy water hosted an array of vessels, big and small. I padded along the bank, my boots crunching over rocks and frozen bits of mud.

Teenagers hung out in clusters along the river's edge guzzling cheap beer and laughing at vulgar jokes. Some took advantage of the darkness to kiss. I skirted a group that sat around a bonfire smoking pot. No one bothered me because no one heard me. No one saw me either. I could have fed on that fresh youthful blood but I chose to leave the kids in peace. Maybe Damien was rubbing off on me after all.

The bus route had taken me in the opposite direction of the Margaret Bridge so I backtracked along the coast. Once I reached the bridge, I flew to the top of the huge metal structure. Gazing out over the water, I studied the vehicles in traffic. So many people, so many lives. The medieval castle on the hill drew my gaze and I found my thoughts drifting to Arsham. What was the symbol of his medallion doing on the wall of the labyrinth?

I flew to the flat an hour before sunrise to await my lover but he never showed. Damien wasn't there when I awoke the next night. I dressed for hunting then descended upon the city like a giant bat. *The Angel of Death*. Some vampires relished playing the role of destroyer.

Bloodlust. We all experienced it in the beginning. Our insatiable thirst and primal instincts pushed us over the edge, like sharks in a feeding frenzy. With time, we learned to become cautious and deliberate. Bloodlust could be controlled and enjoyed, particularly when derived from our sire's blood.

Pure magic flowed through Arsham's veins. The mere thought of his royal ancient blood made my mouth water. It also filled me with longing...

I wandered through the Christmas market located by the magnificent basilica of St. Stephen. Saturday night meant families and baby strollers everywhere. A pair of musicians performed on a makeshift stage and adults crowded around to listen, their children twirling in tune with the music.

While surveying the scene, one woman in particular stuck out in the crowd. The color and style of her hair resembled my own. Sharp delicate features framed a lovely heart-shaped face.

Deep blue eyes met mine and I couldn't help returning her pretty smile. Surely she was thinking the exact same thing. We looked so much alike that we could easily pass for sisters. Two children ran up to the woman and she turned her attention to them. A man arrived with a pair of cups brimming with steaming hot mulled wine. His left hand bore a gold ring. He pecked his wife's lips before offering her one of the cups.

Having never experienced the joys of motherhood or a loving marriage, I watched the couple with a pang of envy. The woman looked at me again and smiled. This time, I sneered and turned my back on her.

I headed toward the shadowy rear of the church where I met a pair of lesbian punk rockers. I asked them for a cigarette before striking up a conversation. They chatted and I pretended to listen while compelling them to offer me their throats. I drank my fill and left them in each other's arms. I took one last drag from my cigarette before letting it fall from my fingertips and crushing the butt with the tip of my boot.

Feeling rejuvenated by the blood, I scaled a nineteenth century apartment building and skimmed the rooftops of Budapest. In the distance, night ferries and party boats with colored lights glided on the frigid surface of the Danube. Cold wind caressed my cheeks as I stared up at the full moon. The iridescent moonlight rippling across the dark water took my breath away.

Where are you, Damien?

CHAPTER 4

"'Tis better to have loved and lost
than never to have loved at all."
(Alfred Lord Tennyson)

Matthias Corvinus frowned after hearing the reports of his servants uttered in hushed tones. It wasn't the first time they had described bizarre events taking place beneath his roof. It seemed that Vlad enjoyed torturing and killing helpless animals, a hobby which the king found distasteful. His scullery maids would often cry out in alarm whenever they found bits of mice impaled on tiny sticks or dead birds plucked clean of their feathers. These cruel acts were no doubt caused by pent-up anger and boredom. For this reason, Matthias dispatched his prisoner to Visegrád, where he was placed under house arrest. In time, the king found a bonny wife for Vlad. Marriage and children kept the captive prince occupied for several years.

Everything changed one summer night in the year 1475. Vlad awoke from a strange dream to find a tall figure in a black hooded cloak at the foot of his bed. Startled, the prince covered his mouth to keep from crying out and alarming his family.

"It is I, Vlad," said Teacher as he pushed back the hood to reveal his clean-shaven head.

Not having seen him since the night of his escape, Vlad inquired, "My lord, where have you been all this time?"

"Walking the earth."

"You promised to bestow power upon me so that I could destroy my enemies."

"When the time was right, yes."

"Is now that time?"

Teacher's eyes scanned the room and his gaze settled on a copper chalice resting upon the bedside table. Taking hold of the vessel with one hand, he bit into the wrist of the other. A stream of crimson blood poured from the cut into the chalice. Vlad became fearful when the wound magically healed before his eyes.

Teacher held out the vessel. "Drink."

Vlad took the chalice with trembling hands, hesitating only an instant before consuming its contents. Teacher's blood burned down his throat, endowing him with incredible vitality and power. Sinister images accompanied his newfound strength, and the prince quickly understood how he could use the blood to his fullest advantage.

Teacher witnessed the mortal's partial transformation with an appraising eye. "Vlad, the time has come for you to cease calling me Teacher. From this day forth I am your Master. Tomorrow, you will leave this place and take up your sword to fight the Turks with the newfound vigor I have bestowed upon you. The Ottomans have failed to honor me, and I will now have my vengeance through you."

"Yes *Master*."

***

I decided to see Caleb after feeding on the lesbians. My first stop was the pub but he wasn't there, so I went to his flat. Answering the door in a pair of jeans and a dark green hoodie, he resembled a college student rather than a professor.

"Nora. This is a nice surprise. Please come in," he said, waving me into a sleek modern living room.

Oversized black and white photos of historic Budapest adorned the walls. A shaggy carpet in shades of taupe and white sectioned off the room. A laptop, books, and sheets of paper were scattered on a big dining table. One book was open to a page depicting the famous portrait of Vlad Tepes.

"Am I interrupting your work?" I inquired, taking in Vlad the Impaler's unusual mustache.

Caleb followed my gaze. "Doesn't look very intimidating from the painting, does he? You came at the perfect time, actually. I was about to take a much needed break."

"Great."

"Everything patched up between you and ah—what's his

name, anyway?"

"Charles," I improvised. "I'd rather not talk about him."

"Okay." Strutting into the kitchen in his athletic socks, he scooped two wine glasses from the cabinet. "Will you join me?"

"I've already had way too much mulled wine at the Christmas market," I lied.

He poured the ruby liquid into two glasses anyway. "Here, it's only a splash. Which market?"

I placed the vessel to my lips but did not drink. "The one by St. Stephen. Did you tour around with Elek again today?"

Grimacing, he replied, "No but I went to the Terror Museum this morning. Have you been?"

"Not yet."

"Heavy stuff." He paused. "Are you celebrating Christmas in Budapest?"

I shrugged. "Are you?"

"That was my original plan, although I thought it would be with Jennifer."

"Do you have any family back in Scotland?"

Regarding me thoughtfully, he replied, "I do, but I'm not answering any more of your questions."

"Why not?"

"You know a lot about me but I know nothing about you."

"I'm not that interesting, I assure you."

"Are you kidding me? You're the most interesting woman I've ever met. Judging by your stylish clothing and jewelry, you're successful. Your life seems to be one long extended holiday. Despite your youth, you reject technology and keep yourself off the so-called grid. Do you know what I think?" Lowering his head to peer over the tops of his glasses, he declared, "You're a spy."

"That's quite a theory, I'll give you that."

"It's not like you would admit to being a spy."

"If I did, I would need to kill you."

"Hmm. Not a fan of that scenario."

"Nor I. Tell me more about your research and your book."

"Back to talking about me, are we? Okay, here's another

story for you. Do you know the legend of the golden chalice?"

I did know it but shook my head nonetheless. "Tell me."

"Vlad Tepes placed a golden chalice in the main square of his town. At the time, he ruled over an estimated sixty thousand people. He declared that anyone could drink from the chalice but no one could remove it from the square. The vessel remained untouched throughout the entirety of his reign. The townspeople were terrorized of him, yet today he's seen as a hero in Romania. Go figure."

"Is that your next stop? Transylvania?"

"Actually, I was there for a few days before I came here. Lovely country, great food, hospitable people."

"I agree."

"You've been to Romania too?" I nodded and he continued, "I don't want to pry into your personal life but what do you do for a living? Now that you've denied being a spy, I'm curious."

"Maybe I'm a highly paid assassin."

He laughed aloud. "No one would ever suspect such a feminine young woman of being a coldhearted killer." As an afterthought, he added, "Do you even know how to use a gun?"

"I know the basics," I replied with a straight face. "In answer to your question, I've made some intelligent investments." It was a partial truth. Decades of purchasing good stocks had made me quite rich.

"I see. Thus the ability to travel." Caleb refilled his empty wine glass. "You've barely touched your wine."

I set the glass on the counter. "I can't finish it."

Caleb checked his phone then rubbed his neck. "I had planned on visiting the little bath house at the foot of the hill tonight for a quick soak. After a day of writing, I need it."

I stood. "I won't keep you—"

"Don't go. I was about to invite you to join me. We can continue our talk as we soak. What do you say?"

"I'll get my swimsuit."

The clever Turks had built the Király Bath in 1565 within the walls of Old Buda. In times of pestilence, war, or siege, they could still enjoy a good soak. Time had created rusty patinas on the stone. Believing the discolored streaks to be a sign of ruin rather than centuries of mineral deposits, uninformed tourists usually avoided this particular bath.

I, on the other hand, loved it.

"The Turks knew what they were doing," Caleb said softly while easing himself into the warm water.

The acoustics were such that even whispering could sound jarring to the ears.

"Definitely," I agreed.

"The last several weeks have been difficult for me. My ex and I used to do everything together, and now she's living her life across the ocean in Nevada—without me."

"Was she a former student?"

"Yes. Things were great between us until she got homesick." He shrugged. "Have you ever had your heart broken, Nora?"

Shattered into thousands of pieces. "I have. A long time ago, before Charles."

"A long time ago?" he repeated, amused. "You're twenty!"

I feigned chagrin. "I guess you have a point."

We watched an old man shuffle out of the steam room and plunge into the cold pool.

"There's a hot pool over there," he said, pointing to a spot across from where we sat. "Shall we try it?"

"Sure."

We exited the thermal water and entered the tiny hot pool tucked into the side of the room. We were the only two people.

"The Romans loved their baths too," Caleb commented. "They dug into the earth to create pools of different temperatures. There was the *tepidarium, frigidarium*, and the *caldarium*."

"Warm, cold, hot."

"Let me guess, you can speak Latin."

I was fluent in modern languages and almost fluent in Latin. Arsham, on the other hand, knew all the languages, including the ancient ones.

There you go again...

"I studied Latin in high school," I lied.

"Why not Spanish" It's much more useful."

"Latin lies at the foundation of our Western culture so I figured..." I trailed off, pretending to be shy.

"Charles is a fool." Staring at my mouth, he said, "This may be crazy but, can I kiss you? I'm not trying to be a pervert or anything. I'll tell you why in a bit."

At my nod, he leaned toward me. Meeting my eyes, he smiled slightly before kissing me chastely on the lips.

He leaned back against the wall. "Thank you."

"What was that all about?"

"*Now* it feels like Jennifer and I have officially broken up. You see, I've never cheated on her during the three years that we were together."

"So kissing another woman is closure for you?"

"I know, it's stupid..."

I moved forward and took his face into my hands. "It's not stupid, Caleb."

Pressing my lips to his, I snaked my arms around his neck. Caleb opened his mouth to me and I offered him a proper kiss. Eventually, I pulled away and eyed him expectantly.

"Wow," he whispered.

***

Damien sauntered into the living room. Seeing me on the sofa with a book in my hand, he paused. "Hello."

"Hi," I replied coolly.

He quirked an eyebrow while reading the cover of my book. "*Vlad the Impaler*. Really?"

Ignoring his comment, I asked, "Where have you been?"

"Terrorizing the Hungarian countryside and feasting on peasants. What have you been doing in my absence besides reading up on Romanian legends?"

I snapped the book shut. "I'm not amused."

"I thought it was pretty funny."

"Look, I don't need to know you're every move but it *is* courteous to let your mate know your whereabouts before disappearing for a week."

"It's only been five days and we're not officially mated."

His comment stung, but I shot back, "I'm a vampire, not some weak mortal woman. My concern is for your safety, nothing more. Slayers exist in most major European cities, and apparently so do shifters."

"I was the best slayer in London, remember? I know all the tricks, but it's nice to know that you worry about me." He paused. "Wait, what did you mean by that last comment? Have you come across a shifter here in Budapest?"

"I sniffed one out the other day. Male. Feline."

"What did he look like?"

"Young, black hair, pale. I didn't see a slayer."

Damien's mouth went hard as his brow creased in thought.

I asked, "What's wrong?"

He shook his head briskly. "Nothing." Pulling me toward him, he added, "I'm sorry for the other night."

"Have you noticed how often you apologize to me?"

"Things have been tense between us, huh?"

"Tense would be an apt description."

Closing the gap between us, he said, "I've missed you."

Holding me led to kissing me and the inevitable lovemaking. He still touched me with the urgency and passion of a newborn vampire. Greedy, rough. How I missed the mortal Damien who knew how to play my body like a finely tuned instrument.

There's another male who once stoked my passion, and he knows my body as well as his own...

Damien regarded me thoughtfully before kissing my brow. "What's going through that pretty head of yours?"

"Us." The lie felt bitter in my mouth.

"You think of me with disappointment, don't you?"

"Honestly, yes, because you fail to embrace your true nature. I realize this life was forced upon you and you're angry, but we must try to make the best of it. Understand that I say this for *your* sake, not mine."

"There's something that troubles me."

"You can talk to me about anything, Damien. Tell me."

"What happens when we get tired of traveling?"

I looked at him blankly. "What do you mean?"

41

"You know, when it gets old. When we become bored."

"There's so much to see and do in this world, so many things to learn, so many books to read. I don't think we'll ever get bored. I know I won't."

He sighed in frustration. "I'm not like you, Angelique. I was raised to be a fighter not a scholar."

"I'm not a scholar."

"You know what I mean."

His confession saddened me. I had hoped that his passion for life, nature, art, and adventure matched my own so that we could derive some pleasure from our immortality.

My mind raced with ideas. "Maybe what you need is some excitement. We can go parachuting in Tuscany or hang gliding over the Grand Canyon. We can deep sea dive in New Zealand with great white sharks. There are many dangerously fun things to do, and the best part—we can't die! How does that sound?"

"Look, immortality may be a blessing to you but not to me. I never wanted this."

Another blow. Pity that he didn't share Caleb's outlook or that he wasn't more like the fictional Lestat.

I gave him a measured look. "So you're telling me that you'll never make the best of your situation."

"I'm not the 'make lemonade when life gives you lemons type' if that's what you're asking."

Ironically, his lemon analogy instantly soured my mood. "Suit yourself, Damien. I'm truly sorry that you feel that way. Don't expect me to be miserable alongside you."

"Don't worry, I won't."

I said nothing more.

CHAPTER 5

"A distant enemy is always preferable to one at the gate."
(Emil Cioran)

From 1475 to his death in January 1477, Vlad Tepes fought against the Turks with a ferocity that made him famous throughout the European continent. The Romanian prince's cruelty became a topic of conversation in the peasant markets and noble castles. Thousands of men had been savagely impaled on stakes, their corpses left to rot. "Vlad the Impaler" was rumored to enjoy dining amid the dying, dipping his bread in the blood of his enemies. Stories like these made even the most seasoned soldiers cringe with fear and disgust.

Tales of Vlad drinking blood before venturing into battle made noble lords uneasy. People began speculating on the forces behind this unholy behavior, eventually drawing the attention of the clergy who frowned upon these vile methods.

Some say Vlad's death was a result of an ambush. Others claim that he fell off a horse and died from his wounds. One thing was certain: no historian dared to mention the dark hooded figure that whispered into prince's ear at night. Only a fool would attract such an evil demon to his doorstep.

***

The weekend was upon us once again and parties abounded in Budapest. Damien wanted to stalk the big commercial bath houses packed with tourists.

"Let's go to Géllert," Damien suggested while slipping on a shirt. "Christmas is only two days away so everyone will be partying like crazy. The pickings will be easy tonight."

Selfie-sticks. Noise. "I don't like that place."

"We can go to the Lukács."

Another bath house that hosted mega parties. "I don't like that place either."

He spread out his hands in supplication. "I'm trying here."

"I'm not in the mood for a wild party."

"It's not like I can feed in a library, sweetheart."

"Go on without me."

Damien stared at me blankly, then vacated the flat without further ado. The relief I glimpsed in his eyes before he left compelled me to follow him. To my surprise, he went in the opposite direction of the bath houses he had mentioned. Keeping a safe distance between us, I melted into the shadows.

Where are you going, Damien?

I tracked him to the New York Palace Hotel. Perplexed, I watched as he entered the café and made a beeline for a table at the back. Edging closer to the windows, I saw him take a seat across a stunning woman—the same raven-haired beauty whom I had seen a few days ago.

What the hell?

Damien leaned back and smiled while the mysterious woman dove into conversation. The level of comfort between them indicated that their relationship had been going on for quite some time. He took her hand into his own at one point and laughed, seemingly delighted by her words.

I studied the woman. Clad in tight leather pants and red lipstick, she looked sexy—and really young. Resisting the urge to jump to conclusions, I forced myself to remain calm. After all, I also nurtured a friendship with a human. Caleb wasn't anywhere near as sexy as this woman, but still…

Not wanting to get caught spying, I scaled the building across from the hotel and monitored the entrance from high above. I sat frozen like a statue for over an hour before they exited the café. Damien embraced his comely companion, then escorted her to a white Volkswagen Beetle. I thought he was saying goodbye until he got into the passenger seat. They drove straight to the Géllert.

My silent landing on the establishment's glass roof went unnoticed by the throng of people milling about below. Carefully skirting the edge, I peered down into the big thermal pool. A party was underway with plenty of wet firm flesh on display. Bodies gyrated in tune to deafening rap music while a few couples shamelessly made out in public. Colored strobe lights, trendy drugs, and alcohol completed the contemporary Bacchanalia.

Damien eventually entered the pool in his stylish swimming trunks, leading his date by the hand. Blessed with curves in the right places, the woman's bikini couldn't be tinier. Only three red triangles and a bit of gold dental floss held the revealing swimsuit together.

They were engaged in what seemed to be a serious conversation with heads bent close together and eyes shifting to the crowd. Damien eventually moved away from the woman and, to my astonishment, began hunting for prey. Within moments, he was feeding on someone.

My eyes slid to where Damien's date sat watching him with a studious expression. *No shock? No hint of fear?* There were only two reasons why a vampire groomed a mortal for eternal life: special talent or love.

I studied the young woman with renewed interest. Either she possessed extraordinary abilities or Damien had fallen in love. Naturally, the second scenario was the most likely one. Given our current state of perpetual discontent, it made sense for him to seek a mate better suited to his personality.

Intellectualizing the matter didn't make it any easier to swallow. The thought of Damien cheating on me was both offensive and hurtful. Erika's words came to mind: *"Heal your heart and make it strong. Learn to love yourself and your own company. Never again give in to a man so easily."*

My sister had offered me that sage advice after Arsham had broken my heart. That was over two centuries ago.

Damien fed on a bleached blonde drug pusher, then waded through the pool toward his date. She appeared to ask him several questions, which he patiently answered. Between the glass and the howling wind, I couldn't hear what they were saying but I could read their lips whenever their faces were in full view. Sure enough, Damien was describing the hunt in detail. They eventually began talking and laughing with an ease that provoked my resentment.

I didn't want to stick around to see more so I flew back to Old Buda. Not wishing to be alone, I decided to check the pub down the street. Luckily, Caleb sat at the bar making conversation with an old man. At the sight of me, he smiled and excused himself from his elderly friend.

"Hi, Nora."

The old man at the bar eyed me with curiosity, then inquired in broken English, "She girlie friend?"

Caleb shook his head. *"Friend."*

"Beautiful," the old man said.

"Yes she is," Caleb agreed, his green eyes twinkling behind the lenses of his glasses. "Can I buy you a drink?"

"No thanks. Actually, would you walk with me?"

He paid for his beer then accompanied me outside. We said nothing for several minutes as we strolled down the street.

Finally, he asked, "Fighting with Charles again?"

"Is it that obvious?"

"Almost midnight and you're out wandering the streets alone and upset—doesn't take a genius to figure this one out."

"Ah, but your IQ is higher than that of the average person," I said to lighten the mood.

Chuckling, he played along. "Well, that *is* true. Have you noticed that we tend to laugh whenever we're together?"

"Now that you mention it…"

He reached for my gloved hand and gave it a friendly squeeze. We climbed the Fisherman's Bastion and gazed across the Danube. The clear night allowed for a breathtaking view of the Parliament.

In an attempt to push Damien from my mind, I said, "Have you seen the Hungarian crown? It's a Byzantine masterpiece. There's a copy of it on the upper floor of the Matthias church. Have you been inside?"

"Yes and yes. Amazing." He hesitated. "There's something I need to tell you…Jennifer called me today. She wants to give us a second chance."

"How do you feel about that?"

46

Caleb squinted, his gaze on the river. "I still love her."

The icy wind tousled my hair and I ran my hand through the tangled locks. "In that case, what have you got to lose?"

"I don't want to risk getting my heart broken again."

"May I offer you a bit of advice?" When he nodded, I continued, "Heal your heart and make it strong. Learn to love yourself and your own company. Never again give in to a woman so easily. Follow those rules and you'll be fine."

He gave me a measured look. "Those are wise words for one so young."

"They aren't mine. Someone gifted them to me."

"A good friend, obviously."

"The best, but now she's gone."

"I'm sorry."

"So am I." I turned to admire the view once more. "Is Jennifer willing to live in Scotland?"

He smiled. "Good memory. Jennifer told me that she misses me more than she ever missed Nevada."

"Smart girl. Good men are hard to find nowadays."

"Thank you for the compliment."

"You've earned it."

"She's departing tonight from the US and will meet me in Scotland. I'm leaving Budapest the morning after Christmas."

"So soon?" I said, disappointed.

"I'll be home on Christmas Day finishing up some work and packing. Promise me that you will stop by to say goodbye. I would hate to go without seeing you."

"I promise."

***

Damien arrived at the flat in a cheerful mood. "Hey," he said, removing his jacket and draping it over a chair.

"Cutting it close," I pointed out while brushing my hair. "The sun is going to rise in less than an hour."

"I wish you could have been there tonight. Fun party."

I seethed inwardly and said nothing as I set down the hairbrush. Crossing the living room, I locked the door since he had forgotten to do so, then got into bed.

He slipped in beside me. "Hey, are you okay?"

Turning my back on him, I made no reply. Nuzzling my ear, he made it clear that he wanted me. Normally, the feel of his hardness against my thighs filled me with lust. My lack of sexual response made him pause.

Urging me to flip over so that he could look into my eyes, he said, "You're not being fair. You told me to go out without you and now you're punishing me."

"I followed you tonight. I saw *her*."

His eyes widened in surprise. "I see. I wanted to tell you about Jeanne."

"I bet you did," I snapped.

"Angelique—"

I cut him off. "Allow me to quote your exact words, 'the only time we need to go near humans is to feed, and we should select those deserving of punishment.' Do you remember saying that?"

"I do but Jeanne is an exception to the rule."

"Oh? Why? Because you like her? All this time you've been lecturing me about associating with humans and here you are sneaking with one behind my back. You're a hypocrite!"

Leaning up on this elbow, his eyes traced the contours of my face. "You have every right to be angry."

"You bet I do."

"You're gorgeous when you're jealous."

I had to refrain from punching him. "I'm hardly jealous of some slut you're grooming to become a vampire."

To my chagrin, he laughed. "I highly doubt that Jeanne Sauvage will ever be a vampire."

Sauvage? "Wait, are you saying—"

"She's my half-sister."

Stunned, I asked, "Is she a slayer?"

"Not really."

"Not really or not yet?"

He shrugged. "She's only a kid."

I sat up in bed. "She didn't look like a kid to me."

"Jeanne is barely nineteen."

"You've never mentioned a sister. How long have you known of her existence?"

"Not long," he replied cryptically. "I've always assumed that I was an only child. Apparently, my father fell in love with another woman during his marriage. Thankfully, my mother never found out."

"Why didn't you tell me about Jeanne? Why keep something important like this from me?"

"Are you kidding me? You have far too many ties to the London lair. I couldn't take that kind of risk with my kid sister."

Kid sister. He made a valid point. "Fair enough. What is she doing in Budapest?"

"I told Jeanne we were coming here. I figured it was a safe city where we could meet and catch up."

"Those nights that you didn't come home—"

"I was hanging out with my sister." Pulling me into his arms, he added, "I bet you were imagining all sorts of horrible things."

His hands moved along the planes of my body, igniting my passion. I bared my throat, allowing him to bite me. The sensuous act felt so good that I moaned in pleasure.

"I love when you make that sound," he murmured against my skin before drinking deeply of my blood.

Damien moved over me and entered my body. I received him, moving in tune with his powerful thrusts.

Putting his lips to my ear, he whispered, "What male on Earth would ever cheat with a female like you in his bed?"

By the time the sleep of the undead claimed me, I felt better. I shouldn't have doubted Damien.

We woke up in each other's arms the next night. After exchanging kisses and sweet words, we got dressed.

"I have many questions pertaining to what you told me yesterday," I said while zipping up my boots. "Does Jeanne know about me?"

"She knows the whole story of us."

"She watched you feed on someone at the Géllert."

"Jeanne is well aware that you and I don't kill our prey. I even explained our unique capacity for providing humans with pleasure when we feed on them. She's cool with it."

I slipped on my coat. "Your association with her is dangerous regardless of whether or not she's cool with it. If Arsham finds out—"

"Fuck Arsham. Do you honestly believe that I care what he thinks?"

"No…but you should."

"Nobody is going to keep me from seeing my sister."

"Half-sister," I corrected.

"Jeanne is the only living relative I've got and vice-versa. She's an orphan."

"My point is that we need to be extremely cautious. Arsham has spies everywhere."

Ignoring my warning, he said, "She wants to meet you."

"Why?"

"I've told her all about you." When my eyes narrowed suspiciously, he added, "She knows you're my lover." He shrugged into his coat, then stroked my cheek. "Come on, let's go hunting outside of the city. I want to take you to this little village I discovered in the countryside."

"I'm really in no mood for loud parties and seedy bars."

"We're not going to either of those places. Tonight, I want to go hunting like old times."

This surprised me. "What's the occasion?"

Once again, I glimpsed a flicker of guilt in his eyes. "You deserve it. I know I've been selfish lately. Relationships are about compromise, right?"

***

Damien had arranged for me to meet his half-sister on Christmas Day. We descended from Old Buda and crossed the river to the main city after sunset. Families strolled through the streets in an attempt to burn off their decadent holiday lunches. I smiled at a pair of toddler twins dressed in identical lavender coats. Each little girl toted a Barbie doll.

Damien placed his arm around my shoulders. "You always did have a soft spot for children."

"I like their innocence."

50

"Yeah. They're cute."

A baby buggy passed and the heavily swaddled infant within it stared at us with guileless eyes.

Damien inquired, "Have you ever fed on a baby?"

I whipped around to stare at him. "No!"

"Never been tempted?"

I frowned at him. "Never. Arsham strictly forbids it."

"Why would Arsham care about the lives of infants?"

Despite being the only Elder who knew the secrets of our sire's past, I said nothing.

Damien studied my face. "You know the reason. Tell me."

I hesitated, then confessed, "Arsham experienced the joy of fatherhood as a mortal."

"You're joking." When I remained silent, he said, "That poor kid must have been pretty messed up. Imagine having a narcissistic psychopath for a father. What other secrets do you know about Arsham?"

"That's it," I lied.

Although he didn't appear convinced, he dropped the matter. "I want to ask you something and I need you to answer honestly."

"Okay."

"Do you miss Arsham?" I hesitated and he removed his arm from my shoulders. "Never mind. I already know the answer."

"Damien—"

Scowling, he sped up his pace. "Come on, we're late."

Catching up with him, I explained, "I spent over two hundred years with my sire and brothers. You can't blame me for thinking about them once in a while—or missing them, for that matter."

"Maybe you should pay them a visit."

The suggestion was made in such a nasty manner that I bit my tongue in order not to argue with him. Some fights simply weren't worth the effort.

Jeanne awaited us in a cozy pub located below street level. The vaulted ceiling of mellow bricks and rough stone walls appeared to be at least five hundred years old. She sat at a quiet

51

table in the back of the dimly lit room. A perfect choice for meeting two vampires in public.

Her face melted into a smile for Damien. "Hey bro."

He kissed her cheek. "Jeanne, this is Angelique."

I sat down. "Hello."

Staring at me in an odd manner, she said, "I've been looking forward to meeting you ever since Damien let me read the Sauvage journal."

My gaze shifted to Damien. "He let you read that?"

"Of course. I *am* a Sauvage," she reminded me crisply.

Damien added, "Jeanne was surprised to learn that you're a French noble."

She asked, "You're a duchess, right?"

"My title no longer carries any weight but, yes. I am a former member of Louis XVI's royal court."

"You were part of the aristocracy that oppressed the people."

Despite her rude assessment, I said pleasantly, "Some of us did, most didn't. I've never oppressed anyone."

"Guilt by association is still guilt. The French Revolution was inspiring."

My eyebrow shot upward. "How so?"

"To punish the oppressors of humanity is clemency; to forgive them is cruelty."

I resisted the temptation to roll my eyes. "You quote Robespierre's words—a man whom I have met on more than one occasion."

Her eyes grew wide. "What was he like?"

"Arrogant, idealistic, and self-righteous." Her dubious expression, prompted me to add, "Professors teach a warped version of history nowadays to push political agendas."

"Revolting against the elite class is always a good thing."

I stared down the girl. "The French Revolution may have begun as a noble cause, but it quickly evolved into something sinister. Armed with their perceived moral virtue, the peasants believed themselves immune to corruption. It didn't take long for these ignoramuses to form angry mobs. They terrorized the city, destroyed historic buildings, and desecrated precious artworks. Worse still, they brutalized and killed innocent people in cruel ways—including the elderly, children, and infants."

Parisian gutters overflow with shit and blood. No one is immune to the vile stench. Not even vampires. Aristocratic babies are torn apart by ravenous dogs. Bloodthirsty mobs cheer them on beneath flickering street lamps. The darkness of night fails to hide their sins. A toddler looks to me for help before being swung against a wall by his tiny feet. Toothless peasants laugh as brains and blood spatter the faded bricks. The little eyes still haunt me… 'Vive la France! Vive la France! Vive la France!'

Jeanne's voice disrupted the disturbing memory. "That's the price to pay for freedom."

I eyed the moronic girl and laughed coldly. *"Freedom?* Robespierre ended up a victim of his own sadistic creation, the guillotine. The French Revolution gave way to violence, famine, and staggering poverty. Then came Napoleon…"

Jeanne was about to challenge me again when Damien, seeing the look on my face, prudently intervened. "I think it's safe to say that Angelique is the expert on this subject given that she actually lived through it."

I returned Jeanne's arrogant stare, daring her to make another ignorant comment.

Steering the conversation toward benign shores, Damien began asking his sister questions about Yorkshire, which allowed me time to study the impertinent girl. I could see the resemblance between Jeanne and her brother. Similar eye color, black hair, high cheekbones. Jeanne's long legs were encased in thigh high boots and she wore a red knit mini dress. The layers of kohl around her eyes and harsh red lipstick failed to hide her youth and lack of sophistication.

Jeanne made an attempt to include me in their conversation. "Have you ever been to Yorkshire, Angelique?"

"Yes and I find it quaint."

"I find it boring. I'm thinking of moving to London to help—"

"Can I buy you another drink, Jeanne?" Damien interjected

loudly while pinning his sister with a hard stare.

Tapping her fingers against her lips, she said nothing more. I noticed that her nails bore chipped blue polish. A look of complicit understanding passed between the siblings.

Finally, she said, "There's going to be a mega Christmas party at Club Play tonight. There will even be a special guest DJ from Ibiza. We should go."

Damien nodded. "I'm up for it but I doubt Angelique will join us. She has to say goodbye to her professor friend."

Jeanne appeared confused. "A vampire?"

"Human," he replied.

She gaped at me. "You have human friends?"

"I made an exception."

She looked to Damien, who explained, "This guy is supposedly famous. What's his name? Carl Morgan?"

"*Caleb* Morgan," I corrected.

Hearing this, Jeanne gasped. "*The* Caleb Morgan?"

Damien frowned. "You've heard of him?"

"You haven't? He's a famous vampirologist who wrote a couple of cool books." Jeanne turned to me and added, "You've got some balls, lady."

Damien shot me an accusatory look. "A fucking vampirologist?"

I said, "He specializes in European folklore surrounding our kind. He writes about other creatures too."

Jeanne inquired, "Does he suspect what you are?"

"No." I was about to say more, then stopped myself.

"I know that look. Tell me," Damien prompted.

"It's just that…He claims to have seen a vampire in London. I think he saw a newborn. A seasoned vampire would never be so careless."

Damien laughed. "Oh this is good."

"No, it's not," I snapped.

"Has he told anyone?" Jeanne demanded.

"He's thinking of including the sighting in the book he's writing now," I replied.

My lover stared at me in shock, then laughed harder.

I looked around to make sure no one was eavesdropping on our conversation. "This isn't funny, Damien."

"It's actually hilarious," he countered.

Jeanne said, "I guess you'll have to kill your friend."

I scowled at her suggestion. "I'm not going to kill Caleb."

"Defying Arsham's law, are we? This night keeps getting better and better," Damien said with glee.

He suddenly stopped laughing and eyed me closely, as though an idea had popped into his head. I couldn't guess what it was but the look on his face made me uneasy.

Jeanne studied her brother's expression before removing a cell phone from her purse. She began texting someone. "I need to let my friend know where to meet us later. Angelique, you really should consider coming with us."

I said, "Thanks but no. Who is your friend?"

She shrugged. "No one you would know."

I understood Damien's desire to foster a relationship with his newfound relative, but I found the girl insufferable.

Jeanne began discussing party plans for New Year's Eve. I listened with detached interest for another fifteen minutes, then stood to take my leave.

"Going already?" Jeanne asked with a private look in Damien's direction.

"It was nice meeting you," I lied.

Damien said, "See you later."

Both of them stared at me as I exited the pub. I stepped out into the cold night and went straight to Caleb's flat.

His face blanched when he opened the door. "Nora!"

"Caleb, is everything okay?"

"Ah, yeah," he replied, still blocking the doorway.

I peeked over this shoulder into the living room. "May I come in?"

"Sure, sure. Come in."

I attributed his strange behavior to anxiety. He was about to reunite with his estranged girlfriend. Offering him a smile, I said, "Merry Christmas."

"Oh, right. Merry Christmas…"

A neat stack of sheets piled on the dining room table drew my gaze. "Did you finish your book?"

"I did. I've already contracted a freelance editor to comb through the manuscript."

"Congratulations. I look forward to reading it."

Smiling nervously, he said, "I ah, I..."

"Caleb, tell me what's going on."

"Oh...Jennifer called earlier."

"Did she change her mind about going to Scotland?"

"No, no. It's not that." He eyed me for a long time, then said, "Wait here."

I watched him go into his room and emerge a moment later with a small box.

Surprised, I said, "Is that a gift? I'm afraid I have nothing to offer you in return."

"That's where you're wrong."

The manner in which he said this made me wary.

"Open it," he urged.

I tugged at the green ribbon and tore the red floral paper. When I pulled the lid off the box, I froze. Inside was a pretty lapis charm attached to a gleaming silver chain.

Shit.

"I chose lapis to match your eyes," he explained in a taut voice as he took a few cautious steps toward me. "Now I see that they are actually darker than the stone."

Arsham always referred to my eyes as midnight sapphires.

I forced a smile. "It's lovely. Thank you."

"Put it on." When I hesitated, he lifted the chain from the box and the offensive metal dangled near my skin. "Here, let me put it on for you."

"I'll wear it tomorrow," I said, pushing his hand away.

"I would prefer you wear it now."

"Caleb—"

Suddenly, he threw the necklace at me. I ducked away from it as quickly as I could without arousing suspicion. The silver chain nicked my cheek, instantly searing the skin. Caleb's face paled in terror as my flesh began healing right before his eyes.

I heard him breathe the word *vampire*.

I had him pinned against the wall by the throat faster than he could blink. "Are you fucking crazy?!"

"Oh God! Please don't kill me! Shit!"

His feet dangled above the floor as I applied pressure to his windpipe. "Do you realize what you've done?"

"You're a vampire!"

"Shut up, Caleb."

"Oh God, oh God…Shit."

"Calm down. *Now*."

"Okay, okay." He exhaled a deep breath. "Don't hurt me."

I relaxed my grip. "Why did you do that?"

"To confirm my suspicion, why else?"

I let go of him abruptly, causing him to stumble to the floor. He clutched his throat and coughed several times. I made no attempt to help as I eyed him coldly. "Any other vampire would kill you right now."

"I'm sorry!"

"Don't *ever* do that again. Do you understand me?"

He nodded so hard that I thought his neck would snap.

"Get up," I said.

He scrambled to his feet and went into the kitchen. Positioning himself behind the counter, he whispered, "Shit."

"Calm down," I snapped while glancing at the ceiling. "Who lives in the building?"

"The old woman who owns this flat lives downstairs and she's practically deaf. Her daughter lives upstairs, but she's vacationing in Fiji so the place is empty."

Relieved that no one had heard him, I said, "What you did to me just now was incredibly moronic."

"Can you blame me? I'm a vampirologist for Christ's sake!"

"What made you suspect my true nature?"

He pointed to a white envelope on the counter. "Someone slipped *that* under my door a moment ago while I was packing my suitcase in the bedroom. I assumed it was a joke at first until I started thinking…Since I had already purchased the necklace yesterday—and I knew that vampires are supposedly allergic to silver—I wanted to test my theory."

Allergic. I almost chuckled at the understatement. I snatched envelope and extracted the note. The slanted, flowery script suggested a female hand. *"She's only out at night. She doesn't eat or drink anything when you're together. She speaks with wisdom far beyond her years. Silver burns her skin. What does that make her?"*

I glanced up at him. "Who gave this to you?"

"I haven't the slightest idea."

"What about the handwriting, do you recognize it?"

"No."

Shit. "If you tell anyone about this—"

Caleb reached for a kitchen knife and wielded it in a most pathetic manner.

I sighed. "Put down the knife. I'm not going to hurt you."

"How can I be sure?"

Grabbing the edge of the kitchen counter, I leaned forward. "After all the wonderful conversations we've shared these last couple of weeks? Trust me, you'd already be dead if I wanted to kill you."

"You were enraged a moment ago. You pinned me against the wall and growled at me. My throat still hurts."

"I only did that to frighten some sense into you."

Warily, he set down the knife. "Isn't there a vampire law forbidding you from exposing yourself to humans?"

"Yes, and this is the part where I'm obliged to kill you, but I'm choosing to overlook it for the sake of our friendship."

"You realize this is the most thrilling discovery of my entire academic career—of my life!"

"I do realize that, but now you've placed me in considerable danger. Yourself too, for that matter. We're only allowed to befriend humans whom we intend to turn into vampires."

His face fell. "I don't want to be a vampire."

My eyebrow shot upward. "You recently sang praises to the concept of immortality. What happened to being like Lestat?"

"I thought about our conversation later that night. Jennifer hates vampires. She finds them scary and so do my parents. I would lose all of my loved ones and be forced to spend eternity alone. Please don't turn me into a vampire."

"I won't."

"Are humans usually given the choice?"

"No."

Eyeing me steadily, he concluded, "I would be put to death for refusing the gift, wouldn't I?"

"Yes."

Caleb exited the kitchen in a pensive state. Wearing a sheepish expression, he bent down to pick up the necklace and placed it on the counter. "I'm sorry Nora."

"I understand why you did it. If I were in your shoes I probably would have done the same."

My confession prompted him to indicate the sofa. "May I ask you some questions?"

I nodded and sat down, then watched in wry amusement as he took the seat farthest from me. "I can smell your fear."

"Predatory trait," he commented, morphing back into scholar mode. "What else can you detect?"

"I can hear your heartbeat. You should take a deep breath before you pass out. I can also sense that you find me more attractive now than you did when you believed me to be human."

"How do you—?"

"Pheromones give off a particular odor. Also, I'm old and experienced."

Caleb swallowed hard and crossed his legs. "I've always dreamed of coming face to face with a vampire. Never did I imagine…I'm at a loss for words."

"It's normal. Take your time."

He stared at me and I read several emotions in his eyes. I imagine encountering an extraterrestrial would incite the same response. Awe, fear, shock, curiosity…

His gaze settled on my gloved hands. "Your hands are always covered by leather gloves. Now that I think of it, the only time I've ever touched your bare skin was at the Turkish bath when we kissed. You felt warm because of the hot water.

Am I correct?"

I removed one of my gloves and moved toward him. Using my vampire charm, I compelled him to remain still as I pressed my icy palm against his cheek.

"Ice cold," he whispered. "Undead."

Retrieving my hand, I said, "Undead, Demon, Monster, Angel of Death...I've been called every one of those names."

"I have a million questions."

"Of course you do."

Adjusting his glasses, he inquired, "How long have you been this way? A vampire, I mean."

"Over two centuries."

His eyes grew wide as saucers. "Holy shit! Sorry. You said you were born in France, is that true?" At my nod, he continued, "Were you there during the Revolution?"

"I lived in the countryside but I was well aware of the horrors taking place in Paris."

"Have you met or seen any famous historical figures?"

"Several."

"I should get my tablet to take notes," he said excitedly as he stood. "No one is going to believe this—"

I prevented Caleb from moving by standing in front of him, only I'd done it so fast that it startled him. "You cannot reveal anything that has taken place here today to anyone. Not Jennifer, not your parents, not the university...*no one*."

"You're a living, breathing history book. This is amazing!"

"Yes it is. I defy every law of nature, I know, but you cannot tell anyone. Please repeat that line back to me."

"I cannot tell anyone."

"Good."

His face lit up in realization. "You've seen and done more than anyone on the planet."

"Not really. There are vampires who are older than me."

"How old?"

"My sire is nearly one thousand years old."

His mouth dropped open then he closed it. "Impossible."

"Believe what you want."

He doubled over and clutched his head. "This is surreal."

"Breathe, Caleb."

"How can you be so calm?"

"I've had over two hundred years to process this whereas you've had less than an hour."

"I need a drink."

Caleb went into the kitchen and poured himself a shot of whiskey with trembling hands. After gulping it down, he poured himself another and looked at me. "Would you like one?" Catching himself, he blushed. "Sorry. All those times I offered you food and wine...I feel like an idiot."

"You didn't know. Besides, alcohol has no effect on me."

"Should I offer you my blood or something?"

I allowed him a glimpse of my fangs, instantly making him regret his words. "If you're offering..."

He blanched. "I only meant...I was trying to be polite."

"I'm teasing you."

Caleb laughed nervously before gulping down the second shot. He debated pouring a third.

Reclaiming his seat, he inquired, "You told me that you were twenty years old. Is that when you were bitten by a vampire?"

"Yes. My sire bestowed immortality on me in order to save me from a life-threatening situation."

Caleb obviously wanted me to elaborate but when I refused, he went on to the next question. "What did it feel like? After you were bitten, I mean. I'm curious about the transition from human to vampire."

I gazed into the distance, recalling my first impression of vampire life. "The initial bite hurt me but in a pleasant manner. It's hard to describe. I blacked out and when I woke up, I felt different. My senses were heightened to a degree unfathomable to humans. The world around me sprang to life and everything became a thousand times more vivid. I could hear things from a great distance and see clearly in the dark. My strength had increased at least twenty fold. I knew things too. Vampiric perception is keen to a fault. Then I felt the painful burn in my throat—the agonizing need for blood. It's indescribable."

His eyes glazed over with wonder. "Wow."

"You would be a valuable addition to our coven, Caleb."

"The agonizing pain and need for blood sounds dreadful."

"In time, you learn to manage the thirst and the pain gradually subsides." I paused. "Are you sure you don't want to join our ranks?"

His face paled. "I'm sure."

I stood. "Very well. I should go."

Glancing up at me, he said, "Please don't go."

"I must." For some reason, a sickening feeling settled in the pit of my stomach. A premonition, perhaps? I stared at him long and hard. "There are thousands of vampires in the world. Our population may be small but we are potent."

"You mean deadly."

"Exactly. Vampires don't take kindly to things like this leaking out into the public. Our kind can hunt down anyone, anytime, anywhere. *Remember that*."

"Are you threatening me, Nora?"

"I'm only warning you, my friend." I went to the door and opened it. "Have a safe trip back to Scotland. I wish you and Jennifer much happiness."

"Can I at least give you a hug?"

"It's best if you don't."

Fear crept into his eyes. "Oh."

I smiled slightly. "Take care of yourself, Caleb Morgan."

I closed the door.

"Wait!"

By the time he exited the flat to chase after me, I had already vanished into the night.

CHAPTER 6

"Profit is sweet, even if it comes from deception."
(Sophocles)

The roof across the street afforded him an unobstructed view of the townhouse and its large windows. He tracked her graceful movements through the glass panes with hungry eyes. She paused before the mirror to brush her hair and his fingers ached to touch the silken strands of burnished gold. His gaze dropped to the reflection of her mouth. Closing his eyes for a brief moment, he recalled her scent, her taste…

New Year's Eve in Budapest demanded fashionable attire, yet she selected a shapeless black dress from the armoire. Watching her divest of the white satin bathrobe caused a stirring in his loins. She was the physical embodiment of perfection until she donned the unflattering garment. Damien Sauvage had managed to dampen her feisty spirit *and* her sense of style.

The insolent slayer was becoming a bigger thorn in his side than he had originally anticipated. There were times he wanted to kill his progeny. Gut him and splay his organs as a hunter would a wild boar. The Elders were aware of disturbing things going on in Budapest. At the last meeting, everyone voted to maintain a discreet distance in order to glean more information. Spies had already been dispatched, and Rahim had admonished him to wait and see.

Wait and see.

Damien was keeping secrets and, sooner or later, Omar's spies would bring everything to light. They had been instructed not to follow the duchess, who would easily detect them and blow the cover off the entire operation.

He had secretly crept out of the coven earlier for a mere glimpse. Now, it was time to go. Tearing his gaze from her lovely face, he flew into the night.

***

Damien and I celebrated New Year's Eve at a popular night club in Budapest. The Artemovsk 38, commonly called A38, was an old military ship with an interior big enough for concerts and an open air deck for parties. Jeanne had chosen this unique venue and Damien had insisted that I accompany them in order not to offend his sister. I complied for the sake of peace. Besides, I had never attended a party on a military ship.

Cocaine and other drugs flowed freely as people rubbed against one another on the dance floor. At one point, the lights dimmed and the music slowed for a few heartbeats. Fog machines worked together with neon lights to create a visual spectacle. The music picked up, the driving beat heightening the drug-induced trips of hardcore partyers. One drunk woman lifted her shirt to expose her fake breasts. A nearby scumbag took full advantage of her inebriation to enjoy them.

I stood in the corner studying the crowd with disdain. How many parties had I experienced throughout the decades? Drugs, fashion, and music changed from one generation to the next, but not the people. *Never* the people. Humans were predictable.

I caught sight of Damien sauntering through the throng of dancing bodies. He feasted on the blood of various humans, morally justified that his victims were social derelicts—at least according to his definition.

Jeanne, on the other hand, spent most of the night flirting with a cute bartender and throwing back shots of tequila.

When the clock struck midnight, Damien materialized beside me and planted a kiss on my lips. "Happy New Year."

"Happy New Year," I said with a smile.

Placing an errant strand of my hair behind my ear, he asked, "Are you having a good time?"

"Sure," I lied.

"Thank you for coming with us tonight. I know this isn't your scene."

"It hasn't been my scene since that horrible night at the Ministry of Music." Rather than kill me for committing treason, Arsham had locked me inside the punishment coffin.

64

"No wonder you hate coming to these places."

I nodded slightly. "Bad memories."

"Why didn't you tell me sooner?"

I shrugged in response. Scanning the room, I saw that Jeanne had disappeared. "Hey, where's your sister?"

"Maybe she went to the bathroom."

I spotted Jeanne speaking with a woman who struck me as familiar. Then it hit me—red wool coat at the New York Palace.

Grabbing Damien's arm, I demanded, "Do you know that blonde speaking with Jeanne?"

He followed my gaze and shook his head. The DJ slowed it down and he led me to the dance floor. "Come on."

"Are you sure you've never seen her?" I insisted.

"Positive." As we swayed to a romantic song, he asked, "Where should we go next?"

"Don't you like Budapest?"

"I do, but I want to be in a city where I can at least understand the language."

In all fairness, Hungarian was difficult. Mastering languages took time—even for vampires. So far, Damien had learned French and Spanish.

"We can return to France," I suggested.

"I've already spent several years there."

"True. You've already traveled through Spain too. How about Chile or Brazil?"

"I was hoping for English."

"We can go to the United States. Have you ever been to New York or Miami?" He made a face so I added, "There's Australia, New Zealand, Canada…"

"I've never been to Yorkshire."

My eyes shifted to where Jeanne stood watching us. The blonde had vanished. "Yorkshire?"

"Yeah, where my sister lives."

I should have guessed. "Two Sauvage siblings so close to London—not a good idea."

"Why not?"

"It's dangerous."

"We'll be careful."

"If you care about Jeanne you won't put her at risk. There's also the fact that she can't stand me."

"You haven't even given her a chance." When I hesitated, he added gently, "At least say you'll try. *For me*."

"What if I hate it there?"

"We'll go somewhere else. I promise."

My nod earned me a kiss on the forehead.

***

Jeanne lived on the outskirts of Staithes, a charming village in North Yorkshire with a sizeable fishing port. She had recently inherited a spacious stone cottage from her mother, and the quaint home sat alongside an empty barn on a large piece of fertile land.

I adapted to the solitude and peace of the windswept countryside with an ease that surprised me. Days easily melted into weeks and, before I knew it, a month had passed.

One night, I found Damien and Jeanne sparring with katanas inside the barn. At the sight of me, they stopped. My gaze shifted from one guilty face to the other. "What's going on?"

"We're messing around," Damien replied.

My gaze settled on the katana in Jeanne's hand. "That's a replica of Damien's ancestral weapon. How did you get it?"

"Christmas gift from big brother," she replied in a challenging tone.

Puzzled, I turned to my lover. "Damien, may I have a word with you in private?"

He cursed under his breath. "I'll be right back, Jeanne."

We walked outside in silence. When we were well out of human earshot, I said, "You're training her to be a slayer."

"She looks up to me and wants to know about our family. I'm teaching her the Sauvage legacy."

At least he didn't insult my intelligence by trying to deny it. "You're playing with fire."

"What's that supposed to mean?"

I got in his face. "You know *exactly* what it means."

"You're blowing this out of proportion. She's only a kid."

"Stop calling her a *kid*."

"Seriously. This isn't what you think."

"Are you sure about that?"

"Come on, Angelique. Jeanne can't even fight." When I made a face, he added, "Stick around and watch so you can judge for yourself."

"I will."

We went back into the barn where I watched them spar for about an hour. True to Damien's word, the girl could barely wield the sword. At one point, he gave me an "I told you so" look that almost made me chuckle.

Convinced of Jeanne's ineptitude, I left the pair to their own devices and sought my new favorite spot. Located about a mile from the cottage, the swell of verdant land faced the sea.

If I arrived at the hill directly after sunset, I could still hear seagulls calling out to one another before seeking shelter from the night. Sometimes, the watery horizon boasted faded streaks of red, orange, and plum. Having only experienced sunlight for two decades of life, I often tried to recall the colors of the sea during the day. I imagined the rocky coast in shades of glistening gray and brown. The water in turquoise, dark blue, and green. My eyes found the moon nestled between two navy clouds and I smiled slightly at the reigning Empress of Night. She cast the colors of the world in a gossamer veil of silver.

A dog barked in the distance and my eyes focused on a man limping along the shore. The dog had managed to get swept up by a wave and would soon drown in the merciless current. Desperate to save his pet, the man entered the water. I flinched when a violent wave toppled him over and threatened to drag him out to sea.

"Get up, get up," I whispered.

The old man stood on shaky legs only to fall again when a huge wave crashed against him. Barking hysterically, the frightened dog receded further from the shore.

I sighed, debating what to do next. "Shit."

Moving too fast for the human eye, I grabbed the animal and placed him on a large rock where he could reach solid ground.

Next, I jumped into the sea and dragged the old man to shore. Even the moonlight couldn't disguise his blue lips.

"Come on," I said before pumping his chest.

Water spurted from his lips and he groaned. I judged him to be somewhere in his sixties.

"Are you all right?" I inquired.

In response, he gripped my hand. Having been in frigid water, his hand was as cold as mine. "Oh Lord!"

Helping him to his feet, I said, "You shouldn't walk along this rocky coast. It's dangerous."

"My dog...Gracie!" His head swiveled left and right as he squinted in the gloom. "Gracie, where are you?"

The collie barked and carefully picked her way along the rocks to the shore. Wagging her tail, she came to stand by us.

"Bad dog!" Turning to me, he added, "She ran after a seagull that was feeding on a dead fish..."

The ornery dog repaid my kindness with a menacing growl. I stared into the animal's eyes until she flattened her ears. Putting her tail between her legs, she whimpered and crept to her owner's side.

The old man frowned. "What's wrong with you, girl? She's usually friendly with people. Sorry about that."

"You and Gracie should go home before you catch cold."

He pointed eastward. "I live past that ridge over there. My wife makes a wonderful kidney pie if you'd like to join us for supper. It's the least I can do to show my gratitude."

Most vampires would jump at the opportunity to feed on the couple. I merely shook my head. "Thank you but no."

"Well, God bless you."

I watched as he retreated along the shoreline. In my world, God was dead. I flew back to the cottage in a thoughtful mood. Jeanne had finished her practice with Damien and was now in the kitchen preparing a late dinner.

She froze at the sight of me. "You're dripping wet."

"I saved your neighbor," I explained.

"Which one?"

"Old man with a collie named Gracie."

Her face darkened. "Mr. Larson. Fuck."

"What's wrong?"

"His wife is a notorious gossip. You didn't tell him that you were staying here, did you?"

"Of course not."

She stirred a pot of what appeared to be neon orange pasta. "Nobody knows that you and Damien are my house guests and I'd like to keep it that way."

I glanced at the box of Mac-n-Cheese on the kitchen counter. How anyone could eat that stuff remained a mystery to me. "You should create some kind of back story for us in case anyone comes poking around here."

Pouring the contents of the pot into a bowl, she said, "Maybe that's a good idea."

"Where's Damien?"

"He went out hunting," she replied before placing a spoonful of orange pasta into her mouth.

I shuddered in disgust. "I'm going to get changed up."

I took a shower, then wandered into the guestroom that Damien and I shared. I was in the process of dismantling and cleaning one of my guns when Jeanne materialized in the doorway. This time, she had a beer bottle in her hand.

She took a sip then asked, "What kind of gun is that?"

"Glock 43."

"Do you have others?"

"Several. Knives too."

"Cool."

"The world only knew pistols when I was your age." I held up the gun and admired its design. "I can only imagine what Louis XVI would have done with this technology."

"What kind of a childhood did you have?"

The question caught me off guard and I paused for a moment. "My mother died giving birth to me. My father pawned me off on my aunt, whom I adored. The years I spent with her were the best of my human life."

"Are you as deadly as Damien says you are?"

"Most vampires would say yes."

"What do *you* say?"

"I trained for many decades and know how to use every hand weapon known to man. I served as a personal bodyguard to my sire and kept my coven safe."

She took a long sip from the bottle, eyes glued to mine. "Will you teach me? Train me to be like you?"

"To hunt vampires?"

"Yes, but not the ones like you and Damien. You guys are cool because you don't kill humans."

"Teaching you to fight my own brethren would be a huge betrayal to my coven."

She nodded pensively. "Until the day when humans are spared, I prefer to fight vampires."

"I understand your position, Jeanne."

"Then help me."

"I can't."

"Damien said that Arsham and your brothers kill people. The fact that you love them despite this makes you guilty too."

Lowering my eyes, I said, "That's not fair."

"Oh no?"

"You can't expect sharks or cheetahs to not kill their prey. Predators hunt to eat. That's our nature."

"There's a big difference between animals with inherent instincts and sentient beings with the power of choice."

Touché. "You're absolutely correct. I foster the hope that Damien and I aren't the only ones who believe in sparing the lives of mortals."

"Well?"

"I still can't help you."

Frustrated, she nodded and said nothing more.

Damien strutted into the cottage and approached us. "Hey. What's going on?"

Jeanne tilted her head in my direction. "Angelique is a hero. She saved my neighbor and his dog."

He quirked an amused brow at me. "Really?"

I rolled my eyes and offered him brief details.

Jeanne eventually said, "I'm going to bed. See you guys

tomorrow."

After she had shut herself inside of her bedroom, I said to Damien, "It's only three in the morning. That's early for you."

He shrugged. "Maybe I want to spend time with you."

"That's pretty rare these days."

"I know, and I'm sorry."

How many times a week did he apologize? "Jeanne asked me to train her. You told the girl I was a warrior."

"I spoke the truth. You should have seen her face. She really admires you."

I doubted that but kept silent.

He continued, "Are you going to help her?"

"You know I can't."

"You mean *won't*."

"I refuse to betray my coven."

"You mean betray your sire."

"Damien, knock it off. I'm not going to train a slayer."

He laughed but it sounded forced, almost rehearsed. "She's not a slayer, Angelique. She's only a kid who wants to learn a few self-defense moves from a pro who has been at it for centuries. Can you blame her?"

Damien's insistence on the usage of the word "kid" grated on my nerves. Resisting the urge to shove him across the room, I said, "If all she wants are self-defense moves, you're more than qualified for the job."

"Whatever. I don't know why you hate my sister so much."

I chose not to dignify the rude comment with a reply.

***

Being so close to London, it was impossible not to think of Arsham. If he knew that Damien was training a slayer, he would be furious. Duty demanded that I try and put a stop to the madness—or at the very least report it to the coven.

Damien made another attempt to convince me to train Jeanne. I refused and it led to an argument. Disgusted, I sought my spot on the hill to calm down. The rhythmic sound of the waves and crisp salty air soothed my frazzled nerves.

Arsham...

Gorgeous, lethal, and stubborn were apt descriptions for the arrogant vampire prince. What was he was doing at the moment? When the twins were alive he would go out on the town with them almost every night. Deirdre and Chiara had served as his constant companions; pretty playthings that drew the attention of mortals. Dressed to impress in expensive clothing, the trio had frequented the best bars and had enjoyed the most exclusive VIP lounges in the city. Throughout the years, they had gorged on the blood of London's elite.

Now that Deirdre and Chiara were dead, I couldn't help wondering who had taken their place. Who warmed my sire's bed? Certainly, there had never been a lack of stunning vampires willing to please their handsome leader.

What do you care what Arsham is doing or with whom?

No one was in the barn or the cottage when I returned from the sea. Jeanne had left her laptop on the coffee table so I surfed the web for a bit and checked to see if Caleb's book was available for purchase. It still hadn't been published so I would need to check back at a later date. There were many "Caleb Morgan" forums listed under his website, so I clicked one of the links. It took me to a page announcing a lecture in anticipation of his upcoming book, *Vampire Mythology*. The talk was scheduled for tomorrow evening at a cultural salon in Edinburgh that often featured writers and musicians.

Reservations were requested in advance and could be made online. My finger hovered over the "RSVP" option button for only an instant before I pressed it. Feeling giddy, I went into the guestroom to decide what I would wear for the event. Naturally, I revealed my plans to no one.

I meandered through the cobbled streets of Edinburgh the next evening in a pair of slim jeans, brown leather boots, and wool blazer. Blending in with the graduate students and locals at the cultural salon, I made my way toward the back of the room where I wouldn't be noticed by the speaker. Bookshelves and tasteful paintings adorned the walls, and a baby grand piano occupied a corner of the room. When the space was filled to maximum capacity with standing room only, a young man in a knit turtleneck and jeans stood before the audience.

"Good evening everyone," he said, pausing to allow people to take their seats. "My name is Robert Kramer and I'm Dr. Morgan's Teaching Assistant. Tonight, the professor will be offering a lecture on the folklore surrounding two mythical creatures: vampires and werewolves. Light refreshments will be served in the foyer afterward. Now, it is my pleasure to present, Dr. Caleb Morgan, Head of Parapsychology at the University of Edinburgh."

I applauded along with the rest of the people as Caleb strutted out in a casual wool blend suit and V-neck sweater. Stylish yet not pretentious. New glass frames highlighted the pleasant features of his face.

"Hello everyone and thank you for coming," Caleb said. "Tonight's lecture will appeal to your imaginations..."

People by the doorway moved to allow a latecomer. Instantly, I was overwhelmed by the stench of cat piss and incense. Wrinkling my nose, my eyes darted to Elek as he took a reserved seat up front beside Robert, whom I presumed was "Rob the TA."

Elek's eyes scanned the room, presumably searching for me. I remained semi-hidden behind several people while Caleb extrapolated his theories on my species. The shifter appeared annoyed throughout the entire presentation. Obviously, my vampiric scent drove him crazy.

Caleb was mobbed by people at the lecture's conclusion. Some wanted him to sign his last book and others wanted him to pose for selfies. I melted into the background and patiently waited for an opportunity to speak with him. The moment he was alone, I circled the room in order to approach my friend from behind.

"Hello Caleb," I purred.

The skin of his nape prickled at the sound of my voice. Slowly, he turned around to face me. Elek came over to us at once. I stared at the shifter, who glared at me in return. His youthful inexperience was clearly reflected in his fearful eyes. I compelled the shifter to calm down with my vampiric charm.

Caleb inquired, "What are you doing here, Nora?"

"The same as everyone else. I came to listen to your lecture."

He laughed nervously. "How did you know about it?"

"I saw it on an online forum and couldn't resist." Indicating Elek, I added, "Aren't you going to introduce us?"

"This is Elek, the graduate student who gave me the tour of the labyrinth in Old Buda. I told you about him."

I extended my gloved hand to the shape shifter. "Nice to meet you."

Elek reluctantly shook my hand.

Caleb said, "I'll be mentioning him in my author's note in the book. Elek's help has been crucial to my research."

The shifter narrowed his eyes at me. "Dr. Morgan said you were interested in vampires."

"It's a topic near and dear to my heart," I replied smoothly.

Rob appeared and urged Elek to exchange notes over glasses of wine in the foyer. I watched the shifter walk away with a neutral expression on my face.

The moment the young men were gone, Caleb led me to a quiet corner of the room. "I haven't stopped thinking about you since Christmas…I still have so many questions."

"I'm sure you do. How are things with you and Jennifer?"

"Couldn't be better. She was hired by a real estate firm last week and had to work late tonight, which is why she's not here."

My eyes shifted to where Elek stood watching me from the foyer. "You *do* know what he is, right?"

Puzzled, he followed my gaze. "Are you referring to Elek?"

"He's a feline shape shifter. I suspect he'll tell you what I am soon enough."

Startled, he demanded, "How do you know?"

"That doesn't matter."

"You're natural enemies."

I shrugged. "Shifters work with slayers, so…"

"I'm surrounded by supernatural beings," he murmured, awestruck.

"Lucky you." Extracting a book from my purse, I said, "Would you sign my book?"

"*Night Creatures*. You really are a fan. This book was inspired by my dissertation."

"I know. I downloaded your dissertation and read that too."

He reached inside his coat for a pen and scribbled on the inside cover of the book. "I'm flattered, to say the least."

"Others want to speak with the famous vampirologist and here I am monopolizing your time."

His mottled green eyes met mine. "There's no one more captivating in this room than you, Nora, and I mean that."

I smiled at the compliment. "I know you do, my friend, but I should go."

"Please don't. We can get a drink when I'm done here. Well, I'll drink and you can pretend."

"Tempting but no."

"Are you still in Budapest?"

"No."

When I didn't offer any more information, he said, "I know, you can't tell me. I hope to see you again soon."

I placed my face so close to his that his pupils dilated with excitement. Showing him the tip of my fangs, I whispered, "My offer is still open…"

A touch of fear colored his features as he shook his head.

I retreated. "Goodbye Caleb."

I cut through the throng of people and headed toward the exit. Looking over my shoulder, I caught Caleb staring after me with a wistful expression.

Catching sight of Elek in the foyer, I approached him. "Do me a favor and take care of him, will you?"

The shifter flinched. "Who?"

"Caleb, of course."

"Don't worry about that."

"Thanks. He means a lot to me."

Elek gaped at me as I exited the cultural salon. I stepped into the chilly night and hurried up the street with quick steps. I darted into an alley to read what Caleb had inscribed in my book. *Nora, meeting you was one of the highpoints in my life. Thank you.*

CHAPTER 7

"War scenes are less difficult than love scenes."
(Jean-Jacques Annaud)

I arrived in Yorkshire before dawn and tiptoed into the cottage. Jeanne slept peacefully in her room and Damien wasn't yet home. Crossing the expanse of the living room, I noticed his jacket draped over a chair. My gaze was instantly drawn to a single strand of golden hair on the fabric. It wasn't uncommon for human hair or makeup to get on our clothing during a feeding. Unfazed, I brushed it off and continued to the guestroom. There was no sign of my lover, and he wasn't in bed when I woke up the next night. I went in search of Jeanne and found her foraging through the refrigerator.

"Hi. Have you seen Damien?"

"Not since he left last night." Closing the refrigerator door, she studied me. "Don't you know where he is?"

"Do you?"

Her eyes twinkled. "I'm sure he'll be home soon."

Something about the way she said this rubbed me the wrong way. Convinced that she knew of Damien's whereabouts, I pressed, "Are you sure he didn't tell you?"

Scooping her car keys off the counter, she replied, "Why would he? None of my business. Going out, be back soon."

Red tail lights lit up the front yard as she pulled away from the dirt driveway. I ventured out into the darkness toward the hill where I could sit and think. The tumultuous sea indicated a coming storm. Wind tugged at my hair as I studied the slow course of a commercial fishing vessel heading toward the port.

I smelled the dog long before she began barking.

"Stop that, Gracie!"

To my relief, Mr. Larson walked his dog along the hill's crest rather than the shore. Not wishing to be seen by him or anyone else, I zipped down to the shore below and sat on the farthest rock. The waves crashed around me and I relished the sound and feel of their power.

After a couple of hours, I took off toward the village. By then the wind had died down. The quiet before the storm. People lingered in front of shop windows as I casually strolled down the main avenue. A brightly lit coffee shop brimmed with college students. I studied the young people with a discerning eye. What a blessing for them to have been born in an age of wondrous technology. Human youths were healthy, flaunting shiny hair and unblemished skin. No warts or pustules or missing teeth before the age of twenty-five. Many of them wore silver and gold jewelry, precious metals that only the nobility could afford in my day.

I continued down a side street past a dingy bar catering to fishermen. Peeking through the mullioned windows, I spotted Damien leaning against an old juke box.

I went inside and walked up to him. "What are you doing?"

"Hunting," he replied, his eyes darting nervously.

"Where have you been?"

"I can ask the same of you."

I hadn't told Damien about my meeting with Caleb in Edinburgh. I wasn't in the mood to argue with him so I reached into my pocket and fished for a coin. Pushing it into the slot, I selected a song. Loud music poured from the speaker.

A nostalgic smile touched his lips. "I remember that song playing in the background while making love to you in the bedroom of my old flat in London."

"Felicia almost walked in on us," I reminded him.

"I miss those days," he confessed huskily.

"Me too."

Damien's eyes were drawn to the window, compelling me to turn my head. I glimpsed a blonde retreating from the bar.

"Are you expecting someone?" I inquired.

"What? No." Damien gathered me to his chest and nuzzled my neck. "Let's hunt."

Eyeing the inebriated crowd, I nodded in response to his

suggestion. We poured more money into the jukebox and selected songs that would appeal to the salty men and women who lived by the sea. Their suntanned faces bore deep lines, and their dull gazes reflected the physical and mental hardships endured by fishermen.

I wandered to the bar and selected a seat beside a ruggedly attractive bearded man. His gnarled hands were no doubt a result of pulling up heavy nets.

He glanced at Damien before giving me a measured look. "Did you fight with your lover boy over there?"

"Maybe."

"Looks like he doesn't miss you."

Damien was already chatting up a woman in a skirt much too short for her age.

I shrugged. "I don't care."

"In that case, I'll buy you a drink."

I reached for his whiskey and placed the glass to my lips. "I'll have a bit of yours if you don't mind."

Leaning back, he frowned. "You're not from around here."

I set the glass on the scarred wooden bar, then ran my fingers along his thick wrist. Meeting his eyes, I compelled him to kiss me. When he moved forward, I avoided his lips and bit him on the side of the neck. I drank very little, certainly not enough for him to pass out. To anyone watching, I was simply sharing a secret. In a flash, I healed the wound and held him until his dizziness passed.

Damien eyed me from across the room and indicated the exit with a slight nod of his head. I slid off the stool and we left the bar together.

***

I woke up alone the next night. The lights were on in the barn and I heard the familiar clash of katana blades. I had only watched Jeanne practice on a couple of occasions, and I wondered if her skills had improved under Damien's tutelage. Exiting the house, I made a beeline toward the barn. A revolting stench accosted me and I spotted a feline shape shifter slipping through the barn entrance.

"Shit," I cursed, hastily scanning the area for slayers.

"Harry! Come in."

I froze at the sound of Damien's friendly greeting. How did they know each other? I crept to the back of the barn and positioned myself beside a dirty window to spy on them.

"Felicia sends her greetings," said the shifter.

Felicia? Of course! I peered through the dusty glass and studied the young man with renewed interest. Red hair, pale skin. The resemblance was strong.

"Thanks. I miss her a lot. Hey Jeanne, come and meet Harry. I used to live and work with his older sister." Damien placed a hand on the shifter's shoulder. "I sent Felicia a letter explaining what your role will be to Jeanne."

Harry nodded. "She has been training me."

Jeanne shook his hand. "Hi."

Damien smiled. "It's my hope that you two will work together like Felicia and I did. We made a great team back in the day. Why don't you two spar for a bit? Harry, you can use my katana."

Harry gripped the weapon and lunged at Jeanne in a savage manner. To my astonishment, Jeanne fought back with impressive ferocity. I watched in astonishment as she ducked, lunged, and parried with graceful precision. She knew how to fight, which led me to the inevitable conclusion that she had been faking in my presence.

Damien's complicity in this charade made me sick.

Self-defense, my ass.

I staggered back to the cottage in a troubled daze. Pacing the room, I rehearsed what I would say to my lover the moment he walked through the door.

When Damien arrived to take cover from the sunrise, I confronted him. "You invited a shifter here without so much as consulting with me. I can smell him from here! What were you thinking?"

"*Consult* with you? This is Jeanne's home, not yours."

"You know what I mean."

"It's not like you've been expressing much interest in Jeanne or anyone else for that matter."

"Don't turn this around and make it my fault."

Glancing at the window, he said, "Sun's almost up. We need to sleep. Let's talk about this tomorrow."

"I thought this whole thing was harmless at first—"

"What are you talking about?"

"Training Jeanne to fight. Consorting with a shifter."

"Remember Felicia? That's her brother in the barn. Harry is excited to be paired with the last human Sauvage on the planet so don't ruin this for everyone."

I shook my head in disbelief. "As an Elder, I can't allow this to continue. Arsham would—"

"I DON'T CARE!"

I recoiled as Damien glared at me.

He continued, "If you mention your sire's name in my presence one more time, I'll—"

Jeanne burst into the cottage. Looking from me to her brother, she demanded, "What's going on?"

"Nothing," Damien replied through clenched teeth.

Rather than go into the guestroom we shared, he stormed outside and slammed the door.

***

Harry practiced with Jeanne in the barn during the day, then retreated to his rented room in Staithes at night for a few hours of sleep. Under Damien's supervision, they fought until human exhaustion overtook them. They maintained this rigid schedule for over a week, then Harry drove back to London. I don't know what sort of arrangement he made with Jeanne. Damien offered curt replies to my questions and remained aloof toward me.

One night, I said to him, "I've been thinking that maybe I should take off for a while."

Rather than express dismay, he snapped, "Back to Arsham?"

Admittedly, the thought of returning to the London lair had crossed my mind more than once. "I don't know."

Damien took hold of my chin, forcing me to meet his gaze. "I never intended for things to be this way."

"You've been shutting me out for months and now you're

outright ignoring me. What did you think would happen?"

"I'm not shutting you out, Angelique. You're the one with the problem. You're against Jeanne's training."

"You're teaching her to kill vampires!"

"You didn't have a problem with slayers when you fell in love with me."

Frustrated, I ran my hands through my hair. "You know what? I won't be a bother to you or Jeanne any longer."

He hesitated. "Don't go."

"Give me one good reason to stay."

"I don't like the idea of you taking off alone right now."

"What do you mean by *right now*? What's going on?"

Oddly, he seemed nervous. Suspiciously so.

He shrugged in a contrived manner. "Like you said, I'm training a Sauvage to be a slayer. If anyone finds out, it could be dangerous for you."

"For us *both*," I corrected.

Jeanne ran into the room. "Damien, I need to show you something." Glancing at me, she added, "In private."

I noticed that she held a Kindle e-reader in her hand.

"Can't it wait?" Damien said, his eyes glued to mine.

"It will only take a sec, bro."

"We'll talk about this later, Angelique," Damien said before tracking his sister into the next room.

The door remained slightly ajar. Peeking through the crack, I saw Jeanne pointing to something on the tablet's screen. They shared a meaningful look then retreated outside. I shuffled into the guestroom defeated. The rift between Damien and I had grown into a canyon.

I awoke the next evening to Damien hastily shrugging into his long black leather jacket. "Hunting in the city?"

Sparing a glance in my direction, he replied, "No."

"Why the rush?"

"I promised Jeanne that I'd meet her in the village. I don't want to keep her waiting."

My eyes went to the katana hilt sticking out the back of his jacket collar. "You're taking your katana to the village?"

"Yeah...I need to get it sharpened. Routine maintenance."

"About last night—"

"Don't bother." He tossed a glance in my direction and added, "We'll talk later."

He left the cottage and flew into the night at alarming speed. Something felt wrong. I got ready and took off for the village center of Staithes. The moon played peekaboo with sooty clouds while I searched for Damien. I couldn't find him anywhere. He told me that he was meeting Jeanne, so I checked the eateries and pubs. They weren't there. I did a final scan of the streets before returning to the countryside.

The black windows of the barn and cottage made me uneasy. Where the hell were Jeanne and Damien? I let myself into the cottage and paused. My eyes darted to the door of Jeanne's room and I debated whether or not to invade her privacy.

"Screw it," I said, barging into the room.

I searched for clues in her drawers and desk but found none. After turning on her computer, I checked the browser history and discovered that she had purchased an online train ticket to Edinburgh Waverley station. The train had departed this morning from Staithes at six-thirty. I shut down the computer and stood, perplexed. My eye fell on the Kindle e-reader atop the night stand. She had shown Damien something last night.

Self-publishing has become surprisingly profitable these days...I recalled Caleb's words with a stab of panic. I grabbed the small tablet and swiped through Jeanne's library of electronic books. Featuring Bela Lugosi as Count Dracula on the cover, *Vampire Mythology* by Dr. Caleb Morgan was included in the collection. The new release bore yesterday's date and already boasted several five star reviews.

"Oh no..."

I clicked on the vintage cover and skimmed through the digital pages of the book. Not only did Caleb include the vampire sighting in London, he dedicated a chapter to me: *Nora the Vampire*. I threw the tablet on the bed and dashed out into the night. Hopefully, it wasn't too late.

***

My first stop after arriving in Scotland was the University of Edinburgh. It didn't take long to locate the engraved brass plate on the office door that read: DR. CALEB MORGAN. I picked the lock and slipped into the dark room. A large window ledge supported a row of healthy plants and smooth beach stones. Caleb's diplomas and credentials were featured on the wall behind his desk, but the opposite wall boasted a huge vintage black and white print of Sir Christopher Lee as Dracula.

The faint scent of Caleb's aftershave clung to the fabric of his ergonomic chair. I rifled through the papers on the desk while cursing the man's stupidity. Once I found his address and located it on Google Maps, I descended into the city. I knew that Damien and Jeanne were prowling the area in search of vampires so I employed extreme caution. My anger and resentment at having been tricked by the Sauvage siblings bubbled to the surface as I crossed a cobbled street.

Damn them both!

Something moved in the shadows. Fortunately, it was only a stray dog. I proceeded toward Caleb's apartment building with mounting anxiety. The historic edifice was four stories tall with a red brick face. I checked the names on the doorbells and noted that "Morgan" occupied the third floor. The apartment was devoid of light. Pushing away the disturbing images cramming my head, I forced myself to picture Caleb in a cozy Scottish pub having dinner with his girlfriend. I imagined them laughing over pints of beer and having a good time.

It was wishful thinking, of course, for the nocturnal breeze carried the unmistakable stench of death. Rather than use the stairs, I scaled the outside of the building and crawled through the window. The odor of the initial stages of human decomposition accosted me as I stealthily tiptoed through the living room. I visually traced the silhouette of two corpses seated upright on the sofa. Closer inspection revealed that they were Caleb and a woman whom I presumed to be Jennifer. Their necks bore tell-tale puncture wounds, their bodies bled dry. Judging by their state of decay, they were killed a couple of hours ago. Had I not wasted time looking for Damien in

Staithes, I could have probably saved them.

Damn it.

Angling my body, I stared into Caleb's eyes. Once full of life and humor, his empty gaze filled me with grief. What a terrible waste of a brilliant mind. Had he heeded my warning, he would be celebrating the success of his book.

The air in the room shifted slightly and my skin prickled. Turning around, I spotted two male vampires clad in black. I didn't know either of them.

The one closest to me stepped forward. "Angelique de Nuit you are under arrest for the crime of treason."

"What?"

He grabbed my arm. "You must come with us."

"Get your hands off me. Is Arsham here? You need to take me to him."

The other male grabbed my free arm. "Please don't make this more difficult than it already is, my lady."

I snarled at them. "Arsham may be in danger, you fools!"

My words fell on deaf ears. Furious, I wriggled free and kicked one of them hard in groin while shoving the other away from me with such force that he slammed against the wall and shattered the plaster. Newborns were no match for me.

Throwing open the door, I fled the flat and ran down the hallway. Before I could reach the stairs, a solid mass stepped into my path. Two big hands gripped my shoulders, forcing me to an abrupt halt. I knew that scent anywhere.

I was no match for the powerful vampire who held me.

"Angelique."

The two males ran out of the apartment and Arsham shook his head slightly, signaling for them to back off. They retreated to the opposite end of the hallway and stood like a pair of sentinels, their eyes burning into my spine.

Arsham searched my face. "What are you doing here?"

"Damien Sauvage and his half-sister are in Edinburgh…I have reason to believe they're looking for you."

"*Looking* for me?"

"Hunting you," I admitted, averting my gaze.

Taking hold of my chin, he forced me to look at him. "What made you befriend a man like Caleb Morgan in the first place?"

I stared at him incredulously. "Did you hear what I said, sire? There may be a shifter with them."

"A shifter? I see. Why wait until now to warn me?"

His eerie calmness unnerved me. "I only discovered their wicked plot a few hours ago. I came here as fast as I could."

"To save your friend or to warn me?"

I hesitated then confessed, "Both."

"Were you unaware of Caleb Morgan's profession? Really, Angelique, a vampirologist of all people?"

"He is—*was*—an impressive scholar who stimulated my intellect," I replied, cleverly evading the first question.

Arsham quirked an eyebrow. "Had your slayer been up to the task you wouldn't be in this compromising position."

I lowered my head in shame for I couldn't defend Damien.

He continued, "I imagine that a man like Caleb Morgan must have proved a refreshing change from your own personal Savonarola. Don't you find your lover's angry tirades tedious? I imagine it must be difficult to sit through countless lectures on morality and the vileness of vampirism."

My brow creased. "How do you know...?"

The faintest smile touched his sensuous lips as he finally loosened his grip on me. "I know many things, my child— things of which you are still unaware."

"How did you find out about Dr. Morgan's book? That's what drew you here in the first place, right?"

He nodded, his eyes narrowed. "My hackers are always on the lookout for things like this on the Internet. Dr. Morgan's book was red flagged."

"Had I known that Damien and Jeanne were planning to come here and stalk you, I would have stopped them."

"I believe you, but that doesn't excuse many of the things you've done these past months—or rather, *not* done. You failed to see the potential danger. You've become careless."

"I've failed in many things, it's true. I don't deserve your forgiveness," I admitted contritely.

He put out his hand. "I'll be the judge of that." He watched as I genuflected and kissed the blood ruby on his finger, then continued, "I was disappointed that you didn't come home when I retracted your banishment. You could have shown your gratitude with a brief visit. Remember, you are still an Elder."

"I meant no offense, sire."

"So here we are," he said with a wave of his hand. "Damien Sauvage is once again involved in a plot to assassinate me, and he has embroiled you in his scheme. He knew you would try to rescue the professor and he predicted that I would be here for two reasons…First, to interrogate and kill the man who wrote the book and, second, to confront you about it. He must know the danger in which he's placed you, and how badly this makes you look in the eyes of the coven."

The same thoughts had already crossed my mind. Damien had conspired behind my back with Jeanne without any regard for how it would affect me. "I have no defense other than ignorance."

He regarded me thoughtfully before marching me outside to where my brothers stood across the street. I wanted nothing more than to embrace them both, but now was neither the time nor the place for such displays of affection.

Micah, devoid of contact lenses, stared at me with his reddish albino eyes. "Sister, it gladdens my heart to see you even in dire circumstances."

Beneath our sire's scrutiny, Valerio hid his happiness to see me with a tight smile.

"Greetings, brothers. Where's Omar?"

Micah replied, "He remained in London with Rahim. What are you doing in Edinburgh?"

"I came to warn our sire," I replied.

"You openly renounce the slayer?"

"As you know, I am loyal to Arsham and his coven."

"That's not what Micah asked you," Valerio said while taking a step closer to me. "This is the second time Damien has plotted against our sire. It is time for you to break ties with him—*forever*."

Micah added, "The Elders demand that you be brought to trial for treason."

Not another trial. "No…"

"We don't manage thousands of vampires by allowing crimes to go ignored and unpunished."

"No treason has been committed," I protested.

Micah narrowed his eyes at me. "You must have been aware of certain things, yet you deliberately kept them from us."

"I never thought Damien would stoop this low."

Valerio's perfectly groomed eyebrows knitted together in concern as he placed a hand on my shoulder. "You're still an Elder and must be held to a higher standard. It's your obligation to put the coven first."

I nodded in agreement to my brother's words. "I admit that I turned a blind eye to certain matters that I perceived as trivial, but there's a lot that I didn't know."

A white windowless van sped down the street and parked in front of Caleb's apartment building. Three vampires carrying cleaning supplies exited the vehicle and filed into the edifice. The dead bodies would be eliminated and everything in the flat would be spotless within the hour. Our professional cleanup crew consisted of former police officers and detectives who knew a lot about deleting evidence.

Micah said to Arsham, "Two tickets to Malta were purchased using Dr. Morgan's credit card. We also sent an email from his account informing the college administrators that he'll be taking a much needed holiday."

Valerio added, "Our hackers are on social media performing damage control. They're mocking Morgan's book to destroy his credibility. A few of his students are already calling him a fraud and others are suggesting a mockumentary about vampires."

Arsham nodded his head in approval. "Good."

Valerio's gaze settled on my face. "That ghastly book put us all in danger. What kind of name is Nora, anyway?"

"One of my aliases. How did you know it was me, anyway?"

"Who else would dare befriend a vampirologist?"

Micah interjected, "Did you know he was going to include a

87

chapter on the vampire feeding he had witnessed in London?"

"No," I lied.

Crossing his arms to show disapproval, he accused, "You revealed yourself to him."

"Not willingly," I protested. "Dr. Morgan threw a silver necklace at my face, then saw my skin heal instantaneously."

My brothers stared at me in horror.

Micah said, "Had you not spoken with him in the first place, he would never have had the chance to act upon his suspicion. This is why Vampires should only approach humans to feed. I shouldn't have to tell you this, Angelique."

Damien told you the same thing countless times…

"I met Dr. Morgan by chance in Budapest. He informed me that he was doing research on Vlad Tepes during the Romanian prince's imprisonment by King Matthias Corvinus."

At this, Arsham flinched but said nothing.

I continued, "Dr. Morgan's knowledge and passion for folkloric legends intrigued me. I confess, I'm a fan of his work."

Micah rolled his eyes. "There's nothing wrong with admiring talented humans from afar. You crossed the line."

"We met only a few times during my stay in Budapest and I was always cautious, I swear."

"Not cautious enough, apparently. We need to know what you told him. Exactly, word for word."

I went on to describe the harmless topics that I discussed with Caleb. My sire and brothers listened with stoic expressions on their chiseled faces. I stopped speaking when the cleaning crew emerged with two black body bags. I watched in dismay as they dumped Caleb's corpse into the back of the van.

Oh Caleb…

The vehicle detached from the curb and sped into the night. I stared at the red tail lights until they vanished around a corner. Three sets of vampire eyes studied me in the ensuing silence.

Finally, Valerio said, "Seeking human company is a sign of loneliness. Come home, Angelique. We miss you."

Micah added, "London is where you belong. You should be with your own kind. It's safer, not to mention easier."

Arsham stepped between me and my brothers. "Enough!"

Micah and Valerio retreated and said nothing more.

Arsham turned his dark eyes my way. "There is only one way to rectify this wrong and avoid a trial."

"Tell me and I'll do it, sire," I said.

"You must prove your loyalty to me and to the coven. I will accept no less from you."

I glanced nervously at my brothers before inquiring, "What do you want me to do?"

"Show us through your *actions* that you had no knowledge of this plot."

"Sire—"

Arsham held up his hand to silence me. "Before you say another word, think hard on the matter. This is your chance to redeem yourself, keep the peace within the coven, and be reinstated as an Elder without incident…"

"What are you asking of me?"

"You must be the one to hunt down the slayers."

CHAPTER 8

"It is not enough to conquer; one must learn to seduce."
(Voltaire)

My mission of redemption required that I change out of my impractical dress and heels. I broke into a clothing shop and found what I needed: black tights, rubber-soled black boots, and a black jacket. I was now able to move without restriction and blend seamlessly into the darkness.

Taking on both of the Sauvage siblings at once would prove challenging. The wisest course of action would be to track the human first. After scaling an apartment building, I jumped from rooftop to rooftop in search of Jeanne. Pausing at the top of the highest building, I scanned the area. My eyes and ears were meticulously in tune to every sound, every movement. The imposing Edinburgh castle stood atop a hill silhouetted against pewter clouds and an iridescent moon. The wind howled like a banshee, whipping my hair into a mass of tangles. Inhaling deeply, I caught the overly-sweet drug store perfume favored by Jeanne. It came from the direction of Mary King's Close.

Fog settled upon the Old Town as I prowled the narrow cobbled streets like a stealthy shadow. In the distance, a clock tower struck midnight. A few pubs were still open at that late hour, and the occasional laughter and silly chatter of drunkards floated upon the breeze. Faint beeping sounds pierced the night and I tracked them to Jeanne's hiding place. Crouching within the entrance of Mary King's Close, she texted someone on her cell phone.

Swooping in, I grabbed her from behind. "Hello Jeanne."

She dropped the device, cracking its face. "What the fuck?!"

I kicked her cell phone across the street. "The trail you left may as well have been a neon sign. Maybe you're not as bright as your big brother has led you to believe."

"Piss off, Angelique. Why don't you go and kiss Arsham's ass? That's where your loyalty lies, isn't it?"

Tightening my grip, I said, "My sire's name is unworthy of your tongue."

Flailing her arms wildly, she screamed at the top of her lungs. A light went on in the building across the street, compelling me to drag her into the shadows.

"Shut up," I said, clamping my hand over her mouth.

She liberated one of her hands and managed to unsheathe her katana, cutting into my wrist. The deadly blade sliced so deeply into my flesh that I was forced to temporarily loosen my hold on the brat. Apparently, Damien had taught her some useful tricks. I shoved the girl away from me, making her stagger toward the curb.

I caught movement out of the corner of my eye and turned my head in time to see a male slayer racing toward me with a raised sword. I ducked and reached for my Glock, only to realize that I had foolishly left it at Jeanne's cottage. Thinking quickly, I scaled the wall and flipped in the air to land behind him. The fool spun toward me and I roundhouse kicked him in the face. Arms flailed as he fell flat on his back. I grabbed the sword from his grip and plunged the blade into his belly. The man grunted in pain as he expired in the street.

Jeanne came at me with her katana and I slashed at her arm with the dead slayer's sword. As she staggered toward a nearby wall to assess the damage, an ear-piercing yowl echoed in the darkness. Seconds later, a giant cat sprang out of the alley. Scratching my face, the shifter jumped onto my back in order to give Jeanne a chance to recuperate. The crafty animal clawed at my head and shoulders while kicking up a racket. Pinching the fur behind the cat's neck, I whipped it against the side of parked car. I did this more than once. The badly injured beast fell to the floor and shifted back to its human form.

"Elek?" I expected to see Harry, not the Hungarian graduate student.

Jeanne came at me again. I ducked when she lunged, then punched her hard in the stomach. The air escaped her lungs so violently that it made a whooshing sound when she doubled over. I took the opportunity to wrestle the katana from her hand. The weapon fell to the ground with a soft clang.

"You bitch!" she croaked, reaching for the dagger tucked into her boot.

In a daring move, she threw it at me. Catching the weapon in midair, I then flung it downward so fast that she didn't have time to react. The sharp blade sliced through her jeans and lodged itself in her thigh.

"Ow!"

"I said *shut up*."

I ended the brawl with a final punch to her face. I admit, it felt good to hit the Sauvage brat. Blood spurted from her broken nose as she fell onto the slick cobblestones in a pathetic heap.

Elek pulled a gun on me. "Freeze."

Before he could blink, I broke his hand and he dropped the weapon. Terror crept into his eyes.

I aimed the gun at him. "Who put you up to this?"

He shook his head. "No one, I swear. I arrived this morning to see Dr. Morgan. He's having a party tomorrow to celebrate his book release."

"Liar!"

"I saw you from the alley…Something compelled me to intervene. Call it instinct."

"And the gun?"

"I ah…I…"

Deception oozed from his pores so I snapped his neck.

Tears gathered in Jeanne's eyes as he dropped to the ground. "Please don't kill me."

"How long have you been working with him?" I demanded, ignoring her melodrama.

"I never saw him before."

Eyeing the dead slayer in the street, I added, "I bet you don't know him either, right?"

"Yeah, I knew him. You'll pay for what you've done."

"Your threats mean nothing. Face it, sweetheart, you're no match for me."

The familiar sound of an ancient blade being unsheathed made the skin of my neck prickle.

"She's not, but I am."

"Don't do this," I said over my shoulder.

"Turn around and face me."

"This will only end badly. Walk away."

"I've been walking away for a long time, Angelique."

I finally turned around.

Damien stood twenty feet from me with his katana drawn. His eyes were on Elek. "Who the hell is this?"

"Don't know," I replied.

Seeing the dead slayer, he cursed. "You killed Jake."

"Jake tried to kill me," I shot back.

His gaze shifted to his half-sister. "Get up, Jeanne."

"I can't," she said, pointing to the knife hilt sticking out of her thigh.

He frowned. "Jesus Christ. Did you have to do that?"

I shrugged, unrepentant. "This is your fault."

Damien said, "Get up, Jeanne. *Now.*"

My eyes slid to Jeanne as she desperately tried to retrieve her katana. In a flash, I kicked the weapon out of her reach.

He took a step forward. "Angelique, don't you dare!"

My muscles coiled, ready to strike. "You said she wanted to be a slayer. Well, I'm presenting her with a real fight."

He hissed in anger. "Goddamn you! Jeanne, run!"

Jeanne scrambled hastily to her feet and began limping across the street. "Oh it hurts…it hurts!"

The moment I turned to chase after her, Damien flew at me with his katana raised above his head. I only had a split second to decide: go after Jeanne or fight Damien. I allowed the girl to escape as I blocked the slayer's savage blow. The gun fell from my hand and I had the good sense to kick it far from us so that he couldn't use it against me. Damien lunged at me again and I parried defensively. A swooshing sound made me look to where Jeanne had stood only three seconds ago. The girl was gone!

"Where did she go?" I demanded, scanning the area.

Damien ignored my question. "You just had to save him,

didn't you?"

I ducked his punch. "You set me up!"

"You shouldn't have come here."

"Damn it, Damien! How could you?"

"This has nothing to do with you."

Furious, I shoved him. "It has everything to do with me."

"Arsham and your brothers have always taken precedence over me in your heart. Well, my sister casts a shadow over *your* spotlight. How does it feel to be in second place?"

I picked up Jeanne's katana and wielded it with the expertise that came from decades of training. We were both excellent fighters but he had given himself ample time to prepare for this betrayal, whereas I had not. That alone was enough to afford him the advantage, yet he fought with a savagery that shocked me. Slamming me against a crumbling concrete wall, he ground his body into mine.

He wrestled the katana from my grip and said, "Do you know what the best part is?" I struggled to free myself but he placed the wicked blade to my throat. "You don't want that pretty head of yours to fly, do you?"

"There's no best in anything you've done here tonight," I shot back through clenched teeth.

"Oh but there is...*You* are the one who gave us this opportunity. For once, I'm actually grateful that you befriended a human. By the way, that fool's blood is on your head."

"Shut up," I snapped, despite the fact that he was correct. Caleb's murder was indeed my fault. Jennifer's too. "You failed tonight. As for your sister, she's probably bleeding to death around the corner."

"Sooner or later, I'll succeed."

The katana's honed blade gleamed in the moonlight. I stared into the slayer's eyes; I saw fury, guilt, remorse...

Suddenly, he shoved me to the ground and flew into the night. My face hit the cobblestones hard enough to split open the skin. I rose up on my elbows and surveyed the empty street and darkened apartment buildings. No witnesses. I stood and placed my hand on a nearby wall to steady myself. Blood oozed from a deep wound in my arm and I applied pressure to staunch the flow.

"Hurry up and heal," I whispered as red rivulets streamed down my pale fingers.

The two males who had accosted me earlier in Caleb's apartment emerged from the alley. Silent and efficient, they removed the pair of dead corpses from the street.

A lone figure emerged from an alley. Smooth white hair shone like ivory under the glow of a street lamp. He picked up Jeanne's damaged cell phone and Elek's gun, then came over to me. "You've lost a lot of blood."

"Micah, how long have you been there?"

"From the beginning." He bit into his pale wrist and held out his hand to me. "Here."

Beads of blood glistened like rubies in the moonlight. I latched my mouth onto the wound and sucked only enough to recuperate my strength before relinquishing Micah's wrist. I left him and went to the corner in search of Jeanne.

He ran after me and grabbed my arm. "Come on, let's get you cleaned up."

I shook him off. "I need to find her."

"Jeanne Sauvage is long gone."

"How? I put a knife in her thigh. She's limping."

"She was rescued by a vampire."

"A vampire?" I repeated. "Who?"

"We need to go. *Now*."

I said nothing more as he led me down a few streets to Old Town Chambers, an establishment consisting of luxury apartments. Arsham occupied the grandest unit in the building. Stone walls, candelabras, tapestries—the spacious flat mimicked medieval style yet came equipped with every modern comfort and technological convenience.

Our sire stood gazing thoughtfully at the night view from the window as two guards granted Micah and I access to his presence. I noticed that he had changed into a designer suit.

Micah cleared his throat. "Sire?"

Arsham turned around, his eyes sweeping over my

bloodstained clothes. His gaze never wavered from my face as he sauntered toward me. Touching what remained of the deep gash on my cheek, he frowned. "It's a sin to mar that face."

Having said that, he retreated across the room to the window with Micah in tow. He listened intently to his son's hushed testimony of what had occurred by Mary King's Close. I overheard every word from where I stood. Micah had indeed been there from the very beginning yet he did nothing to help me. Arsham eventually bade Micah goodnight. My brother crossed the room and headed for the door so I followed him.

"Angelique, stay," Arsham said in a clipped tone.

Micah gave me a pointed look then left me alone with our sire. The silence between us stretched, long and uncomfortable.

Finally, I said, "I'm sorry I failed. At least I managed to kill the shifter and the slayer. I'll be better prepared next time."

Eyeing me steadily, he said, "About those two…"

"The shifter was a Hungarian graduate student who aided Dr. Morgan during his research trip to Budapest. As for the slayer, I don't know his identity."

"The London slayer's name is Jake. As for Elek, you spoke with him here in Edinburgh. Recently, I might add."

The fact that he knew this alarmed me. "That's correct, sire. I was introduced to Elek after attending one of Dr. Morgan's lectures."

Going to the sideboard, he poured blood wine into two chalices. "One of the benefits of co-ruling with my half-brother is unlimited access to this rare and delicious wine."

"I have no idea what Elek was doing here tonight, I swear."

"I know."

"Micah said that Jeanne was rescued by a vampire. Who?"

Not bothering to reply, he offered one of the vessels to me. "Here. You need this."

When I didn't move, he urged, "Drink."

I took a sip, relishing the instant buzz. I did need this.

He continued, "Rahim served this special treat to you when you went to his coven in Russia, did he not?"

I replied cautiously, "Yes…"

Peering into the contents of his chalice, he added, "I like it."

"Sire, are you going to tell me what's going on? Who saved Jeanne?"

Arsham set down his drink and pretended to study one of his gold cufflinks. "Why don't you take a bath and change into some clean clothing."

"You continue to change the subject and ignore my questions. Why?" When he didn't reply, I added, "What about the Sauvage threat?"

He smiled faintly. "I'm in the company of my stealthiest vampire, one of the best warriors our coven has ever known."

Resigning myself to the fact that I wasn't going to get any answers, I said, "I don't deserve your faith in me."

"Only time will determine if that's true or not." Pointing to the shopping bags on the plush sofa, he added, "I'm sure you'll find something to your liking in one of those. The bathroom is through there."

His eyes tracked my steps as I grabbed a handful of glossy bags. Gucci, Prada, Dior—Arsham's generosity was legendary.

Seeing my puzzled expression, he said, "I knew you would come to Edinburgh tonight."

"Did you think I would betray you?"

"Would I have purchased clothing for you if I did?"

I made my way into the bathroom where a lovely copper tub filled with scented water stood surrounded by candles. Peeking over my shoulder, I saw that Arsham had retreated to the spot by the big window. He made no attempt to look at me as I removed my tattered clothing. Easing into the hot water, I sighed in relief and pleasure. Most of my wounds had already healed themselves, including the one on my face. I stretched out at the bottom of the tub, completely submerged. I remained in that position for several minutes.

Damien's betrayal stung. Things had been bad between us, but *this*? His need for vengeance had destroyed our relationship. I had loved only two males in my life, and both of them had hurt me. One would think that a warrior vampire such as myself had no need for human sentimentality. Perhaps my craving for love stemmed from the fact that I had never known that sacred emotion during my human years. My distant father and sadistic husband had treated me as mere property.

My thoughts shifted from my past to the vampire prince who awaited me in the other room. I recalled how easily I had given my fragile heart to him after I became a vampire. Lacking sophistication, I had showered him with the pure and innocent love of youth.

You've never stopped loving him…

Acknowledging my feelings for Arsham was akin to opening Pandora's Box, for the potency of those emotions possessed the power to wreak havoc in my world.

The sobering thought prompted me to sit up in the tub. Slicking back my wet hair, I opened my eyes to find Arsham staring at me. Neither of us moved nor spoke for a long moment. I eventually stood, making no attempt to cover myself. Hungry eyes roamed over my firm wet body but he remained rooted to the spot. To my astonishment, he turned his back on me.

I exited the tub and dried myself off. Reaching for the shopping bags, I noticed that each one contained a complete outfit. I chose a Dior dress in deep blue silk with a pair of gold strappy heels. At the bottom of the bag was a small blood red box and a note written in Arsham's firm hand: *I knew you would pick this dress.* Nestled inside the box was a pair of gold Cartier earrings cradling two gorgeous sapphires.

I dressed then studied my reflection in the mirror. The blood wine had restored color to my cheeks and lips, thus eliminating the need for cosmetics. My luminous skin and shiny hair begged to be caressed.

I exited the bathroom and noted the smug look on Arsham's face. "I'm impressed. How did you know I'd pick this one?"

"I know you better than you know yourself."

His words unsettled me. "Thank you for the dress, the shoes, the earrings…"

"Do you like them?"

"Of course. I don't deserve any of this, sire."

He refilled our chalices. "I believe a conversation between

98

us is long overdue, wouldn't you agree?" I nodded and he continued, "I've been looking forward to this day."

A few hours ago I feared that my sire would punish me. Now, I stood before him in an outfit worth thousands of dollars sipping rare blood wine. Of one thing I was certain: life in Arsham's world was never dull.

He led me to a set of overstuffed chairs facing a fireplace. We settled across from each other and I couldn't help but admire the way the golden light of the flames accentuated the flawless beauty of his honeyed skin.

He said, "Micah informed me that you fought in earnest. I understand why you failed in your mission tonight. I'm not as unreasonable as you may believe me to be. It's difficult to fight—*to kill*—someone whom you once loved."

"That's not why I failed, I assure you."

Long tapered fingers caressed the stem of his chalice as he stared into the flames. The muted light from a floor lamp glinted off the blood ruby, transforming the expertly-cut stone into crimson fire. "There's something I need from you."

"As you wish."

"Your loyalty to me and to your coven must come from your own heart and from your own desire."

I stared at him incredulously. "Sire?"

"I'm talking about free will, Angelique."

This was not the Arsham I knew. "With all due respect, I thought our existence revolved around duty, protocol, sacred laws..."

"I have lived by that code of conduct for nearly a millennium. I don't want that anymore."

I ventured cautiously, "Is this Rahim's influence on you?"

He bristled. "Why would you ask me such a question?"

"It's not like you to dismiss protocol."

"There are thousands of divinities in this world who demand love and exclusive devotion from their worshippers. Is it wrong that I desire the same thing?" He paused, allowing his point to sink in. "I am a god who has thrived on fear for too long."

He had never referred to himself in such a manner and it left me speechless. I glimpsed the weight of eternity in Arsham's eyes and could have easily drowned in those fathomless pools had I not averted my gaze. Did all vampires feel this way after a certain amount of time? Would we all evolve into the realm of divinities? A blood soaked version of Nirvana?

Is this what awaits me in the future?

"Why are you telling me this?" I whispered.

"I've always been able to speak freely with you. Do not deprive me of that pleasure."

"I would never deprive you of anything, sire."

His eyebrow shot upward. "Except your company."

"I didn't think you wanted me back at the lair."

"It may surprise you to know that the ten years you were in the punishment coffin were difficult for me."

"Ten years is nothing to a vampire of your advanced age."

"True, but I had never been away from you for so long…I missed your presence in the coven, as did your brothers. Your behavior hurt many of us."

"I never meant to cause pain to anyone."

He moved forward and touched my cheek. "Do you recall journeying to the East with me?"

Why was he bringing this up now? "How could I forget? We stood on the Great Wall of China before the sunrise. The memory is indelible. One of my fondest, in fact."

"Mine too." He leaned back in his chair and regarded me thoughtfully. "I trusted you with many intimate details about myself that night. I recounted my childhood, and the tragedies which led me into vampirism. Do you remember?"

"I do, and I have never betrayed your confidence."

"Never told anyone? Not even *him*?"

"*Never*, sire."

"You chose Damien Sauvage over your coven. *Over me*."

I lowered my head in shame. "I'm sorry."

"For seeing the folly of your ways now that your lover has deceived you?"

"You have reason not to trust me, sire. Allow me the chance to prove myself. As for Damien, we've been at odds for months.

Long before tonight."

"You still love him."

"Not anymore." Not for a long time.

"I'm relieved to hear this."

Meeting his eyes, I confessed, "I was wrong about so many things, Arsham. I wish I could go back and change the past. I swear that I will strive to be worthy of your forgiveness."

Arsham's eyes glistened in relief, allowing me the slightest glimpse of vulnerability. His stoic mask was back in place a split second later, thus concluding our intimate tête-à-tête.

He opened the drawer of the antique mahogany table nestled between the armchairs. Extracting a manila envelope from the snug compartment, he said, "Earlier this evening you asked how I knew about the current state of your relationship with Damien Sauvage. My best spies have been monitoring him ever since you and he departed from Grand Cayman."

I frowned. "Why would you do that?"

"According to your brothers, you and Damien displayed vastly different reactions to the news of your banishment being lifted. Were they wrong in their assessment?"

"Damien resented—*resents*—you, sire. He detests being a vampire and refuses to conform."

"I know. Micah and Valerio advised me to keep a close watch on the slayer. Insisted upon it, in fact. I allowed them to make arrangements with Omar. Your brothers were extremely concerned for your safety on several occasions, and even attempted to convince me to intervene."

"Why didn't you?"

"I wanted you to come to your own realizations and conclusions where Damien was concerned."

My eyes were drawn to the big manila envelope in his hands. "What's that you're holding?"

Wearing a pained expression, he placed the envelope in my lap and stood. "I'm sorry."

Arsham *never* apologized. I stared at him in confusion as he crossed the expanse of the apartment and exited the room.

CHAPTER 9

"Men's vows are women's traitors!"
(William Shakespeare)

I ripped open the envelope and pulled out a stack of blown-up photographs taken with a long-range camera lens. Damien seated at a café table with an attractive blonde. Damien and the same blonde strolling hand in hand along a moonlit river. Damien and the blonde kissing at a bar. Damien and the blonde holding each other on the deck of a night ferry—*in Budapest*.

"What the hell?" I whispered aloud.

The last photograph in the stack made me gasp. It depicted Damien, the blonde with the red wool coat, and Jeanne seated at a table in the New York Palace café. Caleb and I had been captured in the background. Contrary to popular belief, vampires did cast reflections and these photographs proved it.

I tore my gaze from the disturbing image to stare at the orange and gold flames in the fireplace. My mind spun furiously with the possible ramifications of what this meant. The fire greedily consumed the wooden log in the same manner that Damien had sucked the joy from me these last few months.

I assumed his drastic change after departing Grand Cayman had been due to his lingering resentment of being a vampire. What's more, I foolishly believed that he would get over it with time and learn to accept his fate.

The envelope fell from my lap. All but one photograph spilled onto the floor. I heard the soft click of a door and footsteps coming toward me.

"*Sorellina*," Valerio said, lifting me from the chair and taking me into his arms. "Betrayal is always a hard blow."

It was considerate of Arsham to send Valerio to comfort me. Clinging to my brother, I said, "I'm a fool."

"No, he's an asshole."

I held up the photograph taken at the New York Palace café. "I was there with Dr. Morgan."

"We know."

"I had no idea that Damien was also there, or who Jeanne was at the time."

"We know that too."

"Who is the blonde in the red coat?"

"A Russian vampire by the name of Katya. One of Rahim's Elders. She was an ambassador in the London lair."

"Ambassador?"

"Two alphas governing one coven requires a bit of strategy. Although Rahim is in London right now because of this situation, he spends most of his time in Russia. Some of our London vampires reside in Moscow. Likewise, a few Russian vampires remain with us. It makes for good relations."

"Not to mention the opportunity to spy and keep tabs on one another," I added, knowing full well the real reason for such an arrangement. "Tell me about Katya."

"Rahim often left her in charge of the Russian coven in his absence, until he discovered that she was turning vampires against him. There was a terrible argument and she disappeared shortly afterward." He paused. "How long have things been tense between you and your lover?"

My brow creased in thought. "Everything went downhill after you saw me in Grand Cayman."

"According to our spies, Katya made contact with Damien shortly after we saw you."

I glanced down at the photograph and studied Katya's face with renewed interest. "Why?"

"We believe she wants to challenge the sires."

"That's a serious accusation, Valerio."

"Who else could successfully assassinate two powerful leaders than a Sauvage slayer turned vampire?"

"Damien said he had no prior knowledge of his half-sister's existence until recently."

"He knew of her existence after Katya made contact with him. We believe she may have introduced them. I was there when Damien presented Jeanne with the replica of his katana."

"What do you mean you were there?"

"Disturbing reports began coming in from our spies. Arsham sent me to confirm them."

The puzzle pieces fell into place. "Damien claimed that he needed time to ponder his existence, and began hunting alone a few nights a week. Since he was a young vampire, and we all come to terms with immortality in our own way, I didn't think anything of it. When that excuse wore thin, he drastically changed his hunting habits. I loathed feeding on derelicts so we rarely hunted together."

Valerio winced. "I hate to say it, but he was with Katya when you weren't with him."

I mulled over that sobering bit of information. "If you've known all along that something bad is brewing, why not kill Katya and Damien—and Jeanne, for that matter?"

"We don't know *everything*. Katya is sly and nearly as old as you. She could have already turned other vampires against our coven leaders without our knowledge. There may be spies among us who have been instructed to retaliate if anything were to happen to her or Damien. Arsham and Rahim are employing extreme caution in this matter."

"A prudent strategy."

The door opened and Arsham entered the room. "I take it you've been informed on the current situation, Angelique?"

Current situation. A bland term for my world being brutally capsized. I merely nodded in response to the question.

Arsham said, "Thank you, Valerio. We leave in fifteen." He waited for Valerio to go before giving me an expectant look.

"Katya saved Jeanne tonight, didn't she?"

"Yes."

I showed him the photograph in my hand. "When Damien saved your life by decapitating Severin, I believed there was some hope. I was wrong."

Folding his hands before him, Arsham squared his shoulders and peered down at me. "Immortality doesn't make us perfect. Our instincts, although sharp, aren't totally immune to the contamination of powerful emotions."

I gathered the photographs from the floor, then walked over to the fireplace and tossed them in it. The flames consumed the paper, burning holes through Damien's face. Katya's too. It felt good to watch the pair disintegrate into ash.

Arsham removed a small photograph from his pocket and held it out to me. "Don't forget this one."

I gasped at the sight of Katya standing outside of Caleb's rented flat in Budapest. "She wrote the note!"

"What note?"

"I paid Dr. Morgan a visit prior to his departure. Someone had left him a message insinuating that I was a vampire. He confirmed his suspicion by throwing the necklace at me."

Come to think of it, Jeanne had texted someone at the pub after having discovered that I was Caleb's friend. Could she have contacted Katya? The level of deception and treachery to which the Sauvage siblings had stooped sickened me.

I continued, "How could I have been so blind? So stupid?"

Arsham opened his arms in response and I went into them without hesitation. For the first time in a long time, I felt safe. Nuzzling my cheek against his chest, I sighed contentedly.

He pushed me away. "We're going to London."

"What about tracking Jeanne and Damien?"

"Thanks to you we have Jeanne's cell phone. Micah hacked into it and discovered that she's been in contact with a pair of London slayers. One of them was Jake, the mortal you killed tonight. After what has transpired between you and the Sauvage siblings, I'm certain they'll reconfigure their strategy."

"What makes you think that?"

"Now you're on our side."

***

We arrived from the four hundred mile journey a bit before sunrise. After all these years, I still found it amazing at how quickly our kind can cover great distances. Flanked by Micah and Valerio, I tracked our sire's steps through the maze of the underground lair in London. I ignored the stares and whispers tossed in my direction. The guards turned sharply down a side corridor while the four of us continued to Arsham's chamber.

Once inside, I admired the familiar Oriental rugs, precious antiques, and the great gilded mirror from Versailles. Seeing the latter brought back a flood of memories from the eighteenth century, including the night when I had first met Arsham—the handsome and exotic courtier.

Arsham watched me closely, gauging my expression. Omar joined us a few minutes later.

My brother embraced me. "Welcome back, Angelique."

Arsham placed a hand on Omar's shoulder. "I need to brief you on what's happened." To us he added, "I'll see the rest of you tomorrow evening when the Elders convene."

We filed out of our sire's chamber.

Micah looked at me after our sire closed the door. "I imagine the meeting won't be pleasant for you."

His blunt honesty could always be counted upon.

Valerio took my hand. "Come, I'll take you to your room."

"I no longer have a room," I pointed out.

Micah said, "Valerio has always held on to the hope that you would return."

Valerio added, "You're going to love it."

Leave it to an eighteenth century homosexual to decorate a room to perfection. My spacious chamber boasted the Rococo style, complete with crystal chandelier, frescoed ceiling, and gilded mirrors. Fresh pink roses bloomed in an antique porcelain vase by the bed, and an exquisite hand-cut crystal decanter held a copious amount of delicious blood wine.

"Do you like it?" Valerio asked with an exaggerated wave of his arm. The expensive gold and diamond watch on his wrist gleamed in the soft rosy light of a tasteful lamp.

"Madame Pompadour would be proud."

"I knew you'd come back, Angelique. Although, I thought it would be sooner than this…Better late than never they say."

"I've thought about coming back to London many times."

"Damien is a fool to let a vampire like you slip away."

"I thought…"

When I trailed off, he said, "You're sentimental, which is

rare in a vampire. I suppose I am too."

I flicked my wrist at the room. "Only someone with heart and vision can pull of this kind of amazing interior design."

We both chuckled and he said, "Let me know if there's anything you need."

I looked down at my new Dior dress. "I'll need to get some more clothing. Everything I own is in Yorkshire and I have no intention of going back there."

"Got that covered, *sorellina.*" He threw open the doors of an antique armoire and I gaped at the row of neatly hung garments. "I had fun picking them out for you."

I ran my hand along the beautiful fabrics. "An outfit for every occasion. Thank you."

"Being back in London will be an adjustment for you—"

"I'm grateful for Arsham's mercy and the affection of my brothers. I've been a fool for too long."

"Love can make a fool of anyone."

"Damien—"

"Ah!" Valerio said, holding up his hand to silence me. "We only mention his name when absolutely necessary. Deal?"

"Deal."

"This is a new beginning for you. Everyone is happy you're back—*especially* our sire."

"I feared that I had disappointed Arsham to the point of earning his rejection."

"Our sire loves his creations in a way a father loves his children, but with you it's always been more than that."

"Deirdre and Chiara too," I pointed out.

He smiled wryly. "Not even close. Those two brats were used for his entertainment."

"What was I used for?"

Valerio quirked an eyebrow and didn't reply. Instead, he said, "You should get some rest. I'll see you tomorrow."

The moment he exited the room, I stretched out on the canopied bed and admired the vintage gold brocade fabric. I thought about my brothers and my sire. Emotionally spent, I closed my eyes and drifted off to sleep at sunrise.

I exited my chamber the next evening in a fitted black cashmere sweater, charcoal pants, and black boots. I donned the earrings my sire had gifted me, put my hair up in a chignon, and applied cosmetics with discretion. My outfit was both somber and tasteful. I was under no pretense about this meeting; I knew I would be judged as if I were on trial.

I made my way toward the main areas of the lair where the majority of vampires congregated. A hush fell upon the crowd when they spotted me and a path was cleared for me to pass. Some faces expressed joy, others skepticism. I took special note of those who displayed contempt.

With head held high, I made my way to the spacious octagonal room where my trial was held over a decade ago. Suppressing a shudder, I paused at the doorway and listened to the chatter of the Elders. The moment I crossed the threshold, they fell silent. Micah caught my eye from across the room and indicated the empty chair beside him. Ignoring the stares of those already seated, I made my way toward my brother with confident steps.

Rahim intercepted me. "Angelique."

I stopped and inclined my head in respect. "My lord."

"Allow me to be the first to welcome you home," he said loudly enough for everyone to hear before bringing my knuckles to his lips.

Like Arsham, he dressed to kill in finely tailored suits and smelled divine.

"Thank you," I said, grateful for the warm welcome.

He put his lips to my ear. "Arsham told me what happened last night. As far as I'm concerned, your loyalty is not in question. Some Elders disagree and I'm sure they'll state their opinions today. Please know that not everyone feels as they do."

"I appreciate the warning."

"I've missed your lovely face. I look forward to hearing your insightful views on the impending dilemma before us."

Rahim stepped aside, allowing me to pass and take my seat beside my brother.

"Just so you know, Rahim has always spoken up in your defense," Micah whispered after I had settled in the chair. "By the time this meeting is over, you will have more friends here than enemies thanks to my testimony. Valerio's too."

"I appreciate your faith in me, Micah. I don't deserve it."

"On the contrary. Were it not for you, Rahim would have killed Arsham and—although it pains me to admit this—Severin would have killed our sire if Damien hadn't intervened."

"Damien did that for me, not Arsham. He's regretted it ever since and still dreams of vengeance."

Looking splendid in a tailored black pinstriped suit, Arsham entered the room and took his seat beside Rahim. Both thrones were magnificent; equal in size and value. To my relief, the two alphas appeared to be at ease with their shared role.

Arsham lifted his hand and the Elders fell silent. "As you can see, one of our lost sheep has returned to the fold. The Duchess de Nuit has proven her loyalty to me and to our coven last night in Edinburgh, where she fought valiantly against the Sauvage slayers. Both escaped, unfortunately. She did manage to kill the well-known London slayer, Jake Nisman, and a Hungarian feline shifter whom we know only as Elek."

Whispers and gasps filled the room as several sets of eyes slid my way.

Arsham continued, "Damien Sauvage has been training his half-sister to continue the murderous family legacy."

Rahim said, "He has once again betrayed our coven and Angelique is here to testify."

"Testify? Why should we trust her? Damien was her lover!"

"That's Andrei," Micah whispered in my ear.

I recalled the ex-KGB prick with a grimace. He didn't like me when he had met me in Russia, and he obviously didn't like me now.

I stood and stared at him. "With all due respect, sir, have you never made an error of judgement?"

"Perhaps when I was a human," Andrei shot back.

"I am happy to learn from one as perfect as you."

Some in the audience snickered at my comment but the old vampire offered me a cold smile.

Mayu stood and gave me a dirty look. I recognized her as the same Elder who had doubted me when I had been in Russia.

She said, "Given Angelique's track record for deceit, how can we believe anything she says?"

Arsham replied, "Why not hear the testimony of Micah and Valerio so that you may judge for yourself?"

I gave Micah's hand a squeeze as he stood and recounted his findings over the last several months. I maintained my composure despite the pain of listening to my brother reveal several disturbing things about Damien and Katya. Discovering the truth under such public circumstances served as a blow to my pride. Valerio also spoke on my behalf. The Elders stared at me in contemplative silence by the time my brothers had concluded their testimony.

"It seems to me that Angelique de Nuit is the victim here."

This assessment came from a mature female. I had never seen her before but I would certainly go out of my way to meet my new ally.

"Speak your mind, Jazmin," Rahim said.

Jazmin rose from her seat. "It's obvious the duchess had no knowledge of what Damien Sauvage was doing behind her back. I certainly wouldn't suspect treason from the man who had saved my sire's life." Her comment evoked a few nods before she continued, "Angelique de Nuit is guilty of giving a fellow vampire the benefit of the doubt—a vampire who took advantage of her affection and trust."

I offered the astute Elder a grateful smile.

Rahim said, "I agree."

Arsham gave a firm nod. "I concur."

The sires stood from their thrones, signaling the conclusion of the meeting. Andrei and Mayu appeared annoyed as they eyed me with contempt.

"I've made a couple of enemies," I whispered to Micah.

He followed my gaze. "Those two are difficult. Pains in the asses, actually. Jazmin is a powerful ally. Perhaps you should go and speak with her."

"Good idea."

Jazmin's silver hair and wizened eyes were at odds with her trim figure and modern style. Seeing my approach, she turned toward me. "Hello Angelique."

"I appreciate what you said today."

"I only spoke the truth. I've heard a lot about you, and it's nice to finally pair the name with the face."

"I can only imagine the negative things you've heard."

"You'll be pleasantly surprised to learn that it wasn't all bad." Glancing at Valerio, she added, "Your brothers never gave up hope. They knew you would return to your rightful place someday."

"They obviously know me better than I know myself."

"They brag a lot about you. To some of the newborns you're regarded as a legend. I overheard a few of the young males talking…" She trailed off and chuckled. "They referred to you as the Warrior Goddess."

I shook my head, amused. "Hopefully, I'll soon be training some of them. That's what I did before…"

"Ah." She paused. "Give it some time. It won't be long before you regain what you've lost."

"I hope you're correct."

She tilted her head to the side and changed the subject. "You were in Budapest recently. That's where I was born. I haven't been back in decades."

"Budapest is wonderful. One of my favorite cities, in fact."

Her sad smile spoke volumes. "My parents died during the Great Turkish War when the Duke of Lorraine laid siege on Buda in an attempt to seize it from the Turks. I was destined to perish alongside my family on that fateful day in 1684 but a vampire offered me an alternative to death."

"Rahim?" I inquired, intrigued.

She nodded. "I've been by his side ever since that day."

"Arsham chose each of us for our unique talents. May I ask why Rahim chose you?"

"I can see things."

111

"You're a psychic?"

"I practice divination. In Budapest, I was highly paid by members of the nobility to read their cards and create astronomy charts for their children. My parents began exploiting my talents at a young age."

"Impressive."

"Not nearly as impressive as your skill. I've never met any vampire who could detect shape shifters. You should know that Rahim admires you very much. He's never wrong when it comes to judging someone's character."

"I'll take all the friends I can get."

"Don't be too hard on yourself, Angelique. No one in this coven is above reproach."

"I broke a sacred law and was found guilty of treason."

"You've paid the price for your sin and you've proved your loyalty, so take comfort in that. You're fortunate to have Arsham as a sire. He believes in you."

"I am lucky, indeed," I agreed with a glance in Arsham's direction.

He caught my eye and smiled at me.

Jazmin followed my gaze. "I met your sire for the first time shortly after the merging of the two covens. I also spend considerable time in the London lair."

"Oh?"

She met my gaze and said pointedly, "I've never seen Arsham crack a smile—*until today*."

"His prodigal child has returned," I said wryly.

"Do you believe that's the only reason?"

I shrugged. "Yes."

Jazmin looked at Arsham again. This time, an odd little smile played upon her lips.

CHAPTER 10

"The pattern of the prodigal is: rebellion, ruin,
repentance, reconciliation, restoration."
(Edwin Louis Cole)

During the first week of my return, I kept to my quarters and only crept out to hunt. Valerio and Micah showed up at my door at the onset of the second week.

"You can't stay in here forever," Valerio said once inside the privacy of my chamber. "As fabulous as your room is, you need to come out and socialize with the rest of us."

I shrugged. "I'm allowing myself some time to adjust. I've noticed a few new things in the lair. New vampires too."

"We've acquired some interesting characters," Valerio said while unbuttoning his shirt. "Check this out."

"That's right," Micah said, unbuttoning his shirt too.

Amused, I inquired, "Stripping is your new hobby?"

In response, they bared their right shoulder blades to me. Each one flaunted an identical black scorpion tattoo.

Valerio said, "Omar has one too. One of the new vampires was a celebrated tattoo artist in Italy. He's into ancient Roman history and his obsession is the elite Pretorian Guard."

Micah added, "The best Roman warriors were chosen to protect the emperor, and they distinguished themselves from other soldiers by flaunting black scorpions on their shields. The clever artist suggested to Omar that the Elders should get black scorpion tattoos. I think it was his own way of ingratiating himself into the coven. Rahim didn't like the idea but Arsham loved it. Hence, our scorpions."

Valerio began buttoning his shirt. "You need to get one too."

"Why?" I asked.

Micah replied, "You're the only vampire who can detect shape shifters, and you stood by Arsham's side for decades.

113

You're the epitome of an elite guard."

"If Omar puts me back on Arsham's detail, I'll do it."

Valerio said, "The artist's name is Ace. I'll point him out."

"You two didn't just come in here to show off your body art did you?" I inquired.

Micah said, "Actually, there's someone I want you to meet."

They led me to the old lair, which dated back to the Victorian era. It was the original underground structure built by Arsham after we had moved the coven from France to England in the nineteenth century. White subway tiles punctuated with colorful mosaic designs adorned the walls. I paused to admire them as nostalgic memories flooded my brain.

Touching one of the tiles, I commented, "I didn't think anyone used this wing anymore."

"They don't," Valerio said. "The vampire who spends most of her time here likes the solitude."

"Her?" Both of my brothers grinned mischievously, so I asked, "What's going on?"

We arrived at a stainless steel door and I said, "I don't remember this being here."

Ignoring my comment, Micah pushed the intercom button. "Eva? It's me."

"Come in, my love."

"My love?" I whispered in surprise.

The door clicked open and we entered a huge laboratory outfitted with the latest equipment known to man. Amid the beakers, burners, and glossy monitors stood an attractive vampire in a spotless white lab coat. I took in her reddish blonde hair, porcelain skin, and eyes the color of rainwater.

Micah kissed her lips and said, "Angelique, I'd like you to meet Eva, my mate."

"It's a pleasure, Eva," I said, delighted.

"Likewise, my lady. I've heard so much about you," Eva said in a melodious voice.

I gave Micah a reprimanding look. "I wish I could say the same, Eva."

"I wanted to surprise you," he explained.

"You've succeeded in your mission. When did the happy event take place?"

"I sired Eva five years ago."

Valerio whispered, "She is a genius."

The unassuming female merely shrugged at the compliment.

I surveyed the lab. "What are you working on?"

Eva glanced at Micah, who said, "You can tell her."

She indicated a microscope, its lens aimed over a Petri dish. "I'm creating a serum that will enable us to resist the effect of UV light. Contrary to popular belief, our *unholy* sleep is not a punishment from God but rather a response to chemical reaction. We sleep when the sun rises due to the altered composition of our vampiric bodies."

I digested this information with keen interest. "Are you trying to make vampires immune to daylight?"

"I'm afraid that would be impossible. The serum, if successful, would enable us to remain awake for about an hour after sunrise. Maybe two if we're lucky."

I peered into the Petri dish. "Why are you doing this? *How* are you doing it?"

"Prince Arsham requested that I conduct these experiments on the body of a warrior who had been killed by a slayer. I subjected a piece of the corpse's skin to lethal amounts of ultraviolet light, then compared the sample to the undamaged skin. This allowed me to analyze the chemical reaction that takes place when we are exposed to the sun. I've derived several theories and now I'm conducting experiments to determine which ones can be verified."

"Fascinating, isn't it?" Micah interjected.

"Why would Arsham request this of you?" I demanded.

Rather than answer my question, Eva glanced nervously at Micah. "Forgive me, my lady, but I don't know."

I turned to Micah and regarded him expectantly. "Well?"

My brother made an odd face. "Our sire never revealed his intentions to anyone. You, Valerio, and Omar are the only other people who know what's going on in this lab."

I frowned. "Not even Rahim knows?"

"No."

My eyes slid to Eva. "What sort of scientist are you?"

Shifting from one foot to the other, she replied, "I have two PhDs. One in chemistry, the other in biology."

Micah said proudly, "Eva has worked in various government agencies around the world prior to joining our coven."

"I'm honored to know someone so accomplished," I said.

She smiled shyly at my comment.

Despite my burning curiosity over Eva's experiments, and Arsham's reasons for requesting them, I changed the subject. "How did you two meet?"

Micah placed an arm around his mate. "We met at the London Library on a rainy Sunday evening. Hardly anyone was there. Eva's head was bent over a medieval manuscript depicting popular curatives…She resembled an angel that had fallen from the sky. I wasted no time courting her, and when I revealed my true nature, she didn't even flinch."

Eva added, "I wanted to conduct experiments on him immediately. I am the luckiest scientist in the world. I have my own lab, unlimited resources, and an eternity to conduct research."

"Aren't you forgetting something?" Micah prompted.

"I have you, which is the greatest treasure," Eva said.

I basked in the glow of their mutual happiness despite the epic fail of my own love life.

Valerio added, "Isn't it romantic?"

"What about you?" I inquired of my Sicilian brother.

Micah took it upon himself to reply. "Valerio is a playboy."

"A man whore, actually," Valerio admitted while checking his flashy designer watch. "Which reminds me, I have a date with a sexy newbie."

I watched him go, amused.

High pitched beeps echoed throughout the lab.

"My timer is going off. Excuse me," Eva said before scurrying toward the machine.

"What do you think of her?" Micah whispered.

My brother had remained alone for centuries, which meant

that Eva must be truly special. Her studious nature matched his own. They were solitary creatures, preferring the company of books to the company of others. "I think she's perfect. Beautiful and intelligent, like you."

Taking my arm, he escorted me into the hallway and closed the lab door. "I owe you an apology, you know."

"For what?"

"I didn't want you to see those photographs of Damien and Katya, but Rahim insisted that you should."

"What about our sire?"

"Arsham thought so too."

"You should know me by now, Micah. I'll take the harsh truth over an easy lie any day."

"I know."

"Are you coming?"

"I'm going to stay with Eva for a bit. I'll see you later."

I left the old lair and headed toward the modern section. Although I found Eva's serum intriguing, I wondered how resisting our unholy sleep for an hour or two could be of any benefit to Arsham or anyone else. A potion making us immune to daylight—now *that* would be a miracle.

Omar and his wife, Dani, sat chatting in one of the lounges and I stopped to exchange pleasantries with them. Originally from Ethiopia, the exotic female possessed strength and grace. A worthy match for the great warrior, Omar.

At one point, I said to my brother, "If there is any way that I can make myself useful to you, please let me know."

Omar pulled me aside. "Have you kept up your training?"

"Not as much as I should have," I admitted.

"You know where the training facility is. I'm sure you can entice one of the newborns to spar with you—go easy on them."

"I'm not *that* rusty." I hesitated. "I can train them for you."

"Arsham and I are still discussing matters."

"Matters meaning *me*."

"Yes," he replied while averting his gaze.

To think that I had once been the most illustrious vampire in the coven. "I understand, Omar. I don't expect for things to be how they were before…"

"Don't take it personally."

"I won't but if you need me on his personal detail, my sense of smell is as strong as ever."

Omar met my eyes and nodded.

I wished him and Dani a pleasant evening before returning to my room. How could I have allowed this to happen? My emotions had ruined what I had worked so hard to achieve within the coven: *respect* and *trust*.

* * *

In the days that followed, I made a concerted effort to show my face more often and speak with other vampires. Some within the coven still whispered and stared whenever they saw me. Arsham monitored my movements and whereabouts through his spies, but he made no attempt to spend time with me. In fact, I got the distinct impression that he was going out of his way to avoid my company.

I had barely stepped foot out of my room one night when Arsham materialized before me. Surprised, I inclined my head.

"I'm meeting with Omar tomorrow to revise our security protocols and I expect you to be there." At my quizzical expression, he added, "I'm reinstating your former position on the Security Team. I want you close to me."

I took in this information while studying the perfectly executed tie knot at his throat. The costly silk mimicked the color of blood. "How does Omar feel about that?"

"He's the one who suggested the idea."

"I am honored. Thank you, sire."

Arsham tilted his head back, his eyes scanning the room. "When was the last time you fed? You seem pale."

"Three nights ago."

"Of course. Erika. She also had the habit of going days without feeding. Claimed it made us stronger. I tend to disagree."

I shrugged. "I like the challenge."

"Rebel blood. She had it too." Meeting my gaze, he added, "It would please me if you accompanied me on a hunt tonight.

Are you up for it?"

Arsham asking instead of commanding? "It would be my pleasure."

We chose one of the secret exits and slipped into the cool night. A half-moon greeted us from a cloud-ridden sky.

Arsham said, "I want to smell the sea."

"Do you have a specific place in mind?"

"Brighton."

The coastal city was about fifty miles away. We flew side by side in silence, two shadows in the night sky. We arrived undetected beneath the cloak of night.

Illuminated by electric lights, the Brighton Pier stood out in stark contrast to the blue-black water. People strolled the historic pier beneath the moonlight, some kissing, others speaking softly. Arsham offered me his arm and I slipped my hand into the crook of his elbow. Blending in with the humans, we mimicked their pace, their glances, their movements.

At length, he inquired, "How are you settling in?"

"Fine, sire. There have been a few changes in my absence."

"Such as?"

"Micah and Valerio showed me their tattoos the other day."

"Ah, the black scorpion. I'm sure your brothers explained the meaning behind it."

"They did."

"Do you not like the idea?"

"On the contrary, I like it very much."

"They felt the desire to symbolize their loyalty to me."

I hesitated. "Why have you not commanded me to obtain a scorpion tattoo?"

"I didn't *command* any of my other children. They did it of their own free will because they respect and love me."

"I see."

"*Free will*, Angelique."

I made a note of that, then changed the subject. "I also had the pleasure of meeting Eva."

"She's an exemplary vampire and a valuable addition to our coven. It's good to see my son so well-matched."

119

"I agree." I paused. "She's working on a serum to keep us from being claimed by sleep at sunrise. *At your request*."

"That's right."

"May I ask why?"

"You may not, and I'm sure Micah explained that you are sworn to secrecy."

"He did."

"Only my children know. I haven't even informed Rahim."

"I won't breathe a word of it to anyone."

He stopped to admire the antique dome of the Brighton Marine Palace. Frowning in thought, he ventured, "June 1899?"

"May," I corrected. "I believe the pier's grand opening was held on the twentieth."

He resumed our stroll, urging me to keep pace. "Your memory is fresher than mine because of your youth. We aren't completely immune to the ravages of time."

Surprised by his rare display of humility, I teased, "I'm practically a child in comparison to you."

"You *are* a child. *My* child."

I took advantage of the intimate moment. "Have you ever regretted offering me eternal life?"

"Why would you ask such a thing of your maker?"

"Because I've disappointed you, sire. More than once."

"I admit, you try my patience at times. You're the most unruly of your siblings. My rebel."

"It's not my intention to cause you grief."

He shot me a disbelieving look. "Is that so? More often than not it feels like you go out of your way to provoke me. In answer to your impertinent question, I have no regrets."

We walked in silence, our eyes on the water.

He said, "You need to reconcile yourself to the fact that the slayer is out of your life. Permanently."

"I've accepted that fact long before what happened in Edinburgh. Even before I met Dr. Morgan."

"There's no turning back this time, Angelique. If you betray your coven again—"

"That won't happen—"

Placing his forefinger on my lips to silence me, he continued, "If it does, you will be banished from the coven and from London altogether. I will never again look upon your face. Do you understand?"

"I do, sire."

Music and laughter poured from the big Victorian venue built on the pier for people to rest, eat, and drink.

Arsham glanced at the building and casually inquired, "Do you remember the parties we attended during Queen Victoria's reign?"

This was the second time he brought up the past with me. "Vividly. We danced in grand ballrooms on smooth parquet floors that smelled of beeswax and gleamed like gold beneath the candlelight. Crystal chandeliers sparkled like stars above our heads…"

"You describe the scene exactly as I envision it in my mind." He stopped to inhale the salty air and gazed up at the sooty sky. "I miss those days. Life was simpler, people were simpler. Fashion and the arts were elegant…" Lowering his head to look at me, he added, "I miss *you*."

His honest confession caught me off guard. "I'm not going anywhere. I vowed to put the coven first and I meant it."

"Do you put me first?"

"I would die for you."

Taking hold of my chin, he stared deeply into my eyes to discern if my words were true. When his dark gaze dropped to my mouth, I braced myself for his kiss. Instead, he smiled slightly and moved forward along the pier. "Your brothers have repeatedly expressed their joy to me."

"They're glad that I'm in London." A couple passed us with hands entwined. I waited until they were out of earshot. "Are *you* happy that I'm back?"

"My feelings are inconsequential. The only thing that matters is the well-being of the coven, of which you are a part."

Stricken by his reply, I deliberately turned my head to study the moonlight on the rippling waves. I didn't want Arsham to see my face or the disappointment etched across my features. In truth, I wasn't sure what surprised me more: his reply or my reaction to it.

He continued, "I'm giving you the opportunity now, tonight, to confess anything that could compromise your position on the Security Team. You've been gone for nearly two years. My spies are thorough but not perfect. There may be something they've missed. This is your chance to come clean. I don't want any secrets between us. You can tell me anything."

"Anything?"

"Judging by your tone and the look on your face, I'd say you have something grave to confess."

"I'm wondering if you would pay me the same courtesy."

Narrowing his eyes at me, he said, "Quid pro quo?"

"Something like that." At his curt nod, I continued, "Dr. Morgan photographed the inside of the Old Buda labyrinth beneath the castle of King Matthias Corvinus. The area where Vlad Tepes had been kept as a prisoner bears a peculiar wall carving."

"I'm sure those prisoners carved all sorts of things into the stone out of sheer boredom."

Arsham wasn't wearing a tie and the first two buttons of his shirt were open, thus allowing a glimpse of his gold chain.

My eyes were drawn to the metal flashing against his skin. "This particular carving was an exact replica of the Faravahar featured on your medallion."

Arsham's eyes hardened for only an instant before he forced a slight smile. "What are you suggesting?"

"I find it an uncanny coincidence that the man whose savagery earned him the bloody legend of Dracula would imprisoned within the vicinity of a Zoroastrian, a *Persian*."

He stared at me for a long moment, his jaw clenching.

I continued, "Was it you?"

The silence stretched.

Finally, he said, "I had my reasons for wanting revenge upon the Ottomans…I used the Romanian prince as my weapon."

Horrified, I said nothing.

He continued, "I see judgement in your eyes, Angelique."

"Those humans suffered unfathomable pain."

"At the time I was filled with rage. I admit, I have since regretted my actions."

"What were you doing there? Were you a prisoner?"

"Yes. It's a long story and I don't feel like divulging details."

"How did you even…?"

"I allowed Vlad to drink my blood."

I gaped at him. "Without biting him first? Sire, your blood would drive a human into madness."

"I assure you that Vlad Tepes was a psychopath long before we met. I only encouraged him to embrace reality and live up to his full potential."

"You're responsible for the cruel deaths of countless men."

"Whom I perceived as unworthy," he shot back.

"My God," I whispered, looking away.

Arsham frowned and grabbed my arm, forcing me to meet his angry eyes. "Are you referring to the God whom Vlad worshipped? The one that wiped out entire tribes of men and even the world itself with the Great Flood? The Bible is full of cataclysmic events caused by divine intervention. Tell me, how am I different from that God?"

At length, I admitted, "You make a valid point, sire."

We stared at each other with the implicit and unspoken understanding that I could never reveal to the coven what I had learned. Releasing his hold on me, he continued walking and I tracked his steps in thoughtful silence.

At length, he said, "Your turn to confess."

Do you dare tell him about what really happened the night Erika was murdered?

I simply couldn't take the risk. "There is something I need to confess and it will surely displease you."

"I'm granting you impunity so speak freely."

"I prefer to show you." At his curt nod, I added, "Not here."

Mist floated in from the sea creating a hazy film over the city. We retraced our steps along the pier and wandered through the streets of Brighton. The late hour meant fewer people, thus diminishing our choice of prey.

I spied a young man exiting a pub with swaying steps. "Wait here and watch carefully."

Arsham scowled. "Where are you going?"

"Watch."

He stood across the street, eyes fixed on me.

I went up to the young man and asked, "Excuse me, can you tell me how to get to the pier?"

The moment the mortal looked into my eyes, I had him. Vampire beauty and preternatural charms were hard to resist. I lured him away from the brightness of a street lamp and pushed him into a deep doorway. Leaning in closer, I brushed my lips against his neck and he made no move to flee. My fangs pierced the skin and my mouth filled with blood. I drank enough to satisfy but not to kill. Piercing my finger, I applied my blood to the wound so that it healed instantly. I left the human leaning against the wall in a state of euphoric oblivion, then crossed the street to where Arsham stood.

His hands were balled into fists and fury radiated off his body. "You dare to defy yet another of our sacred laws?"

He moved with lethal intention toward the human to finish the job, but I stopped him. "Wait, sire."

"Angelique, you try my patience like no other vampire."

"Wait."

The mortal eventually gathered himself together, shook his head as if to clear it, and continued down the street as if nothing happened. Arsham tracked my prey in disbelief. In fact, we followed the young man back to his flat where his friends were outside waiting for him with pizza. Grinning and hungry, he made no mention of being bitten by a vampire.

Astounded, my sire whispered, "What have you done?"

"Sire?"

"How long have you been allowing your prey to live?"

"Since my newborn bloodlust settled."

My confession caused several emotions to flit across his face—outrage, incredulity, disappointment, bewilderment—but it was fear that caused me concern.

Regarding me closely, he demanded, "Who else is doing this

behind my back?"

"I've always done it alone and never told anyone."

"What of Damien Sauvage?"

"I taught him how to feed like me."

He said nothing while glaring at me.

"Arsham—"

"How do you do it?" My face must have expressed disbelief, for he added, "I'm serious."

"Do you mean to tell me that in all the years you've been a vampire, you've never allowed a single human to live?"

My tone made him defensive. "We kill them to protect ourselves…it is our way."

"It is *your* way. As you have yourself witnessed, there is another way. A kinder way."

"How do you do it? I command that you tell me. Now."

Chuckling softly at the irony, I replied, "*You* ask this question of *me*?"

"What's that supposed to mean?"

Like the fallen angel Lucifer, Arsham was the most glorious among us. "You possess more charm and beauty than all of your progeny combined. You are more desired, more precious than any other vampire in the coven. If anyone can pull this off, it's you. Granted, not killing humans requires us to drink from more than one in order to slake our thirst."

"How many?"

"Two, maybe three." I touched his arm and his eyes settled on my hand. "If every vampire spared the lives of their prey, there would be no need for slayers. Think of it, Arsham. We wouldn't have to live in constant fear or suffer painful losses when one of our own is brutally decapitated."

"Teach me."

"I've already shown you—"

"Bite me." I hesitated and he frowned. "Do it!"

My fingertips caressed his nape of Arsham's neck before sliding down his broad shoulders. Pressing against him, I gently pierced the fragrant skin of his neck with my fangs. His delicious blood entered my mouth and I wanted to drink until I burst, but I wisely refrained. My head swam from the powerful effect of my sire's potent blood.

Elixir of the god.

"That's how you do it," I whispered in a trembling voice.

Arsham knew that his blood was a powerful aphrodisiac. He tilted his head toward mine and stared at my mouth with longing. The instant I moved forward to press my lips to his, he retreated from me. The Arsham I once knew wouldn't have hesitated to take advantage of me in this vulnerable state.

"I want to try this technique of yours," he said.

Shocked by his rejection, I allowed him to lead me down the street. We turned a corner, then another.

"There," he said, eyeing a woman who was in the process of unlocking the outside door of her apartment building.

I watched with mixed emotions as he repeated my exact moves on the unsuspecting woman. Of course, the mortal melted under his alluring preternatural spell. The feeding was over quickly. He propped her into a sitting position on the stoop afterward, then returned to where I stood. The woman eventually opened her eyes and groggily rubbed her head. No screams, no panic, no drama as she let herself inside the flat.

"Incredible," Arsham whispered. "They really have no memory, do they?"

"It's not quite like that…"

Alarmed, he demanded, "What do you mean?"

"If you don't mesmerize them first, they will likely remember your bite."

"How do you know this?" he inquired suspiciously.

"Because I bit Damien when he was human. He already knew that I was a vampire and wanted to know what it felt like."

I didn't dare confess to also having bitten Gilles Sauvage, the slayer who had decapitated my dear sister, Erika. That horrible secret would never be revealed, for I was willing to wager there was no impunity for such a grave sin.

"Hearing such treacherous words spill so casually from your lips distresses me to the core. Frankly, I am astounded by your disobedience and your total disregard for my commandments.

Have you no fear of consequences?"

"Forgive me," I offered contritely.

He held up his hand. "I asked for your honesty and you have accommodated my request. I must now ponder this matter and experiment with it myself. In the meantime, you must not speak of this night. No one can know what has transpired here. That means that you must kill humans in the presence of other vampires in order to keep our secret."

"I understand, sire."

"Perhaps it is best for you to hunt alone. That would be the wisest course of action in order to avoid any complications."

"There's something else you should know."

"What now?" he snapped irritably.

"Our bite is addictive and pleasurable to humans...even an aphrodisiac."

The corners of his lips twitched. "The way my bite is an aphrodisiac to you?"

"Exactly."

"So, not only can we feed on them without their knowledge, we can provide them with pleasure?" Rubbing his chin pensively, he added, "Perhaps we should finally come out of hiding and announce our presence to the world. Human politicians may grant us asylum—better yet—special protection as an endangered species. Think of the possibilities."

"Surely, you jest."

"I do."

I sagged in relief. "I thought you'd be furious right now."

"I *am* furious. You are incorrigible and, according to our sacred laws, deserving of death. Lucky for you, I cannot imagine a world without you in it."

Had I not thought the same thing of Arsham when Damien confessed his desire to kill him? "You've changed, sire."

"Have I? For better or worse?"

"Better."

Closing the gap between us, he stared me down in a manner that would make any human woman blush. "Enlighten me."

"You're pensive and serious...less indulgent. You're

127

different than how I remember you."

He slowly traced my bottom lip with his forefinger. The sensuous gesture made my knees grow weak and conjured memories of the carnal intimacies we once shared. I tried in vain to block the sexy images of his powerful body twisted amid satin sheets...

"Less indulgent? Are you saying this because I haven't yet savored the sweetness of your lips?" he whispered provocatively while his gaze swept over me. "Or is it because I'm not holding your delicious body in my arms?"

"Both," I replied breathlessly.

"You're in the throes of bloodlust right now."

"Yes..."

Pulling me close, he inhaled my scent in a primordial manner that made me ache for him. "It would be so easy to indulge right now." His finger moved from my mouth to my jawline, then traced a path down my neck to the hollow of my throat. Allowing the tip to linger there, he said softly, "Alas, I cannot. I made a promise to myself."

"A promise?" I heard myself say through the dizzying haze of pure lust.

"A vow, actually. One that I have every intention of keeping—despite the temptation." He backed away from me and offered no further explanation.

"I don't understand."

"Someday you will." Glancing up at the sky, he added, "We should start heading back to London."

CHAPTER 11

*"You will never do anything in this world without courage.
It is the greatest quality of the mind next to honor."*
(Aristotle)

Omar possessed a file full of data that had been gathered by coven spies. Placing a folder before me, he said, "Here's what we know for certain: Katya is working Damien and Jeanne, who are in turn working local slayers. Katya may be planning to assassinate Rahim. Arsham too."

I leafed through the documents. "That's a serious accusation to make and a lot of stress to place on the Security Team. For the record, I'm not saying this out of any sentimentality for certain parties involved."

"Noted," Omar confirmed, his black eyes glued to mine. "For the safety of our sires and the coven, we must err on the side of caution and be ready for anything."

"Agreed. Do you believe Damien is in on this?"

"Why wouldn't he be? You said yourself that he resents our sire and still wishes to wreak revenge. I believe they'll wait for the right time to carry out the act, but we don't want to eliminate them before we know what's at stake."

Eliminate. Damien. I shuddered. He brought this upon himself. I refused to go down with him. "Why does Katya want the sires dead?"

"She was Severin's lover—"

"Wait, what? I thought Severin was Rahim's lover."

"Severin was bisexual. We have reason to believe that Katya and Severin were eventually planning to kill Rahim so that they could take his place." At my confused expression, he elaborated, "It was Severin who initially seduced Rahim and planted the seed in his sire's mind to destroy his half-brother, Arsham. It was also Severin who went in search of Damien after he had been turned into a vampire."

"I was in Marseilles when they met."

Omar nodded. "We're aware of that. Given Katya's recent disappearance and what had transpired beforehand, we think she's picking up where Severin left off. Damien's unfulfilled desire for revenge is being exploited to the fullest advantage."

"I get that. What I don't understand is *why*."

"We have a theory that we're keeping secret."

"Who is *we*?"

"Micah and I."

"Are you going to share it with the rest of the Elders?"

"Only with you, Micah, Valerio, and Jazmin. We'll discuss the theory once the sires arrive. You'll find out when they do."

I nodded in understanding, respecting protocol. I asked after his mate and listened as he described in detail his new passion for oil painting. When the door opened, we grew silent and inclined our heads in respect as the sires took their seats.

Jazmin and my brothers entered the room and we settled around the long white marble table dominating the space. Polite greetings were exchanged and then Omar got down to business.

Opening a file on an untraceable tablet, he flipped through a series of photographs depicting Katya and Damien speaking with known slayers here in London. My brow creased in confusion as I tried to discern what this meant. Arsham cleared his throat and glanced pointedly in my direction.

Omar said, "I know we've discussed possible theories but the one I am about to propose seems the most likely. After going through the data again and interviewing our spies, I've come to the conclusion that Katya is trying to create an army of slayers. *Undead* slayers."

Jazmin leaned forward in her chair. "Vampire slayers?"

"Like Damien Sauvage," Omar replied.

Rahim's eyebrow shot upward. "How absurd! They'll never go for the idea."

Omar said, "Are you sure about that, my lord? They're offering eternal life and a chance for slayers to kill what they hate most—vampires. In their minds, they would be doing humanity a favor by preventing countless deaths. A win-win situation."

Jazmin rubbed her chin pensively. "What if you're wrong?"

Omar's eyes bore into hers. "What if I'm not?"

"I believe Angelique should weigh in on this theory," Micah suggested with a look in my direction. "She would know better than anyone how a slayer-turned-vampire thinks and behaves."

I glanced around the table. "Damien Sauvage has been a vampire for about a decade. He has despised and resented every single minute of it."

"Which is exactly why Katya chose him to implement her plan," Omar said, arriving at the logical conclusion.

"If slayers become vampires, they will need to kill humans to survive. It defeats their purpose," Rahim insisted.

"Not necessarily," Arsham countered.

His comment made Jazmin's eyes light up with anticipation. "What do you mean?"

Rahim added, "Do you know something that we don't?"

"I know of another way," Arsham replied.

Rahim frowned. "What are you talking about?"

Tossing a quick glance in my direction, Arsham replied, "We do not have to kill our prey in order to feed."

Shocked silence followed the bold statement.

Rahim's eyes narrowed. "You're joking."

Arsham lifted his proud chin. "I am not. There is another way for us to survive in this world that would completely eliminate the need for slayers."

Rahim threw up his hands. "How can we possibly allow our prey to live? The humans would seek revenge, alert the authorities, discover and destroy our lairs."

Arsham shook his head. "Not if it is done correctly—"

Rahim pounded his fist on the table. "This is blasphemy! What you're suggesting goes against our sacred law."

Arsham stood, unfazed. "Perhaps it's time to change the sacred law."

Rahim also stood. "That would place the entire coven in grave danger."

Everyone eyed the two powerful males facing each other in a stand-off.

Arsham rested his hand on Rahim's shoulder. "You are reasonable and wise. I have learned much from you, my brother. Now I ask that you grant me the opportunity to teach you something in return. Come hunting with me tonight so that I can show you what I am proposing."

"And dispel my concerns?"

"That too."

Rahim's eyes slid to Jazmin. "You have been at my right hand for centuries, Jazmin. I trust you above the other Elders. What are your thoughts on this matter?"

Jazmin glanced at Arsham and then, surprisingly, at me. "I think you should be open to anything that could benefit the coven and keep it safe. The only reason that our species has survived this long is because we possess the capacity to evolve. Perhaps the time has come to implement change, sire."

Rahim regarded her thoughtfully. "Very well. Arsham, you and I will hunt together and I promise to keep an open mind."

Casting a discreet glance my way, Arsham urged Rahim toward the door. My heart swelled with pride.

The two sires exited the room and a discussion broke out in their absence. Jazmin remained quiet, her wizened amber eyes fixed on mine. She indicated the door with a subtle nod, compelling me to stand and follow her out of the room.

"We need to talk but not here," she said.

Jazmin led me to her private chamber. I was greeted by an explosion of vibrant colors when I entered the room. Intricately woven carpets, multi-shaped Moroccan lamps, and exotic antiques filled the pleasant space. An Indonesian desk and chair flaunting inlaid mother of pearl designs drew my attention.

"Lovely," I said, running my hand along the desk's surface.

"Thank you. Everything you see is from my travels."

She motioned for me to pass into another room where an ancient lacquered Chinese screen served as a headboard to a huge bed decorated with satin pillows.

Jazmin closed the door and invited me to sit on a plum velvet sofa. "May I offer you some blood wine?"

"Please."

She poured the deep red liquid into a crystal goblet and handed it to me. "Rahim added his blood to this special wine at my suggestion, making it palatable for us to drink."

"An excellent idea."

"Are you feeling tipsy yet?"

"Yes, and its delightful, but you didn't bring me here to discuss the origins of blood wine."

"I know your secret, Angelique. By the look on your face, I'm willing to bet that you know what I'm talking about."

"I do."

"I hope Arsham can convince Rahim. As I said in there, progress means evolution and we vampires are long overdue for change. I admire your courage. It must have been terrifying to make that confession to your sire. I've never admitted my sin to Rahim because I fear losing his approval."

Surprised, I inquired, "You've fed without killing?"

"More than once."

"Why did you do it?"

"You are known throughout your coven as being the most humane vampire, whereas I am known in mine for my practicality. I did it in order to escape persecution from slayers rather than sentimentality toward mortals."

"I don't want to kill needlessly. Life is precious."

"I believe the two philosophies are complimentary instead of contradictory, wouldn't you agree?"

I nodded, grateful for her willingness to work in unison.

Jazmin continued, "I will do everything in my power to persuade Rahim to implement this new way of hunting into our Codex. I know you will do the same on your end with Arsham. Together, we can work toward ushering in a new age for vampires. One that is free of fear and danger."

"Nothing would please me more."

She touched the rim of her glass to mine and we drank a toast to our shared mission. "You can rest assured that whatever is discussed within these walls will not leak out. I know the importance of secrecy."

"Thank you, Jazmin."

I turned to go and she stood. "Wait." Obtaining a velvet pouch from a drawer, she added, "Will you indulge me?"

She opened the pouch and scattered its contents upon the red velvet coverlet on the bed.

I picked up one of the worn pebbles. "Rune stones?"

"Correct. Ask a question. Anything." When I hesitated, she assured me, "It will never leave this room."

"What will happen to Damien Sauvage?"

Jazmin eyed me steadily. "Are you sure you want to know?"

I nodded and watched as she closed her eyes and ran her hand over the ancient stones.

She opened her eyes and whispered, "Death."

My stomach sank. I despised Damien at the moment but I certainly didn't wish death upon him. Deep down, I secretly fostered the hope that he would change and beg forgiveness from the coven.

Seeing my reaction, she said, "I've given you bad news."

"Unexpected news," I corrected.

"Don't you want to know what the future holds in store for you?" Before I could reply, she ran her hands over the runes again then smiled confidently. "The answer is yes."

"I didn't ask you a question."

"You didn't *verbalize* the question but you communicated it clearly through your eyes."

"I should go," I said, shaken.

"Don't worry. Your secret is safe with me."

Forcing my mind on the events at hand, I pushed Jazmin's prophecies to the farthest corner of my brain. My brothers were still discussing the matter at hand when I returned to the table. I feigned ignorance and made non-committal comments to their speculations on what Arsham had suggested. I wanted to confess the truth to them but my sire had instructed me to not speak on the matter.

I retired to my room feeling elated and apprehensive. Would Rahim be open to the idea of changing sacred law?

The sires engaged in several private discussions throughout the week. Knowing what was at stake, I kept my distance from Arsham out of respect for his position and the heavy responsibility upon his shoulders. I bade my time by discreetly keeping tabs on everything he did. I noticed that he forsook the company of females. On more than one occasion I caught several beautiful young vampires salivating in his presence, yet he didn't spare a glance in their direction.

One night, I stopped what I was doing to simply admire him. Other females paused to do the same. Clad in slim black pants and a fitted black dress shirt that showed off his perfect body, he looked absolutely amazing. He sauntered down the corridor like a sexy panther.

At the sight of me, he paused. "Angelique."

I inclined my head. "Sire."

"You'll be pleased to know that Rahim finally tested your method last night. I admit, it wasn't easy convincing him to even try it. When I first showed him..." he trailed off and readjusted his mask of aloofness. "We will hold an Elder meeting in the near future to discuss our next move."

"This is good news."

"Indeed." Glancing around, he inquired softly, "Omar has you training the newborns. How's that going?"

"Fine."

"Do you like your new chamber?"

"Valerio did a fine job with the décor."

Arsham only chuckled.

Rahim exited one of the rooms and my sire left me to speak with him. I watched him go with a twinge of regret.

Having hunted the previous evening, my intention was to spend the entire night at the lair. I made it a point to engage Rahim's Elders in conversation in order to know them better. Actually, I wanted to erode their prejudices against me. Andrei couldn't be bothered and Mayu offered monosyllables to my questions. Eventually, I gave up.

I also took the time to check out some of the new things

within the lair, like the Steinway & Sons grand piano in the main atrium. It made perfect sense to place the costly instrument in that specific location since the high ceiling provided good acoustics.

Valerio found me hanging out in one of the lounges and made it a point to introduce me to Ace, the tattoo artist.

Sporting blue hair, black eyeliner, and a studded collar around his neck, the punky newborn bowed gallantly before me. "My lady, it's an honor to meet a legend face to face."

I grinned, eyeing my brother. "Legend? What stories are you telling these children?"

Valerio shrugged. "Only the truth, *Warrior Goddess*."

"Very funny."

"My studio welcomes you, my lady," Ace interjected. "Have you thought about a scorpion tattoo for yourself?"

"Actually, yes," I replied.

Valerio gripped my arm. "Let's do it now, Angelique. Are you up for it, Ace?"

"Are you kidding me?" Ace shot back, thrilled by the prospect. "It would be an honor."

I allowed myself to be led to Ace's chamber, which resembled a high-end tattoo parlor complete with Neo-Victorian furnishings and punk rock posters. Red velvet drapes with gold tassels separated the artist's dimly lit personal quarters and the well-lit studio.

I removed my shirt and stood before them in tight black jeans and a tank top. Ace's eyes were glued to my body. Seeing the lust in his gaze, I cleared my throat and scowled at him. Catching himself, he lowered his eyes out of respect. I sat down and turned around, granting him access to my right shoulder.

Rather than get to work, he slowly circled the chair. "Would you stand up for me, please?"

I did as I was told.

"Your back is perfect, my lady. A true work of art." Ace came back around to face me. "I cannot desecrate such beauty with a small tattoo on your shoulder blade."

Valerio and I exchanged glances before I demanded, "So

what are you suggesting?"

"I envision the *entire* back covered in ink," the artist replied while grabbing hold of a pencil and sketch pad. "Your brothers bear a scorpion with tail at the bottom and outstretched claws at the top. For you, I propose *this*."

Valerio and I watched in fascination as Ace sketched my back like a shapely hourglass. He then placed a giant scorpion with claws curved inward on the tops of my buttocks, its body climbing up my spine, and its venomous stinger resting on my right shoulder blade. The sinewy creature appeared to be hovering, ready to strike.

Valerio's eyes widened. "I'm gay and I find that sexy."

Ace nodded. "On a back like this one, *oh yeah*."

"Do you think Arsham would approve?" I asked of Valerio.

"He would *love* it. You're the only female Elder and you're his personal bodyguard. Your tattoo should be different."

I looked at Ace. "Let's do it."

"Your wish is my command," Ace said, slipping on a pair of surgical gloves to protect his hands from ink.

Valerio said, "I'll come back later to see the result."

I spent the remainder of the night stretched out on my stomach in Ace's studio. Vampirism allowed the artist to work precisely and quickly, finishing the skin art masterpiece before sunrise.

Removing the gloves, he said with satisfaction, "All done."

I stood before the three-way mirror and admired his fine work from all angles. The giant black scorpion had been created in such a clever manner that it enhanced the elegant lines and curves of my back. Sexy indeed.

Ace stood off to the side, nervous. "Well?"

"I love it."

***

The lair's library boasted a new wing complete with ancient texts and first editions. Long reading tables with cushioned chairs invited book lovers to sit and stay awhile. I made a few selections and settled into a chair to catch up on some reading. Someone eventually slipped into the room. I glanced up from the page to find Rahim staring at me.

Closing the book, I regarded him expectantly. "My lord."

He sat down across from me. "How does it feel to be back?"

"It feels good. I only wish that I had returned under better circumstances."

"There may be a way for you to ingratiate yourself to those who still haven't accepted your return."

"I would relish the opportunity."

"I was hoping you'd say that. I have an important mission for you." He paused, eyeing me closely. "I need you to make contact with Damien Sauvage."

I grew wary. "Why?"

"To confirm Omar's theory, of course."

"You don't believe him?"

Rahim considered his next words carefully. "Altering the Codex is no small thing. We need to be one hundred percent sure that your brother and the spies are correct. You're the only one in this coven capable of successfully performing this feat."

"I doubt that Damien is going to trust me after our fight in Edinburgh."

"I heard that you were one of the stealthiest vampires in this coven. I'm sure you can think of a way to meet with your former lover and gather the required information."

"Damien Sauvage isn't stupid, my lord."

"That may be true, but he's no match for your intelligence and cunning. Invent something. Tell him you're confused, make him think that you're still undecided on where you stand."

I stood and returned the book to the shelf before facing him again. "Was this your idea or Arsham's?"

Guilt crept into his eyes. "Your sire doesn't know that I'm asking this favor of you. I would prefer that you not say anything to anyone."

My brow creased. "Why not?"

Rahim sat back and folded his hands on the table top. "When I suggested the idea to him, he was vehemently against it." He studied my face to gauge my reaction, then added, "He refused to put you in harm's way."

"He actually said that?"

"His exact words were, 'she is precious to me.'"

Overcome by conflicting emotions, I said, "I don't think I should go against my sire's wishes."

"If you care about him as much as he obviously cares about you, then you'll do as I ask. Make it appear as if you took the initiative."

"I don't know…"

"This coven may be facing serious danger and we need to take action. *Soon*."

I thought about it for a moment. "All right, I'll do it."

"Good. Our spies have reported that the Sauvage siblings are back in Yorkshire. I want you to go after sunset tomorrow."

I nodded.

Taking my hand, he brought my knuckles to his lips. "I don't need to remind you that this conversation never happened."

CHAPTER 12

"Courage: a perfect sensibility of the measure of
danger, and a mental willingness to endure it."
(William Tecumseh Sherman)

I crept out of the lair the moment the sun went down the next day. Clad in black leather and armed to the teeth, I was resolved to complete my mission as quickly as possible.

I arrived in Yorkshire and approached Jeanne's cottage with caution. The lights were on in the barn so I silently circled the structure and lingered near one of the windows. I sniffed the air for shifters and, convinced that there were none in the vicinity, proceeded toward the structure. Melting with the blackest shadows, I peered through the dirty glass panes. Katya, long and lean, sparred with Damien. She wasn't faster than me, however. I gloated for only a second before turning my attention to Jeanne, who sat off to the side polishing her katana. The blade glistened under the harsh fluorescent light of the barn.

Katya traded places with Jeanne so that she could practice with her brother. I watched them for about an hour until Jeanne announced that she was meeting friends at a pub in the village. She got into her car and drove off toward Staithes.

Katya went up to Damien, kissed him and said, "Jeanne is getting pretty good."

Damien grinned. "She's got a great teacher."

"Humble too. Where do you want to hunt tonight?"

"Let's stay local," he replied before capturing her earlobe between his sharp teeth. "I have plans for us later."

I averted my gaze as they shared another kiss. A moment later, I heard the barn door open and then slam shut. The amorous pair took off into the night and I darted after them without hesitation. I tracked them from a safe distance until they landed in a nearby village further along the coast.

Damien led Katya into a dubious bar and I slipped in after them. Startled, they turned around and gaped at me. Their collective surprise quickly turned to anger. Surrounded by humans, they prudently kept their cool.

Katya snarled. "What the hell is she doing here?"

Damien eyed me frostily. "Did they send you to spy on me?"

Looking from one to the other, I said, "I snuck out of the lair of my own volition to speak with you."

"It's over between us," he snapped.

"I'm not here for that reason," I assured him.

Katya sneered at me. "Why are you here?"

"The sires are speculating about you two."

Damien put his face close to mine. "Who cares what the sires are doing? Katya sees Arsham and Rahim for what they are— tyrants. That's a hell of a lot more than I can say for you."

Katya laughed derisively then whispered in his ear while caressing his shoulder. "I'm going in to feed, babe. Get rid of this bitch."

It took all of my willpower not to slam her face into the wall.

Damien glared at me. "What the fuck is wrong with you? First you attack my sister, now you're stalking me?"

"I'm not stalking you. I'm here to warn you."

"*Warn* me? Ha!"

"You're courting with danger."

He chuckled but the sound rang cold. "As if you care."

"You should ask yourself why Katya wasn't in Russia when we were there. Did you know that she was the one who prompted Severin to convince Rahim to attack Arsham?"

"Of course I do! Unlike you, she cares about humans."

"That's not why, you fool. She was Severin's lover."

Damien seemed surprised to hear this, then he shrugged. "So what? I don't care who she shared her bed with prior to being with me. If I were that type of guy, I would never have touched you knowing that you had been with Arsham."

I let out a heavy sigh. "Katya is only telling you what you need to hear in order to get what she wants from you."

Gripping my arm, he got in my face. "She wants to fight

against tyranny. She wants to end it."

"She's really done a job on you, hasn't she?"

Squeezing my arm, he marched me outside onto the sidewalk and shoved me away from him. "Thanks for the warning, now leave."

"Damien—"

"You know, you should be grateful for what I've done."

"Grateful that you cheated on me?" I cursed myself the moment the petty words escaped my lips.

Crossing his arms, he retorted, "You're back in London with your brothers and your beloved sire. What more do you want?"

Katya exited the bar and pushed me away from Damien. "You had your chance with him. You screwed up, now go."

I regained my balance and stood my ground. "You need to put an end to whatever madness you're planning, Katya. You're an Elder and should know better."

She bared her fangs but I didn't flinch.

Damien said, "Get the fuck out of here, Angelique."

Katya moved to strike me and I kicked her hard in the stomach, sending her sprawling. She was on her feet in a flash and came at me again. I defended another blow and shoved her into Damien's arms. He held her tightly to diffuse the situation as I flew into the night. They didn't bother to follow me.

Upon arriving in London, I decided to clear my head with a stroll before returning to the lair. My brisk steps took me to Soho and I found myself in Damien's old neighborhood. On a whim, I went to his old flat. I took in the Victorian edifice with mixed feelings. The flat was black and had been refitted with modern windows. My gaze dropped to the stone gargoyle out front. The tip of the fat little creature's face bore a chip and it had lost an ear. The ravages of time.

"Hey baby."

I recognized the man's gold-toothed smile despite his eyes being hidden by a pair of Ray Ban sunglasses. The mass of ebony muscles worked as one of the bouncers at the Ministry of Music nightclub.

"Hey," I said, returning the gesture.

"Long time no see, sugar." Lowering his glasses and eyeing me from top to bottom, he added, "Mmm. Fine as ever."

"Thanks."

"No more clubbing?"

"No…"

"Got yourself a jealous man?"

"Something like that."

A text message came in on his cell phone and he checked it. "Ministry is fading fast. New club in town." He glanced up from the glowing screen. "Been there yet?"

The city's night clubs no longer interested me. "I've been traveling and only got back recently."

"Shadow is the name. You should check it out."

"Is it a wild club?"

"Nothing like that. It's real chill. Adults only."

"Cool."

"Tell them Leroy sent you. Catch you later."

I watched him saunter down the sidewalk. The man definitely possessed swagger.

I crept into the lair unnoticed. Someone played the piano and I veered toward the sound of the music. Sporting a glamorous sequined top, a Japanese vampire played Franz Liszt with admirable precision. Transfixed by her nimble fingers as they danced over the ivory keys, I paused to enjoy the performance. Arsham came to stand behind me, drawing the glances of those gathered around the musician.

Taking hold of my arm, he urged me away from the others. "Where have you been?"

"Sire—"

"Answer me."

"Not here," I whispered while glancing at the pianist.

He led me into his chamber and closed the door. "Someone saw you leaving the lair in what he called a *furtive manner*."

"He? Who told you that?"

"It doesn't matter. What are you up to?"

"Nothing."

"No secrets, remember?"

Not wishing to risk Arsham's trust, I confessed, "I was in Yorkshire."

His eyes turned hard. "Why?"

"You wanted me to put the coven first, so I did. Damien and Katya are planning to challenge you and Rahim."

Circling me like a predator, he asked in a deceptively calm tone, "You took it upon yourself to speak with two traitors?"

The unmistakable jealousy in his eyes frightened and excited me. The fact that I went to speak with Damien behind his back was the real issue at hand here.

I edged away from him. "I wanted to get a confession from them, sire. We need to know what we're up against."

"You went alone." Closing the gap between us, he put his face near mine. "Without obtaining my permission first. What you did was foolish, not to mention dangerous."

"Damien is convinced that Katya cares for humans and claims that she wants to fight against the tyranny. Actually, his exact words were 'to end it.' "

He arched a perfect eyebrow. "The tyranny?"

I averted my gaze out of respect. "You and Rahim."

Taking hold of my chin, he forced me to look at him. His eyes revealed anger and something else. "You could have been killed tonight."

"Damien wouldn't hurt me."

"Are you trying to convince me or yourself? You were lucky that nothing happened this time. Your ex-lover is under the influence of Katya now. *Remember that*." Caressing my cheek, he added, "I can't bear the thought of losing you now that you're finally home. Never take a risk like that again."

"I won't."

He dropped his hand and moved away from me. Opening the door, he said, "Tell no one about what you learned tonight."

I exited his chamber and went in search of Rahim. When I found him, we retreated to the library in order to speak privately.

He asked, "Did you go to Yorkshire?"

"Yes, and Arsham already knows. I made it seem like it was

my idea, exactly as you instructed."

"Good. Did you confirm the intentions of the traitors?"

"According to them, they want to end the tyranny. The manner in which they spoke, the hatred in their eyes…I have every reason to believe that they want you and Arsham dead."

Nodding sadly, he said, "So it had come to this."

"I'm sorry, my lord."

"You did well tonight and I'm grateful. Since you've told my brother, I'm sure he will be apprising me of the situation." Regarding me thoughtfully, he added, "There's something I wish to bring to your attention but I feel it's not my place to do so. The last thing I want to do is offend a coven Elder."

"Please speak freely."

"My brother cares about you more than you realize."

I averted my gaze. "Why are you telling me this?"

"You're intelligent. I'm sure you can figure it out."

***

I emerged from my room two nights later to find Arsham and two bodyguards waiting outside my door. I recognized the two warriors as Thomas and Francis, brothers from Cornwall. They were recent additions to the coven via one of Rahim's vampires. Only two human years apart, the stocky males were pleasant and possessed good fighting skills. Under my tutelage, they were fast becoming formidable warriors.

"Sire, is everything all right?" I inquired.

"I want you to come with me." Casting a glance at the two bodyguards, he added in a provocative tone, "I figured you could use some distraction, and it's been a while since you and I have had the pleasure of each other's exclusive company."

"I'm flattered," I said cautiously.

"Come, we must hurry."

We crept out of the lair through a private door known only to Elders. "Why all the secrecy?" I whispered.

"You'll see."

Once outside, Arsham took off into the night as fast as possible and we followed suit. My curiosity burned as we flew over pastures, farms, and villages. We rode a powerful icy current over the North Atlantic for hours. No one spoke. I cast a glance at Arsham's face, which revealed serious intention.

To my surprise, we landed on Diamond Beach in Iceland. Devoid of people, it felt mystical and ethereal. Big clumps of ice scattered along the black shoreline rendered the landscape fantastic, like a scene from a sci-fi movie.

I glimpsed the faint blush of the approaching dawn on the horizon. "Why are we here, sire?"

"I wanted to be alone with you," he said loudly enough for the bodyguards to hear before pretending to kiss my temple. In my ear he whispered, "We must hurry."

Arsham led us to a remote cottage. The contemporary structure had been built on a swell of land facing the water. Thomas and Francis stood watch in the foyer as my sire and I proceeded down a short hallway that led into a large room.

Arsham closed and locked the heavy metal door between the foyer and what I now realized was an oversized bedroom suite. "This is a soundproof door so we can speak freely."

"There are plenty of remote places outside of London if you desired privacy."

"That was only an excuse."

"For what?"

Rather than reply, he extracted a small leather case from the inside pocket of his black wool coat. Setting the case on the table, he proceeded to remove his black leather gloves.

I cast a quick glance around the room. A king-sized bed dominated the space and sheepskin rugs covered the wooden plank floor. To my left, a glass window almost as big as the wall afforded a sweeping view of the beach. To my right, an open door revealed a bathroom with slate walls.

Arsham unzipped the leather case. "What do you think of my cottage? I had it built especially for this occasion."

I froze at the sight of two syringes.

Ignoring my reaction, he said smoothly, "I had that window made to my precise specifications. The tempered glass supposedly blocks UV light. I had layers of anti-UV film applied to the outside and the inside as an extra precaution."

"There's no glass on Earth that is totally resistant."

He reached for one of the syringes and removed the plastic cap from the needle's tip. "I know. Eva paid me a visit last night, and she came bearing gifts."

Realization led me to become alarmed. "You can't do this."

Amused, he said in gentle voice laden with steel, "You dare to tell me what I can and cannot do?"

"Does Rahim know why you're here?"

"Nobody knows that I'm in Iceland except for you and the Cornwall brothers." His eyes darted to the closed door as he carefully rolled up the sleeve of his crisply pressed shirt. "And they believe we're here for an amorous rendezvous."

My chagrin at having believed the same thing caused me to avert my gaze. Arsham lifted my chin with his fingertip and smiled knowingly, deepening the level of my embarrassment.

I held up my hand. "Wait! What if the serum fails? What if the window fails?"

Arsham injected the serum into a vein on the inside of his elbow. "I guess we shall see, won't we? I didn't want to make guinea pigs of my vampires, which is why I told no one of my intention."

To my dismay, there were no drapes or shutters to cover the window. The darkness was fading fast outside. "Maybe we should take refuge in the bathroom."

"Your concern for me is touching, Angelique." Removing the needle from his flesh, he added, "See? I'm fine. The sun will rise soon. You can go and wait inside the bathroom if you wish. I'll call out for you to join me if this works."

I gave him a look of disbelief. "Not a chance!"

I took the remaining syringe and injected the serum into my arm. He watched me with an unreadable expression as I set the needle down and stood beside him.

"We will share the same fate," I said defiantly.

He smirked. *"Warrior Goddess."*

"The least I can do is live up to the nickname."

Arsham offered me his hand and I accepted it. We stood before the glass with fingers intertwined, our eyes glued to the watery horizon. I instinctively flinched as the first rays of burnished gold pierced the sky.

My sire squeezed my hand in reassurance. "It's all right."

The fragile rays grew stronger, casting their gleaming reflection upon the icy surface of the Jökulsárlón glacial lagoon. Tears of emotion blurred my vision as I watched the tip of the sun rise over the horizon. I wiped at my eyes, then glanced at my sire.

Arsham stood, transfixed, his face expressing pure rapture. I had not seen the sun in over two hundred years, but for him it had been nearly a thousand. I didn't dare say a word for fear I'd break the magical spell. He cast a quick glance in my direction and I swore I saw his eyes glistening with emotion. We turned our attention back to the view. We marveled at the sky as it transformed from dull blue-gray to crimson, then deep salmon, and finally pale yellow. The sunlight glinted off the many clumps of ice, making them sparkle like diamonds, thus giving the beach its name. The world exploded with sun-drenched colors as the sun rose over the horizon line.

At length, Arsham whispered, "Do you like my gift?"

"More than you'll ever know."

He placed his arm around my shoulders and kissed the top of my head while keeping his eyes on the view. The affectionate gesture had a warm human quality to it and, for an instant, I pretended that we were a pair of mortals enjoying nature.

A beep went off, abruptly ending my fantasy. Metal shutters, hidden inside the walls, slowly came together to completely block our view. The image of the gleaming orb in the sky had already burned itself into my memory.

Arsham opened the metal door leading to the hallway where Thomas and Francis lay sleeping on the floor. "We will also be claimed by sleep when this wears off." Turning to me, he smiled. "The serum works."

I touched his arm. "Thank you for this, Arsham…I'll never forget this day."

He covered my hand with his own. "We need to rest now."

I glanced at the big inviting bed. How many times had my

sire asked me to keep him company while he slept? Would he ask that of me now?

Cutting into my thoughts, he said, "The second bedroom is through the bathroom. You'll find everything you need there."

It was a dismissal. Disappointed, I only stared at him. He stared back, silent and stoic, making no move to come near me.

"I bid you good rest, sire," I said softly before darting into the bedroom.

True to Arsham's words, the room offered every comfort. I stretched out on the bed and closed my eyes. Vampires watched sunrises in videos or movies but never the real thing. My sire had bestowed a precious gift upon me. One that I would cherish forever.

I awoke the next evening feeling groggy. A side-effect of the serum, perhaps? I recalled the image of the sunrise and smiled to myself. Crossing the bathroom, I knocked on the closed door. At Arsham's invitation, I opened it.

Shrugging into his coat, he asked, "Do you feel strange?"

"I do," I admitted.

The metal shutters were open to reveal the nightscape. "We must go back to the lair. Speak of this to no one."

"How will you explain our absence?"

Arsham smiled and pretended to adjust his cuff. "Gods don't explain themselves to anyone."

"What about Elders?"

"You don't owe anyone the satisfaction." Coming to stand before me, he kissed my forehead. "Thank you for sharing this morning with me."

"Why did you choose me for this special honor?"

He gave me a measured look. "Who else would I choose?"

We exited the cottage in companionable silence. Thomas and Francis waited for us outside. Believing that Arsham and I had shared an evening of unbridled passion, the bodyguards did their best to maintain a neutral expression. Arsham grasped my hand and the four of us flew into the frigid night.

CHAPTER 13

"People do incredible things for love,
particularly for unrequited love."
(Daniel Radcliffe)

Three days passed with no sign of Arsham. I found myself discreetly searching for him everywhere. Although I did my best to appear nonchalant, I desperately craved his company. Seeking distraction, I decided to check out the new night club Leroy had mentioned to me the other night.

I donned the gorgeous Dior outfit Arsham had gifted me in Edinburgh, then ventured out alone. The club's façade had been painted white and the word "shadow" was an actual shadow. The metallic letters were hammered to a board across the street, and set in front of a powerful light. I found the effect clever.

"There's my girl."

I turned to face the big bouncer in shades. "Hey Leroy. You didn't tell me that you were working here."

"Surprise," he said, moving aside the red velvet rope and allowing me to cut the line of people. "Wow! Look at you. Gorgeous to the bone. Have a good time."

Pressing a sizeable note into his hand, I said, "Thanks."

He grinned at the generous tip.

The chiaroscuro interior lived up to the club's name. Cleverly positioned light sources created shadowy artwork and lettering within the complex. Bartenders and waitresses wore black, as did the bouncers. Stylishly dressed adults danced and chatted with a certain level of sophistication. Definitely an upgrade from the youthful madness at the Ministry of Music. I focused on a pair of dancers. The man and woman only possessed eyes for each other.

I tore my gaze from them and wandered toward the bar. A couple passed me in order to claim the last two available seats.

I didn't mind. I stood off to the side as they placed their order with the bartender, then watched as they played "kissy-face" while he created their cocktails.

I wondered if Arsham frequented this place, then caught myself. He haunted my thoughts a lot lately. Too much, in fact.

He's so different now.

Could a vampire of his advanced age really change?

A handsome man smiled at me from the opposite end of the bar, putting my thoughts of Arsham on hold. The mortal's muted green eyes and pleasant features reminded me of Caleb, whose death I still mourned.

No more human friends, Angelique. Lesson learned.

I turned my back on the man to study the other mortals lined up at the bar.

Green eyes suddenly materialized before me, his smile stretching across his defined features. "Hi. I'm Greg."

I smiled at him. "Penelope."

"Pretty name. Would you care for a drink?"

"No thanks."

"How about a dance?"

I studied the well-dressed man. "Sure."

I allowed him to pull me onto the dance floor where we swayed to the music. "You're not from around here are you?"

"No."

"Visiting London?"

"Yes," I replied, running my hands up his arms and allowing them to rest on his shoulders.

My flirtation prompted him to hold me a bit closer. "What do you think of the city so far?"

"Nice architecture. The National Gallery is wonderful."

"Where are you from?"

"Paris."

"There's a cute French themed bar not far from here. It's cozy and quiet. I can take you there."

Resting my head on his shoulder, I said, "I'd like that. We'll go after this dance, okay?"

"You got it."

Inhaling the scent of his pricey cologne, I discreetly pierced the skin of his neck with my fangs.

Gasping, he whispered, "God, you're sexy."

He hardened against me as I sucked his blood. I drank only a little bit since I didn't want him to pass out in front of everyone. Gazing deeply into his eyes afterward, I mesmerized him. Next, I led my prey to a table toward the back of the room where he could recuperate.

"He reminds you of Dr. Morgan."

I spun around to find Arsham inches from my face. "Sire!"

"Did you love him?"

"What are you doing here?"

His eyes roamed over me before meeting my gaze. "I have such excellent taste...I followed you here."

"Why?"

"I had to know where you were going dressed like that."

"I wanted to check out this new place. I haven't seen you in three days."

"You're evading my question."

"I loved Dr. Morgan's mind, nothing more."

Taking a step closer to me, he said, "I didn't kill him."

"What?"

"The vampirologist and the woman were already dead when we arrived at the flat."

My mind spun with this information. "Who killed them?"

"Keep asking yourself that question and it will lead you to the answer." Holding out his hand, he added, "In the meantime, dance with me."

Shaken by what he had told me, I hesitated. He reached for my hand and gripped it firmly before leading me to the center of the dance floor. The DJ played a series of slow romantic songs, dimming the lights for effect. My sire said nothing as I followed his lead, giving me time to digest the disturbing truth.

"You're surprised," he said.

"I'm at a loss for words."

He held me close, making me feel safe. At one point, he leaned toward me and placed his nose in my hair. Inhaling deeply, he emitted a low growl.

"I've missed your scent," he whispered before reluctantly letting go of me. "I'm going back to the lair now so that you may be alone with your thoughts."

With that, he turned his back on me and disappeared into the crowd. If Arsham and my brethren didn't kill Caleb and Jennifer, who did? Katya? Another vampire from a foreign coven? I left Shadow shortly afterward and returned to the lair where I sought the privacy of my chamber.

A knock on the door made me hopeful. "Come in."

Micah poked his head into the room. "Angelique?"

Hiding my disappointment, I said, "This is a nice surprise."

"Wow," he said, checking out my outfit. "Going out on the town tonight?"

"I went to Shadow."

"What did you think of it?"

"I like it better than the Ministry of Music."

"Me too." Taking in the splendor of my room, he grinned. "Valerio's taste is…well, it's over the top, isn't it?"

"Without a doubt."

I took in his charcoal pants and tailored dove gray shirt. Simple and stylish. The smooth white perfection of his albino skin still had the power to impress me. Like Michelangelo's *David*, Micah appeared to be fashioned from Carrara marble.

"I'm glad you ditched the colored contacts," I said, admiring his strange eyes. "Right now they're violet."

"I literally have to fight off the females because of these unique eyes."

"Poor Eva must live in a perpetual state of jealousy."

"What if I told you that she did?" We laughed together, then he said, "I spoke to Omar about an hour ago. He's happy to have you back on the Security Team."

"I'm happy too. It gives me the opportunity to be useful around here, not to mention proving myself to those who still harbor doubts about me."

"Don't let that bother you. It's a shame you didn't come home with us when we went to see you in Grand Cayman.

153

Valerio and I were reluctant to leave you behind."

"It wasn't personal, you know."

"I know. Our disappointment paled in comparison to that of Arsham's. After we returned from London and gave him our report, he didn't say a word but his mood and actions spoke volumes." He studied my face closely. "I'm not sure whether it's appropriate for me to tell you this, but Arsham changed the day he put you in the punishment coffin."

"That was over a decade ago." I didn't like how he was looking at me so I pretended to admire an oil painting depicting wealthy nobles making merry at a feast. "It's understandable that his behavior changed. He was furious at me for having broken a sacred law."

"No Angelique, it's more than that. Our sire mourned your absence for a decade while you were serving your sentence. Imagine what he must have felt when you ran away the day of your release."

I tore my eyes from the painting to meet Micah's insistent gaze. "I hurt his ego, nothing more."

"You *devastated* him."

"You're serious."

"I am."

I pondered his words. "How can I rectify what I've done?"

"Arsham needs to know that you won't run away again."

"I betrayed Damien and Rahim by foiling their plans and uniting the covens," I pointed out in my defense. "That alone should prove my loyalty."

"Did you know that he's been alone since your release from the punishment coffin?"

"Alone as in…?"

"A monk."

Despite Micah's serious tone, I smirked. "You're joking."

"Hardly."

"You're telling me the vampiric Casanova became celibate on my account? That's rather hard to believe given his insatiable appetite for beautiful vampires."

"It's hard to believe but it's true."

"Why are you telling me these things?"

He quirked an eyebrow at me in response.

Silence.

I removed my earrings and bracelet and placed them in a finely crafted wooden jewelry box. "Enough about Arsham and his sex life. It's really none of my concern, is it?"

"Isn't it? Rumor has it that you and he took off together the other night to an undisclosed location."

Forcing myself to laugh, I said, "This coven is like a giant sewing circle full of gossiping old women."

"Does that mean you're not going to divulge any details?"

"My lips are sealed, dear brother." Placing my hand on his shoulder, I added, "Tell me, are you still practicing your sword fighting?"

"I'm a bit rusty but if you fancy a sparring match there's still a couple of hours before sunrise."

"That's exactly what I need right now."

Eyeing my dress and heels, he said, "Change into something more comfortable and meet me there."

Thankfully, Valerio had purchased a few pieces of athletic gear. I changed into a tank top, running tights, and sneakers before heading to the training room. Performance textiles were modern day miracles in comparison to the stiff, heavy garments I wore in the past.

Micah awaited me outside the door. "This sporty look suits you quite well. Actually, you could wear a burlap bag and still make heads turn."

I chuckled while securing my hair into a ponytail. "Buttering me up won't make me go easy on you."

The young vampires whispered at the sight of two Elders entering the training room. Ignoring their curious stares, we headed straight toward the display of ancient weapons and selected two medieval swords. After testing the weight and balance of our weapons with trained expertise, we moved to the center of a large wooden floor. The other vampires retreated and watched in fascination as Micah and I circled each other with calculating steps.

"What are you waiting for, brother?" I taunted.

Raising his sword, he came at me full force. One of the young vampires cried out. I blocked Micah's first blow, parried, and lunged. He ducked and I spun around, placing the tip of the blade at his throat. He laughed, ducked and managed to nick my arm with the edge of his sword. Some of the vampires gasped in horror. Elders spilling each other's blood was not a common sight. Frightened, a young female left the room to report us.

Seeing this, I said, "They think we're serious."

"Let's really scare them," Micah whispered.

I spun around and pierced his side with the tip of my sword, soiling his white t-shirt with blood. "Take that, you rogue!"

Micah came at me with renewed vehemence. The young female returned a moment later with Omar in tow. He entered the space and crossed his arms, watching us the way a parent would when observing two wayward children. Omar leaned over and reassured the worried vampire that Micah and I were only roughhousing. I would make a tough soldier of her yet. I did a quick scan of the room and noticed a few "softies" that desperately needed some hard training. I had my work cut out for me, which was a good thing. I needed to stay busy.

Micah's blade eventually crossed mine and he grinned at me. "It's good to have you back, Angelique."

***

I knocked on Arsham's door one night. At his invitation, I entered his chamber. "Forgive the disturbance, sire."

He eyed me expectantly. "Is everything all right?"

"I haven't seen you since the night at Shadow."

He waved his hand at the room. "I've been here taking care of business."

"Have you and Rahim reached an accord?"

"Not yet," he replied, picking up a document from a table.

"What will it take to convince the other Elders?"

"I don't know," he replied, taking a seat behind a massive mahogany desk. "I'll let you know when I do."

"Damien and Katya may do something drastic if we don't act soon."

Shuffling through a pile of papers, he said, "Your assumption is mostly likely correct. Omar told me that Jeanne Sauvage was spotted in London."

Alarmed, I demanded, "What course of action is Omar taking? Why haven't I been informed?"

"He sent spies to track her movements and he only told me a while ago. I'm sure he'll apprise you of the situation the moment he sees you."

"Good." I paced the room nervously. "Can't the new law be implemented by force?"

Arsham pinched the bridge of his nose. "Rahim and I will consider that option only as a last resort."

"What's left to consider?"

"Angelique, it's not that easy. We need—"

"It *is* that easy!"

My disrespect earned me a harsh look. "Not all of the Elders are ready to accept this new way of feeding. It's a foreign concept to the older ones."

"Well, Jazmin has no issue with it."

"Like you, she's an exception to the rule."

"It's Andrei and Mayu who refuse to budge."

He sighed. "Among the Elders, yes."

"Have you considered the possibility of their implication in this treasonous plot?"

Arsham hesitated. "Placing two of Rahim's Elders in question would divide this coven. Andrei and Mayu have many allies, not to mention their own progeny. I'm proceeding with caution and I'm ordering you to do the same."

"You can count on my discretion."

"Good."

"Does that mean that I have your permission to spy on them? If I find proof, will you implement the law at once?"

"There will be initial confusion among the vampires when this new law is announced. Things need to be done correctly and it will take some time."

"We don't have the luxury of time. I've been to Yorkshire. I've already confirmed what Damien and Katya are planning to do. Tell me, what more do you need?"

His eyes narrowed in anger. "You forget your place."

"Sire—"

"Let me do what I've been doing for centuries, which is to rule." In a softer tone, he added, "I appreciate your insight and your counsel, but now you must leave this matter to us."

Biting my tongue, I inclined my head.

Arsham lifted a sheet of paper from the desk. He clenched his jaw as his dark eyes skimmed over the figures. He now carried the burden of leadership with a solemnity that intrigued me. Picking up a pen, he began to sign his name on some of the documents requiring his signature. Like the rest of us, he used aliases in order to conduct business in the outside world.

He stopped what he was doing and met my eyes. "Is there anything else?"

"No, sire."

Arsham eyed the door, silently dismissing me. Rather than take my leave, I wandered to the desk and stood behind his chair. Puzzled by this, he turned his head slightly to track my movements. Gathering my courage, I placed my hands on his shoulders and began kneading the knotted muscles.

He tensed. "What are you doing?"

"Helping you to relax."

Taking hold of my wrists, he gently lifted my hands from his shoulders. "You should go."

I moved to stand beside him. "I'm worried about you."

Eyeing the document in his hand, he said crisply, "You need not concern yourself."

"Sire—"

"Leave me, Angelique."

Stung by Arsham's rejection, I exited his chamber. I was well aware of the risks involved in loving the powerful prince, but the heart was a treacherous thing that could neither be denied nor tamed. In the last several weeks, how many times had I recalled our intimate conversations? Our lovemaking?

His magic blood…

I returned to my chamber in defeat.

CHAPTER 14
BRAZIL

"Persistence is a secret weapon for everyone."
(Liu Wen)

Katya leaned up on her elbow to look down at Damien's sleeping face. She knew he would wake up at any second, but that brief glimpse of him in blissful peace almost warmed her heart. It was the only time when he wasn't restless. Steel gray eyes suddenly stared back at her, cunning and dangerous. The predatory look of a young vampire.

Older vampires, such as herself, no longer reflected such blatant savagery in their gazes. Time had increased their skills yet mellowed their outward appearances, allowing them to prey upon unsuspecting humans with greater ease.

His hand moved to the back of her head to grab a fistful of blonde hair. Pulling her toward him, he kissed her hard. She welcomed his tongue and his rough lovemaking, greedily matching his passion thrust for thrust.

"I love how you fuck," Katya said afterward.

Damien only smiled at the remark. He really liked Katya, but she irritated him at times. Angelique had never spoken to him in such a vulgar manner.

Damn it.

He swore to forget about the duchess but she often crept into his thoughts. There was no way he would ever take her back, even if she crawled on her hands and knees and begged him.

Katya continued, "I'm not in the mood to search tonight."

He frowned. "We have to search. That's why we're here."

"We've been going out every night and covering several square miles of territory. I need a break." She caressed his cheek. "Let's have some fun, shall we? I'll put on something sexy. We can resume our mission tomorrow night."

Damien's eyes followed Katya's lithe body as she strutted across the room devoid of clothing. She had a great ass. He got out of bed and went to the window of her *cobertura*. Situated in the center of Brazil's megalopolis, the apartment's rooftop terrace graced the highest floor and allowed for much needed privacy. He stepped outside and sauntered to the edge. Staring out at the darkening twilight sky, he tried to remember the sun. He missed the warmth of its rays on his face. He missed sunsets and sunrises. He missed being human.

The busy traffic and crowded sidewalks of the exciting Avenida Paulista pulsated far below. One of the city's main avenues, it teemed with life, street art, comely Brazilians, and violent criminals. There was an old saying that the crime in São Paulo, or *Sampa*, was so bad that the newspaper dripped blood.

Katya had purchased the apartment in Brazil a year ago in order to simplify her search for shifters. According to ancient legends, avian shape shifters once existed in this part of the world. Not having met with success, she returned to Europe. She had resumed the search for two reasons. First, Harry made it clear that he no longer wanted to hunt vampires. The moment Felicia had discovered that Angelique was back in the London lair, she had wisely dissuaded her little brother from pursuing the dangerous and lonely career. Last week, Harry enrolled in university to study computer engineering.

Damien wondered if he shouldn't follow Felicia's example and convince Jeanne to abandon her dream of becoming the next Sauvage slayer. It would probably be virtually impossible since the girl was stubborn. Every time he tried to do something for Jeanne, she exerted her rebelliousness. Was it so wrong for an older brother to feel protective of his younger sibling?

Angelique served as the second reason to continue the search in Brazil. Her ability for detecting feline shape shifters was legendary, but could she sniff out avian shifters? Neither he nor Katya could answer that question, but it was worth a shot. This was their fourth week in São Paulo and they still hadn't found anything.

He retreated into the apartment to slip on a pair of jeans and a black t-shirt. The delicate clicking of high-heeled pumps made him turn around. Katya looked scrumptious in a tight red tank dress.

"I'm thirsty," she purred.

"Let's go," Damien said as he quickly shrugged into his leather jacket.

Five minutes later they were strolling hand in hand through the crowded sidewalk. São Paulo never slept and offered a myriad of thrilling possibilities. New York City paled in comparison to the vibrancy of South America's "Big Apple." Brazilians who lived in the city were commonly referred to as *Paulistanos*. The majority of them were stunning in appearance.

Bossa Nova poured from the speakers of a small bar off the frenetic main avenue. Jacaranda trees created a canopy over the narrow street, and several trendy people hovered around the doorway sipping beers and caipirinha cocktails.

Katya led Damien toward the entrance. She enjoyed blending in with the crowds and dancing with humans whereas he only tolerated it. Pretending to sip his beer at an outside table, he watched his current lover flirt shamelessly with an oversized teenager in a tight nylon shirt. Anabolic steroids and plastic surgery were common among the vain, and the majority of Brazilians were hung up on outward appearances.

A pretty mulatta in a yellow halter top made eyes at him from a nearby table. Uninterested, Damien averted his gaze.

"Viado," the girl whispered to her companion.

Damien knew the term referred to homosexual men.

The mountain at her side chuckled. "Talvez." *Maybe.*

Katya's hearty laugh drew Damien's attention. Like him, she only fed on the dregs of society but she certainly enjoyed fooling around with every good looking man she encountered. Females, too, for that matter. Damien watched as she whispered into the guy's ear. Whatever she said made his eyes widen with surprise. Probably something dirty. After all, she prided herself on being vulgar. Born of peasants in the early nineteenth century, she lacked the sophistication and polish that Angelique possessed in abundance.

Damn it! He did it again.

A couple started dancing to samba music and it didn't take long for others to follow suit. He tried to ignore the fact that Katya was now kissing an inebriated Brazilian hunk. To entertain himself, he imagined how he would kill Arsham. Perhaps binding him with silver cords and tossing him outside in the brilliant sunshine would prove entertaining. Watching the arrogant prick disintegrate into a pile of worthless ash would make his day.

Katya decided to join her lover several kisses later. "Don't tell me you're jealous," she teased in response to his scowl.

"You're free to do as you please but don't expect me to admire you for being a slut."

She laughed. "You're adorable when you're angry."

The growl he emitted failed to frighten her. Instead, she slid her hand beneath the table and rested it on his thigh. "Listen to me, Damien. That guy I was kissing, his last name is *Pena*, which means feather in Portuguese. It's not the most common name and worth looking into, don't you think?

"I think you're clutching at straws. We're wasting our time in Brazil. Avian shifters don't exist."

"You don't know that. Be patient."

The late hour prompted more arrivals, causing people to literally spill out of the tiny bar. A fight over a girl broke out. Someone by the door dropped their drink. Glass shards and beer scattered everywhere. Slurred expletives and threats were hurled through the crowd.

"Let's go," Damien said, disgusted.

They left the bar and headed for Capão Redondo, the most violent of São Paulo's ninety-six districts. Consisting of seedy bars, scantily clad prostitutes, pushers, pimps, and armed thugs, it scared off many people—including the police. Woe to the traveler who wandered into the dangerous *bairro* in error. Like the *favelas* of Rio de Janeiro, strangers entered at great risk of being mugged, shot, or both.

Shifty eyes and unfriendly faces tracked every move made by Damien and Katya, but they didn't care. Strolling through the sea of unpredictable humans, they laughed in the face of danger.

A tough-looking woman in black leather pants and gold bikini top stepped in front of Katya. "Give me your shoes."

Three girls stood behind the woman, each heavily tattooed.

Katya glanced down at the red designer shoes, unfazed. "They're gorgeous, aren't they?"

The woman flicked her wrist. She held a switchblade. "Take them off, *puta*."

Katya frowned. "What did you call me?"

The woman lunged. In a flash, the hand that still held the switchblade lay on the ground. The woman stared in horror at the bleeding stump, her gold bikini top splattered with red droplets. Katya calmly licked the blood around her lips as the wounded woman fainted. Her friends wailed and screeched as they attempted to staunch the bleeding.

"Come on," Katya said to Damien.

Shocked, he demanded, "Was that really necessary?"

She pouted. "I love these shoes!"

"I thought you never killed indiscriminately. You care about humans, remember?"

"I didn't kill her," she protested.

Damien's eyes fell upon the handless woman who had lost so much blood that she was now going into shock.

Katya waved her hand. "Look around, honey. Do you see any upstanding citizens here? They're all scumbags, which is what we feed on."

"Scumbags are still humans, and you weren't feeding. You did that out of spite."

Katya rolled her eyes. "Lighten up, Damien."

Angelique's words haunted him. Could Katya be pretending to be something she's not?

She nudged him. "Are you going to let this ruin our night?"

"No."

Damien led her to a dive bar where couples danced in such a provocative manner that they may as well have been copulating in public. Grabbing Katya's hand, he sauntered to the bar well aware that everyone stared at them.

"Duas cervejas," he said to the bartender.

Damien paid and tipped the man before handing one of the two beer bottles to Katya.

She feigned a sip. "See that thug right there? He's my juice box. I'll be back."

Damien watched as she veered toward a greasy man with the eyes of a serial killer. To his surprise, the pretty mulatta in the yellow halter top from the other bar lounged by the doorway. Staring directly at him, she waved him over. He approached with caution.

She grinned mischievously. *"Oi, tudo bem?"*

"Do you speak English?" At her nod, he continued, "How did you get here so fast?"

"I could ask you the same question." Glancing at Katya, she added, "You're not gay, are you?"

"No," he replied warily.

Placing her sparkly pink lips to his ear, she added, "Not human either."

He gave her a measured look. "Are you a shifter? We're looking for avian shifters to help us kill vampires."

The mulatta laughed. "As if I'd believe you."

"My name is Damien Sauvage."

Hearing this, the girl sobered. *"The* Damien Sauvage?"

"None other."

"Wait here."

He watched as the girl ran over to a huge black man and whispered in his ear.

Katya materialized beside Damien. "What's going on?"

"I think we've found our shifter."

The Afro-Brazilian's height dwarfed that of the petite mulatta strutting beside him. They came to a stop before Damien, each one looking at him expectantly.

Assuming the big man was the slayer, Damien said, "I was once like you, my friend. A vampire changed me against my will and now I want revenge."

The man's eyes bulged then he laughed heartily. The mulatta

laughed too.

Damien and Katya exchanged puzzled glances.

"I doubt you were like me, my friend," the man replied in broken English. "I am shifter. She is slayer."

Surprised, Damien looked at the mulatta. *"You?"*

The girl nodded. "My name is Xoana. My father used to tell me stories about the Sauvage clan when I was a child."

Damien's brow creased. "If you're the slayer..."

Xoana placed a hand on the man's arm. "This is Corvo."

Corvo revealed perfect white teeth when he smiled.

"That means crow," Katya pointed out.

Xoana said, "I've been tracking you for days. You two don't act like other vampires. You don't kill humans."

Katya quirked an eyebrow. "Is that why you spared us?"

"Yes. I've been trying to figure out why."

Damien inquired, "How many slayers are there in the city?"

"Nine, but I'm the fastest. Twenty-three confirmed kills. Of course, that's nothing compared to your track record."

"Still impressive," Damien assured her. "This is Katya."

Xoana and Corvo inclined their heads at the sexy blonde.

"We have a proposition for you," Katya said.

Xoana glanced around nervously. "Not here. It isn't safe to speak in this place." Corvo whispered something into her ear and she added, "Tomorrow is Tuesday, which means extended hours at MASP. Meet us there after sunset and we'll listen to your proposition."

***

Located on the Avenida Paulista, the Museum of Art of São Paulo was a rectangular edifice elevated by bright red concrete supports. Damien and Katya made their way into the modern building after sunset and found Corvo and Xoana waiting for them by the Van Gogh masterpiece, *A Walk at Twilight*.

"Corvo's idea," Xoana explained, indicating the painting. "Appropriate, no?"

Damien smiled slightly. "Very."

"Why did you ask us to come here?" Katya demanded, looking around in slight confusion.

Xoana shrugged. "Don't you like our museum? Corvo is very proud of his sister who works here. He thinks more gringos should visit the MASP."

Seeing the irritation on Katya's face, Damien intervened. "The museum is very nice and I'm sure your sister does a great job, Corvo. We're not visiting your city as tourists, however. We need your help and, since it's rather time-sensitive, we don't have much time to waste."

Xoana looked from one vampire to the other and frowned. "Exactly what kind of help do you want from us?"

"We're challenging the two sires who co-rule the biggest coven on the European continent."

"That's crazy," Xoana said before turning toward Corvo and translating for him.

The big man scowled at us and shook his head. Gesturing toward the museum's gallery, he said, "Visit is better."

"No visit today," Damien countered.

"We're demanding change," Katya explained, her attention focused on the slayer. "The implementation of a new law that prohibits vampires from killing humans."

Xoana translated again and Corvo stared at the vampires as though they were completely insane.

Xoana said, "Good luck trying to change a sacred law."

"Laws are meant to be broken," Damien pointed out.

"Suicide mission," Corvo drawled while crossing his arms in resistance.

"Corvo is right. Besides, we don't have the money to travel to London on a whim," Xoana said.

Katya put up her hand. "Don't worry about money. It's an all-expense paid trip. Are there any more avian shifters like him in the city?"

"Corvo is the only one in Sampa and I'm lucky he wants to work with me. There may be a few left in the Amazon. I don't know for certain."

Damien turned to Katya. "We don't have the time to continue searching. We've already been here long enough."

Katya nodded in agreement. "Damien and I will accompany

you on the international flight to fill you in on all the details."

Xoana and Corvo eventually agreed to help the vampires. Two days later, the four of them boarded a plane for the transatlantic flight. Neither Xoana nor Corvo had ever flown or left their country. Their eyes were glued to the tiny window during takeoff.

"I bet it feels weird for Corvo," Damien said to Xoana.

She chuckled. "Now that you mention it, yes."

Leaning toward her companion, she translated what Damien had said. Corvo met his gaze and nodded, laughing.

Once the pilot reached cruising altitude, the shifter and the slayer began asking questions. Katya did most of the talking on the plane while Damien offered a few replies. After a couple of hours, Corvo and Xoana fell asleep beneath their synthetic blankets.

Katya and Damien unbuckled their seatbelts and made their way down the narrow aisle toward the end of the plane. Fortunately, the rest of the passengers had started watching films and were eagerly anticipating the inflight meal.

Katya whispered, "Do you think Angelique will be able to sniff him out?"

"I don't know. She told me that feline shifters smell like cat piss and incense."

Katya scrunched up her face. "Nasty combination. Well, there's only one way to find out."

"What do you mean?"

"We'll ambush your ex. How else will we be able to discern if she can sense avian shifters?"

Damien hesitated. "I don't know if that's a good idea."

Katya eyed him steadily. "You still have feelings for her, don't you?"

"I resent her for being loyal to Arsham."

"Look, I want Arsham dead as much as you do but he's not what you think he is. Having spent time in London, I studied him. Like Rahim, he's an ancient vampire with a vast knowledge of history, sociology, psychology, anthropology, cultures, languages—his list of accomplishments is long."

"You're telling me that you find Arsham impressive?"

Katya regarded him blankly. "That's exactly what I'm saying. Don't you get it? We're not plotting to kill just any vampire here. Arsham is a god."

"My ass he's a god."

"Damien, you need to see the world for what it actually is and not what you want it to be."

"Next you'll tell me that you want to be with him."

Katya rolled her eyes. "Grow up, will you? I'm not your ex."

She was about to go when his hand shot out to grab her arm. "I'm stressed out, okay?"

"I really like you, honey. You're the best lay I've had in over fifty years. Your cute face and your hot bod turn me on, but you need to get your shit together. You've got hang-ups."

"Like you don't."

"Oh I do, but they don't cloud my perception of reality."

He sighed. "Okay."

She caressed his cheek. "Much better."

He nuzzled her neck. "What did you say about my cute face and hot bod?"

"You're sexy, I'll give you that."

He cupped her waist. "You're not so bad yourself."

They shared a passionate, furtive kiss.

Feeling himself hardening, Damien glanced at the empty restroom and Katya grinned wickedly in response. The flight attendants were gathered at the opposite end of the plane passing out plastic trays laden with plane food. To their mutual disappointment, an old woman shuffled up the aisle.

Reaching the restroom, she inquired, "Is it occupied?"

Katya shook her head and stood aside as the frail human made her way into the tiny bathroom with great difficulty. The vampires eyed the woman's papery veined hands as she grappled with the door.

"Allow me," Damien said, helping the old woman.

When the door was closed, Katya whispered, "No mile high club for us."

Damien shrugged and moved to reclaim his seat.

Katya followed and settled in beside him. "I'm glad that I'll never get old like that."

For the first time since becoming a vampire, Damien shared her sentiment.

***

I crossed paths with Omar in the corridor and he stopped me. "What's up?" I inquired.

"Arsham informed me that he and Rahim will be attending the opera tomorrow night. He insists that you accompany them."

"Of course."

"You'll need to take two bodyguards with you. How about Thomas and Francis? It would be their first real assignment."

I refrained from mentioning that the brothers had flown with us to Iceland. "We're talking about both sires being out at the same time. Are you sure we'll have enough security? I'm tempted for you to come too."

Omar shook his head. "Too many bodyguards may attract unwanted attention. Three of you is enough to provide a personal escort."

"Fine, but I think some guards positioned throughout the theater and a sniper on the roof would be wise." The look he gave me prompted me to add, "Do you think I'm being paranoid?"

"Maybe. It's good that we heighten security during a threat, but we haven't heard anything on the streets in weeks."

The quiet before the storm. "I don't know…"

"Honestly, I think Damien and Katya may have realized the folly of their ways and abandoned their stupid plan."

"I hope you're right, but until we're sure of it, I think it's best to take precautions."

"That's why I'm assigning Francis and Thomas to go with you. A night at the opera will be a good first assignment for them. Easy stuff."

"Shall I brief them?"

"I'll do it."

Clad in identical black suits, the brothers from Cornwall

169

waited for me by the piano the next night. I wore a tailored black pant suit like theirs, only mine was cut for a female body.

"Good evening, my lady," said Francis, the eldest.

"Hello." Their military stance and serious expressions prompted me to add, "At ease, boys."

They relaxed.

Francis said, "Thank you for this opportunity. Thomas and I are truly grateful."

"It was Omar's idea that this be your first *official* assignment. You should thank him."

"We will," Thomas chimed.

The three of us stood tall and straight with hands folded before us as we waited in the main atrium for the sires to emerge from their chambers. The handsome alphas drew many gazes as they crossed the expanse of the lair in gorgeous designer suits with expensive silk ties.

Arsham's eyes swept over me, his face expressing disappointment. "You're working tonight?"

"Guarding you, sire."

"Pity."

Puzzled, I commanded Thomas to walk ahead while Francis and I monitored the rear. Rahim had purchased balcony seats at the Royal Opera House to see Verdi's *La Traviata*.

A driver brought one of our cars around and we piled into the shiny black luxury SUV. No one spoke as we settled in the buttery leather seats. The vehicle navigated the London streets as smoothly as melting butter before pulling up at the colonnaded entrance of the historic theater. The moment we exited the SUV, heads turned. Mortal women ogled the sires with lust in their eyes. A few men stared too.

We entered the main lobby and went directly to the crush room. Red carpeting and crystal chandeliers afforded the space a bit of its original nineteenth century elegance. There, Arsham paid homage to the Italian soprano, Adelina Patti, who had been immortalized in marble. The diva's success was evidenced by the fabulous gown created for her as Violetta in *La Traviata*. A garment encrusted with almost four thousand diamonds.

Arsham gave me a pointed look. He and I had enjoyed her debut performance together, and many others afterward.

"Almost like old times," he whispered, his eyes glued to mine in a manner that made me breathless.

"Like old times," I repeated.

Rahim glanced at us and said, "The show is about to start."

I snapped back into bodyguard mode as we left the crush room and headed for the second floor. A few people loitered in the hallway, others chatted inside the individual balcony nooks. We found our assigned space and the sires took their seats toward the front. I made Thomas stand outside and was about to sit in the back with Francis when Arsham peeked over his shoulder at me and then patted the red velvet seat beside him. I went over and sat down, as instructed by my sire.

Arsham leaned in close. "I wanted you to come tonight as my guest, not my bodyguard."

"I didn't know."

"I told Omar to inform you."

"He did tell me. Neither of us assumed anything more than the normal protocol."

"Next time, you should assume."

Should I? Did he not expel me from his room when I had attempted to massage his shoulders?

He continued, "You're the only female I want by my side."

His words rendered me speechless, which was a good thing since the first act was about to begin.

Rahim leaned forward and offered me a slight smile, his knowing eyes twinkling in the dimness of the theater. I felt like an intruder sitting there with them. Every so often they would put their heads together and whisper to each other.

I scanned the audience for anyone who appeared suspicious while tossing looks over my shoulder at the two young warriors from Cornwall. Although Arsham had intended for me to attend the opera as his date, I had spent the better part of two centuries protecting him from the potential danger of shifters and slayers. Old habits were hard to break.

Convinced there was no imminent danger, I relaxed a bit and

actually enjoyed the opera. Although I had seen the production many times, it never got old for me—or Arsham for that matter.

The lights came on for the intermission and people milled about the theater. I stood and went into alert mode. I was about to go out into the corridor when Arsham took hold of my wrist.

"Stay," he said.

Rahim went out to discuss something with Thomas while I remained beside my sire. Francis stood off to the side monitoring the audience below as well as the people in the seats above our own.

"Next time, I'll make my intention clear," Arsham said, his eyes lingering on my outfit. "I long to see you in formal attire. Lately, you've been wearing nothing but black suits and athletic clothing."

The fact that he noticed this made my heart race. "When I'm not training newborns, I'm protecting the lair. Omar wears black daily too."

"It matters not to me what Omar chooses to wear."

I glanced down at myself. "It's been a long time since I've had a reason to wear something glamorous."

"We'll need to remedy that situation, won't we? A goddess should be worshipped and draped in costly fabrics."

I smirked at the outrageous compliment but his face was serious. "You mock me, sire."

"Never."

"I've been replaying in my mind something you said when we were in Edinburgh....You referred to yourself as a god."

Regarding me levelly, he said, "What would you call a sentient being who has lived for almost a millennium?"

"You make a valid point"

"Who else but a vampire god could gift you a sunrise?"

Although he had said the words in a playful manner, I covered his hand with my own. "I will treasure your precious gift forever."

"I know you will, which is why I bestowed it upon you."

I hesitated. "Do you feel anything different as you approach your thousandth year?"

"It's not about feeling, it's about *being*." He thought for a moment. "I am ancient. I am eternal. I am transcendent."

I stared at him, stunned.

Arsham sat back and said nothing more.

I watched the second act in pensive silence as his last words echoed throughout my mind.

Our party headed toward the theater exit at the show's conclusion. I ran ahead to make a general sweep of the lobby before giving the okay for the sires to descend. I watched them on the stairs while scanning the people around me. Limousines and taxi cabs crowded the front of the theater. Peering through the glass doors, I noticed the SUV parked further up the street. I exited the building to alert the driver. I stepped onto the sidewalk and froze. Muscles coiled. Something felt off. Arsham, Rahim, and the bodyguards exited behind me. I signaled to the latter, who stepped in front of the sires.

Arsham demanded, "Shifter?"

Sniffing the air, I couldn't pick up any strange scents but my skin prickled in a way that suggested that something dangerous lurked nearby. "Nobody move," I whispered.

Thomas and Francis edged toward me while maintaining their positions as human shields for the sires. The three of us scanned the street as dozens of people poured out of the theater. The warm, talkative humans swarmed around us. Luckily, our unnatural stillness wasn't noticed by anyone.

An elm tree across the street drew my gaze. I spotted a black crow watching me from a leafy branch. The creature was larger than normal. *And the eyes…*

I whipped around and said, "Get the sires back inside!"

Thomas and Francis spread out their arms and urged the alphas toward the doorway against the human traffic.

One man cursed. "Wrong way, moron."

I glared at the man and he took off in fear. Rahim cooperated with the bodyguards but Arsham did not. To my surprise, he headed in my direction.

"Angelique, stay here."

"I'm sorry," I said, shoving my sire back toward Rahim.

Moving too fast for human eyes, I ran at the crow at full speed. Grabbing it with both hands, I turned the corner to get it as far from the sires as possible. To my surprise, the bird shifted into an enormous man. The hitch in my step was enough for the experienced shifter to push me into an alley. I felt a cold hard blade at my throat barely a second later. A petite girl held the weapon with the frightening assuredness of a seasoned slayer. I had been cleverly ambushed by the crafty pair.

The bodyguards ran into the alley seconds later. Thomas tackled the slayer but she managed to scramble to her feet with the help of the shifter. Wings flapped frantically, followed by a loud caw. The large creature swooped and pecked at us with impressive speed and skill. Francis cursed as a chunk of his own flesh plopped down by his feet. The crow attacked again, this time tearing off part of his ear.

"Son of a bitch!" Francis cried.

Thomas threw a garbage can lid at the unholy bird, which gave Francis an opportunity to gather his bearings.

Suddenly, a familiar whooshing sound pierced the night.

No, no, no!

The head of Francis rolled toward my feet, compelling me to aim my gun in the slayer's direction.

Where are you, bitch?

No sooner had I spotted her than I was grabbed from behind and yanked out of the alley. I pulled the trigger and heard the girl scream.

"They've killed Francis," I said, struggling to free myself. "I can't leave Thomas there by himself."

"Let him handle it," Arsham said in my ear.

Poor Thomas was left alone in the alley to deal with the deadly pair. Clutching the shoulder where the bullet had entered, the slayer winced in pain. I thought the ordeal was over until she picked up her katana and raised it in the air.

"She'll kill him too," I said, struggling to free myself from Arsham's grip. "Let me go!"

He tightened his hold on me. "I said *no*, Angelique."

I watched, helpless, as she lunged at Thomas. Thankfully,

he ducked and managed to escape his brother's fate.

Another slayer jumped out of a window and landed directly in front of me. Arsham shoved me behind him and tore out the mortal's throat with precise lethality. Wiping his bloodied mouth with the back of his hand, he studied the slayer's face.

"Do you recognize him?" I inquired.

Arsham shook his head and met my gaze. "As of tonight, you are off my personal detail."

"No!"

"Don't argue with me."

I glared at him. "No one can protect you like me."

"You're a target."

Thomas cried out in pain, shifting my attention. He and the female shifter continued to fight in the alley. Raising my gun, I took aim but missed the shot when she dove behind a dumpster. Big claws grabbed hold of the injured slayer's jacket, lifting her off the ground and speedily carrying her down the alley. Their incredible exit left us bewildered.

Thomas exited the alley with several cuts and small chunks of flesh missing from his face and hands. The wicked crow had attacked him the way carrion birds pick over a carcass. Rahim quickly administered his own blood to the wounds in order to speed up the healing process.

"I'm sorry about your brother," I said to Thomas, placing my hand on his beefy shoulder.

Tears welled up in the young warrior's hard eyes as he regarded me. "I want you to train me to be like you. I want to avenge my brother's death."

I slowly nodded in response to his request.

Rahim's gaze fell on Francis's head. "Damn it."

Thomas demanded, "What was that thing, anyway?"

"Avian shifter," Rahim replied with a frown.

Arsham added, *"Imported."*

CHAPTER 15

"Absence makes the heart grow fonder."
(Thomas Haynes Bayly)

An emergency meeting was held immediately after the incident. An avian shifter in London begged many questions.

Standing before the Elders, I described the strange large crow and the petite mulatta who had brazenly held a blade to my throat. The second slayer had no ID on him, so we didn't know his identity.

"I thought you could detect shifters," Andrei said, sneering at me from across the room.

Resisting the urge to curse at him, I met his cold blue eyes. *"Feline* shifters. I didn't pick up any scent on the avian shifter."

Arsham said, "But you did sense *something.*"

Rahim added, "You ran toward it."

"The air felt different," I admitted, trying to verbalize the bizarre feeling that I had experienced. "I can't describe it."

"Odd that the slayer didn't kill you when she had the chance," Jazmin pointed out, her amber eyes narrowed at me.

"He killed Francis," Rahim interjected.

"But not Angelique," Jazmin countered.

"The second slayer tried to attack Arsham and Angelique," Rahim pointed out.

Andrei stood and spread out his hands. "Jazmin brings up an interesting point. As for that second slayer, the duchess described him as a young man with no ID. Does that sound right to everyone?"

Rahim frowned. "What are you implying?"

"Only the most experienced slayers would even make an attempt to tackle two of London's deadliest vampires. Unless this kid was on a suicide mission, this story doesn't make sense." Tossing a sly look in my direction, Andrei added,

"Perhaps Angelique is conspiring with them and this whole thing was nothing more than a set up."

I stared at the odious vampire with unmasked contempt and vowed to wreak vengeance on him at the first opportunity that presented itself.

Arsham and Rahim stared at Andrei too, only their expressions were unreadable.

Jazmin sighed tiredly. "Really, Andrei? Must you be offensive at every opportunity?"

Andrei bristled. "*You're* the one making insinuations."

"The fact that they killed a vampire of lower rank sends the clear message that they could have easily killed Angelique too. *That* is the point I was trying to make."

Valerio said, "They didn't kill her because Angelique is older, stronger, and faster."

Jazmin shook her head. "I disagree. I believe this attack was meant as a warning and should be taken as such."

"A warning from whom?" Andrei demanded.

Jazmin cocked an eyebrow at him. "Isn't it obvious? A warning from our sister, Katya, and her Sauvage lover."

Mayu frowned. "What are they warning us about?"

I met my sire's gaze from across the room. *Now* was the perfect time to make the announcement. As if reading my mind, Arsham stood. I braced myself in anticipation of his words.

"They want us to implement a new law," he announced.

Rahim stood and whispered in his brother's ear. The room erupted with questions and comments. A few chosen Elders had secretly discussed the possibility of feeding on humans without killing them, but the sires had not yet arrived at a decision.

Arsham said, "There is a way to feed on humans that allows them to live and have no memory of the deed."

Rahim added, "Katya and the Sauvage siblings, as well as the vampires who support them, demand that we implement this new way of feeding into our Codex."

The brothers formed a united front, a clever tactic.

Pointing at them, Andrei cried, "Blasphemy!"

Arsham stared down the cantankerous vampire and, rather

than castigate him, made an attempt at reason. "Not killing humans would eliminate the need for vampire slayers."

Andrei's gaze shifted to Rahim. "Sire, tell me that you're not being swayed into this dangerous scheme."

Jazmin shook her head, disappointed. "Brother, do us all a favor and *evolve*, will you?"

Mayu added, "I agree with Jazmin. We have always existed alongside the humans. How else can we blend in with them if not by adapting modern methods?"

Her wise words surprised me. Several Elders nodded but Andrei belligerently shook his head.

Micah added, "Our survival is inherent on our flexibility."

Valerio voiced his support for Micah's words. In the end, the majority of Elders were favorable to the idea of allowing humans to live after drinking their blood. Implementation of new laws into the Codex depended on *all* of them being in accord, however. Rahim and Arsham had their work cut out for them, and I was ready to do anything within my power to help in this endeavor.

Once the meeting had adjourned, Arsham and Rahim remained in the octagonal meeting room. I vacated the space and waited on the far side of the atrium for my sire to emerge so that I may speak with him. I saw Mayu storm out of the room with Andrei in tow. He grabbed her arm and spun her around, then placed his lips to her ear. She pushed him off and made to go but stopped when she saw me.

I walked up to them. "What's going on here?"

"That's none of your concern," Andrei snapped.

Ignoring him, I said, "Mayu, are you all right?" She looked at me with a hint of fear in her eyes so I added, "If you want to make a complaint to the sires, I'll bear witness for you."

"Oh that's good coming from a traitor," Andrei said, getting in my face.

I didn't flinch. Staring him down, I said, "The fact that I helped in uniting this coven and recently alerted Arsham to the Sauvage threat proves that I'm not a traitor."

A derisive laugh escaped his lips. "All that proves is your

innate ability to save your own skin."

Arsham and Rahim exited the room, prompting the three of us to incline our heads.

I left Andrei and Mayu and went after my sire. "May I speak with you, Arsham?"

Although he seemed distracted, he nodded. He led me to his chamber and closed the door. "What's on your mind?"

"Were you serious about removing me from your detail?"

"Yes."

"Have you told Omar?"

"Not yet."

"You're making a mistake." When he said nothing, I added, "You held me back tonight. I wish you had let me help Francis and Thomas…"

"It was too dangerous."

"We lost a good warrior."

"Damn it, Angelique. I'm as upset as you are over this." His eyes caressed my face and I was touched by the tenderness reflected in them. "I didn't allow you to fight because I won't risk losing you."

"Arsham—"

"Is there anything else?" he snapped.

And just like that, his mask was firmly in place.

"No," I replied.

He sat at his desk and cradled his head in his hands. The burden of leadership weighed heavily on his shoulders. I longed to comfort him, to touch him. Instead, I quietly left the room.

Omar intercepted me. "You were right to insist on more security. From now on, you're calling the shots."

"Arsham wants me off his detail."

"That's insane."

"I know, which is why I'm hoping you'll talk some sense into him. How many surveillance cameras do we have set up outside the lair and in the city?"

"I'll have my crew check. Won't hurt to add more."

"It wouldn't be a bad idea to add trackers to the vehicles in case of an abduction."

"Consider it done."

"If I think of anything else, I'll let you know."

Placing a hand on my shoulder, he said, "I'm glad nothing happened to you tonight."

I went to my room in a pensive state. Opening the armoire, I surveyed the collection of clothing by sifting through the velvet hangers. Valerio had chosen several black and dark jewel-toned garments, but one stood out in stark contrast to the rest. I extracted a luscious La Perla satin slip the color of fresh cream. Exquisite Italian lace adorned the hem.

"What were you thinking, Valerio?" I whispered aloud while admiring the elegant lingerie.

I tossed the hanger on the bed, then went into the bathroom to take a steamy shower. My head felt heavy after tonight's events, and I allowed the hot water to melt some of my anxiety.

I applied body cream and perfume, then towel dried my hair before studying my reflection in the foggy mirror. The inky blue eyes staring back at me were almost unfamiliar.

The slip drew my gaze as I exited the bathroom. I donned the lingerie, relishing the feel of its decadent softness against my skin. How Valerio knew that it would fit me perfectly was a mystery. The antique clock on the dresser announced that sunrise was still a few hours away. My eyes slid to the door.

Do you dare, Angelique?

Drawing on my courage, I left my room and crept to Arsham's chamber. My knuckles hovered inches from the door but I didn't knock. Instead, I did what no other vampire would ever do: I barged into his room. Uninvited.

Arsham, who was in the process of unbuttoning his tailored shirt, spun around to see which vampire had invaded his privacy in such an uncouth manner. The sight of me standing in the doorway in a provocative garment rendered him speechless. I glimpsed desire in his eyes before he quickly arranged his face into a neutral expression.

Averting his gaze, he continued in his task. "I'm assuming there is an emergency."

"Not exactly," I admitted, closing the door behind me.

180

After removing his shirt, he draped it over a chair. "Do you think it wise for an Elder to be running around the lair in *that*?"

My fingers itched to touch his chiseled chest. "I didn't run around the lair. I came straight here."

"What do you want, Angelique?" When I hesitated, he undid the latch of his expensive watch. "Funny, I've never known you to be at a loss for words."

"I want *you*."

A heavy silence followed my bold confession.

Turning his face away from me, he said hoarsely, "Go to your room before we do something we shall later regret."

Undeterred, I took a step toward him. "The only regret I have is not coming to you sooner and telling you the truth."

The old Arsham would have swept me up in his arms and devoured me. The vampire who stood before me now remained cautious and skeptical.

Placing the watch atop a dresser, he said, "I'm weary and in no mood for games."

"I'm not playing games."

Dark eyes flashed as he rounded on me. "Why do you torment me? Haven't I been good to you? Shown you mercy?"

My brow creased in confusion. "Sire?"

"For ten years I mourned your absence."

"I didn't *volunteer* to go into the punishment coffin—"

"Silence!"

I bit my tongue and lowered my gaze.

He continued, "You forced my hand. Your blatant disregard for protocol, your rebellious nature, I have never been able to control you. I didn't want to punish you, but it was the only way to prevent your execution."

"I'm sorry for putting you in that position."

"I suffered a decade without your voice, your scent, the sight of you…"

"What's a decade to an ancient like you?" I retorted.

He glared at me in response. "I felt nothing but joy on the day of your release. I even offered you my throat. *My throat.* An honor I've never afforded anyone else. You drank my blood.

181

Greedily, in fact. Do you recall how you repaid my generosity and my affection? *Do you?*"

"Sire, please—"

"You said another's name while I held you in my arms." I placed a tentative hand on his shoulder and he flinched. "On that day, I swore never to touch you again."

"I've loved you since the night you made me what I am."

"Yet you betrayed me and your coven for Damien Sauvage."

I shook my head slowly. "That's not fair…you rejected me. I confessed my love to you, only to be called a foolish child. Don't you remember? You chastised me for expecting a powerful being such as yourself to align your heart with mine. Those were *your* words. Then the twins came and you barred me from your bed."

"Angelique—"

"I overheard the three of you in your chamber. I had never experienced such pain—not even from my sadistic husband, the duke. Fortunately, Erika taught me to harden my heart against the machinations of men…*and vampires*."

"Erika. I should have known." He heaved a sigh, then continued in a gentle tone, "Angelique, you were so young. You had no experience in life and had never known the love of a man. Being vastly older and wiser, I interpreted your infatuation for me as a passing phase. I figured vampirism would change you, as it does us all."

"My love for you never faded, it only lay dormant out of fear. I didn't want to feel the pain of your rejection again. As for Damien, he wanted me whereas you did not."

He shook his head sadly. "That's where you're wrong. I wanted you…more than anything."

"I risked my heart with the slayer because I believed that I had nothing to lose. Tell me that I have something to lose now. Tell me that you want me. I'm here to put the past behind us and face the future—*with you*."

He stared at me for a long time, debating. At length, he said, "We'll talk of this another time."

I closed the distance between us, lifted his large hand to my lips, and kissed the blood ruby. "Let me stay with you tonight."

"It's best if you don't."

"I love you, Arsham."

"Oh my child, you confuse lust for love. My predatory sex appeal and physical beauty trick people into thinking they love me, but in reality they only desire me. I am undeserving of that most sacred emotion."

"I know the difference between lust and love, and you are deserving of the latter."

He ran his fingertips lightly along my cheek. "How I wish that were true. You love who you believe me to be and not who I really am."

"You're wrong."

"Am I? The other day you were horrified when you learned that I was the compelling force behind Vlad Tepes's savage bloodlust—and that's only one of my many sins. In time I would scare you away with my power. Intimidate you with my age. Repulse you with my cruelty."

"Stop trying to dissuade me. I know exactly who you are."

"Do you?" he challenged, his eyes hard. "You barge in here half-naked trying to seduce an ancient vampire whom you claim to love, yet you have entered into the den of a ravenous wolf."

He edged toward me in a menacing manner, forcing me to move backward. "Stop it."

Ignoring me, he continued his advance. "The blood I've spilled throughout the centuries could fill an ocean. Darkness and decay festers within me like a malignancy. Were I not so selfish, so merciless, I would walk to the ends of Earth and wither into a deathlike state to spare humanity from the likes of me. Instead, I continue to consume everything in my path with a vile greed that disgusts even myself."

My back slammed against the wall.

Placing his face close to mine, he demanded, "Tell me, do you still wish to embrace the demon who stands before you?"

"Sire, if you are a demon than so am I, for I am part of you. There is no other vampire in this world more worthy of my love and devotion."

He hung his head and confessed, "I've wanted to hear those words from your lips for a long time."

Lifting a trembling hand, I touched his cheek. "Arsham."

"Do you know how difficult it is to *feel* when you're as old as I am? I spring to life whenever you're near me. It's more than my admiration for you, or respect for your skills, or lust for your beauty…it's the very essence of *you* that I love."

He suddenly plundered my mouth with a hunger that consumed me. I kissed him back, my passion matching his own.

Pulling away slightly, he said against my lips, "Tell me that you're mine."

"I am yours, Arsham," I confessed.

Nuzzling my neck, he ran his hands along the smooth silk of my slip. "My fingers ache to touch your skin."

I allowed him to pull the slip over my head.

His eyes roamed over my nubile body. "A goddess."

I held my breath when he began circling me. Hearing his gasp, I froze in anticipation of what he would say about the tattoo. Only he didn't say anything at all. Falling to his knees, he gripped my hips and admired Ace's masterpiece in silence. Arsham kissed the tops of my buttocks before cupping them with his big hands. I felt his tongue at the base of my spine and he dragged it up every vertebrae, standing to his feet slowly as he did so. By the time he reached my nape, his breathing was ragged and his member fully engorged as it pressed against me with urgency. I growled at the feel of his desire.

Taking hold of my shoulders, he spun me around to face him. "Why didn't you tell me?"

"I had hoped to show you, *like this*. Do you like it?"

A low throaty chuckle served as his reply as a devilish grin stretched across his face. The velvety sound had the power to evoke my desire. Lifting me in his arms, he carried me to his bed. Candles flickered, casting golden pools of light upon the luxuriant black satin sheets.

"The black scorpion is a symbol of loyalty," he whispered before nibbling on my earlobe.

I said breathlessly, "I'm well aware, sire."

184

"Those who bear it have sworn exclusive devotion to me."

"I'm aware of that too."

Grabbing a fistful of my hair he gazed deeply into my eyes. "They would also die for me."

I stretched out on the ebony softness, urging him down with me. "Without hesitation, my love."

To my delight, he took his time worshipping my body. Fingertips possessed memories, for I relived our former unions while running my hands along his firm skin. My sire's lovemaking proved surprisingly tender and unselfish, pleasuring me in ways that no mortal ever could. Only when I writhed in sweet agony did he enter me. I met his eager thrusts with joy and relief until I reached the point of delirium.

"Angelique," he whispered, his body shuddering after a violent climax. Pinning me beneath his considerable weight, he stared into my eyes. "You are mine. From this moment forth, do you understand? *Mine*."

I nodded, surrendering myself completely to my sire. For the third time in my life, I sacrificed my heart on the altar of love.

Twice to the same male.

"I want to make you my queen, my official mate." The ruby ring on his finger flashed in the candlelight as he ran his hand down my arm. A long moment passed before he added, "Your silence is deafening."

"I'm in shock."

"Is it so difficult to believe that your sire craves a mate?"

"No but…"

Leaning up on his elbow, he peered down into my face. "When that avian shifter attacked you, I knew a slayer lurked nearby. The thought of losing you forever…I wanted to gather you in my arms and take you to my bed the moment we arrived at the lair. I couldn't break my vow, however."

"I won't ever barge in on you again," I teased.

"You can storm my chamber in La Perla whenever you wish," he purred, baring his fangs.

I tilted my head back to expose the smooth white skin of my throat. Arsham pierced my flesh with his teeth and pulled hard,

185

sucking my blood while fondling my breasts. The erotic pleasure drove me mad, making me want him again.

He rolled off me and I straddled him. I leaned over and kissed his elegant clavicle, then licked his neck. In a brazen move, I bit him before he even offered his throat. He gasped in surprise, encouraging me to proceed. I sipped his blood carefully to prolong the enjoyment for the both of us.

His strong hands slid up my thighs, cupping my hips. "My Angel of Night."

I pulled away from his throat before claiming his lips once more. Our passionate lovemaking continued throughout the night until the sun's rays kissed the sky. Satiated and wrapped in each other's arms, we slept in blissful peace.

CHAPTER 16

"Life being what it is, one dreams of revenge."
(Paul Gauguin)

An official announcement of our union was made to the coven. The news was met with joy by most of the Elders. Andrei and few vampires who were friends of the late Chiara and Deirdre didn't bother congratulating me, but they did extend kind words to Arsham. I didn't care. There was only one vampire whose opinion mattered, and I would be sharing his bed—and his life—henceforth. I could confess without reservation that I was the happiest vampire in London.

Arsham planned a decadent party to celebrate the event. Naturally, Valerio demanded access into my chamber in order to give his valuable opinion on what I should wear. Going through the hangers, he pulled out a gorgeous formal gown covered in jet beads.

"You would be honoring my Italian heritage if you wore this little number," he said, holding out the dress. "Vintage Gucci. It would also allow you to show off Ace's work. Go try it on."

The backless sheath dress dipped well past my waist to expose my entire back. The slinky fabric clung to my curves then fell to the floor in an elegant line.

Valerio sighed. "Divine."

Someone knocked and I said, "Enter."

The door opened to reveal Thomas. "Excuse me, my lady. Arsham asked me to deliver this to you."

I accepted the blood red box trimmed with gold. "Thank you, Thomas. Convey my thanks to our sire as well."

The moment we were alone again, Valerio said, "Cartier. He has such excellent taste. Hurry, open it."

I gasped at the sparkling set of diamond chandelier earrings. I put them on and went to the mirror.

Valerio came to stand beside me. "Perfect. Now, do your makeup while I go and put on my tux. See you at the party."

He left my room and I sat at the eighteenth century vanity table to better study my reflection. As Arsham's official mate, I would be scrutinized at every turn. I would be the subject of gossip both good and bad. I would also be a target.

I applied cosmetics, perfume and slicked my hair into a sophisticated ponytail. Satisfied with my handiwork, I slipped into my high heels and ventured out into the lair.

Arsham's eyes alighted on me with pride as the room fell silent. The moment I began walking toward him, people noticed my exposed back and whispered about my tattoo. To me, the symbol meant more than a visual pledge of loyalty. My warning to everyone in the coven was crystal clear: *fuck with Arsham and you fuck with me.*

My sire kissed my hand in greeting before leaning over to place his lips to my ear. "You never cease to amaze me."

My brothers paid me lavish compliments before Micah and Omar, who hadn't yet seen my tattoo, praised Ace's fine work.

For the first time since becoming a vampire, I felt true joy. Being at Arsham's side with my brothers made me feel at home. Finally, I had a purpose in life: care for the coven and help it to flourish.

Rahim conducted the binding ceremony. No one spoke or moved as he wrapped a gold thread around our clasped hands. He then cut our wrists and allowed our blood to flow into an ancient golden chalice. The mixed blood was then consumed by me and Arsham in turn. Vampires did not exchange verbal vows, but Rahim did utter a few words to seal our pact before the witnesses present. A kiss and a round of applause concluded the brief ceremony.

Blood wine flowed freely afterward. Vampires in haute couture gowns, smart tuxedos, and glittering jewels mingled around us, offering their congratulations.

Arsham stuck close to my side, his hand on the small of my back, his fingers caressing the exposed skin. At one point, he whispered, "I want to tear this off you and take you right here."

"I'd like that."

"Are you having a good time?"

"I am. This is wonderful, thank you."

"You deserve this and more, which is why I have arranged for a piano concert in your honor."

The Japanese pianist materialized and handed me a printed program containing my favorite composers: Chopin, Strauss, and Rachmaninoff.

Several chairs had been set up around the piano. Everyone sat down to listen, entranced, as the pianist played one piece after another with passionate precision.

Dance music poured from the speakers at the concert's conclusion, inviting everyone to move with reckless abandon. More cases of blood wine were opened and consumed. Inebriated newborns began to party hard.

Several sets of eyes tracked my movements throughout the evening, and I even noticed a few envious looks from females who wanted what I had achieved. In time, I would find ways to draw them in and keep tabs on them.

Always keep potential enemies close at hand.

Being with an alpha male wasn't easy, especially one like Arsham. My eyes slid to my new mate. Despite his prowess, good looks, and generosity, he was difficult, moody, stubborn...a challenge even for a strong alpha female like myself. He caught my eye and winked.

Totally worth it.

"Dance with me," he said, taking hold of my hand.

The music slowed the moment we were amid the dancers. Holding me tightly, we swayed to the tune of an old song from the fifties, then another oldie from the seventies. When an eighteenth century minuet came on, we showed the younger vampires how it was done in my day.

Rahim tapped Arsham's shoulder. "May I?"

Arsham handed me over to his half-brother. "Of course."

I accepted Rahim's proffered hand and he said, "This was the right thing for you to do."

To my surprise, he spun me around in tune to the music

189

before I had a chance to agree with him.

He continued, "I've never seen my brother so happy."

"Never?"

Rahim pulled me close for a slow dance. "I'm going to tell you something and I ask that you keep it between us. Several months ago, Arsham and I had concluded a meeting and I offered him some blood wine. We consumed more of it than we should have. I am immune to the effects of my own blood but your sire became inebriated."

"You are his sire, after all," I interjected.

Conceding to my words with a nod, he continued, "Arsham told me everything about you—from the night he sired you to the time you left the lair for Damien Sauvage." He glanced at Arsham to make sure he was well out of earshot. "He confessed to having made many mistakes where you were concerned. He deeply regretted not having made you his mate a century ago."

I stepped back to meet his eyes. "Did he actually say that?"

"He most certainly did. You must not repeat what I've told you. My brother would never forgive me."

"Why are you telling me this now?"

"I wanted to offer you a gift on this fine night. At first, I thought diamonds were in order but then I reconsidered. In the end, I couldn't think of anything better than letting you know the truth. Is that not the greatest gift?"

"Thank you, my lord. What you have told me is worth far more to me than precious jewels."

***

Arsham and I stumbled to his chamber after the party. Feeling tipsy from the blood wine, we held on to each other as we approached the door.

He placed his hand on the wall and leaned in close to me. "Did you enjoy yourself this evening?"

"Very much so…I particularly enjoyed it when you referred to me as your *queen*."

He growled softly before nuzzling my neck and instantly igniting my desire. "A definite upgrade from duchess, no?"

My fingers found the buckle of his leather belt.

He unlocked the door and we staggered through the threshold sharing a passionate kiss. Giggling softly, I kicked the door closed and was about to wrap my arms around him when his brow creased in confusion.

Gently pushing me aside, he demanded, "What's this?"

Puzzled, I turned around. On the floor was a manila envelope with two words written in bold black capital letters: CONGRATULATIONS ARSHAM.

He moved to pick it up but I stopped him. "Wait, I'll do it. Stand back."

"Angelique—"

I bent to retrieve the envelope and, convinced there was nothing harmful inside, I handed it to him. "I'm still concerned for your safety."

"I'm still your lord and sire."

"And mate."

I ran my hand up his arm in a provocative manner. He smiled at my flirtation as he tore open the envelope. Frowning, he extracted several photocopied sheets of what seemed to be old documents.

I recognized the handwriting at once. "Oh no…"

Arsham's eyes met mine. "Do you know what this is?"

"Unfortunately, I do."

CHAPTER 17

*"Forgiveness is the fragrance that the violet
sheds on the heel that crushes it."*
(Mark Twain)

A shadow settled across Arsham's features as he read the photocopied pages. I retreated to the opposite side of the room in panic. Sickened by the possibility of losing what I had finally achieved, I waited for the oncoming storm. The words of Gilles Sauvage, penned over two centuries ago, had returned to haunt me and destroy my newfound joy.

No secret can remain buried forever.

Arsham read the last page and regarded me with actual pain in his eyes. His expression gradually morphed from hurt, to outraged, to furious.

"I can explain," I began.

He stormed to where I stood and struck me. *Hard.* I fell to the floor and made no move to flee or defend myself. I deserved every bit of his ire.

"I loved Erika," he said through clenched teeth, his hands balled into two fists. "How could you?" He wanted to hit me again but refrained. Instead, he sagged against the wall. "I've never stopped mourning her loss. I miss her so much…"

"I loved her too," I said at length, slowly rising to my feet.

He eyed me coldly, piercing my heart with a single look. "Not enough to avenge her death."

"Sire—"

Lifting his hand to silence me, he said, "That night, on the Brighton Pier, I commanded you to confess anything that would compromise your position on the Security Team. I even gave you full impunity. Why didn't you tell me?"

"I admit, I thought about it but I couldn't bring myself to tell you. I believed I could get away with keeping it a secret. I didn't want to hurt you, Arsham. I didn't want *this*."

"Oh Angelique," he said, placing his hand on his forehead in a gesture of impatience. "Of all my progeny you are by far the greatest challenge to my patience."

I eyed the collection of weapons on the far wall. Mace, battle axe, daggers and swords. I grabbed the deadliest blade and placed the hilt into Arsham's hand.

"What are you doing?" he snapped.

"I've been carrying the guilt of that night for too long." Sinking to my knees, I lowered my head to expose the nape of my neck. "Do what is best for the coven."

A long tense silence followed my words as I braced myself for the execution that I fully deserved.

"Rise," he commanded.

I didn't move, my eyes glued to the floor. "I would prefer to die here and now, by your hand, than to go through a trial only to be executed later. *Please sire*. Grant me this favor for the sake of the love you once bore for me."

"Rise," he repeated.

I rose on shaky legs, terrified that our love was now tainted by my grave mistake. The thought of him despising me throughout eternity filled me with unbearable sadness.

Heaving a tired sigh, he went to the desk and sank into the leather chair. Indicating a seat opposite him, he said, "Tell me exactly what happened that night. Leave nothing out."

I sat down and recounted the events from the time I spotted the feline shape shifter exiting the pub, to Erika's decapitation by the hand of Gilles Sauvage.

Arsham studied my face. "Why didn't you kill him?"

"Two reasons. First, Gilles had been with my father for five years as an apprentice. I smelled death on the old man and, since he loved Gilles like a son, I didn't have the heart to do it."

"And the second reason?"

"I wanted to prove that vampires weren't monsters."

"In his journal, Gilles describes your bite as being *exquisite*. You offered him pleasure in exchange for murdering your sister. I can't accept this."

"Please don't think of it like that."

"How else am I to interpret your actions?"

"Is it wrong to want to change how a Sauvage sees us? To expose him to the possibility of vampires being more than mindless, unholy, blood-sucking monsters?"

"The Sauvage family continued killing our kind after Gilles died, so your mercy toward the slayer proved useless."

"I know. I'll confess to the Elders and willingly stand trial if you don't want to kill me yourself. I'll accept their verdict without question or fight."

"Are you certain?"

"The well-being of the coven comes first. Eternal life without you would be a worse punishment than death, anyway."

He stared at me for a long time. "Spoken like a true queen."

"Sire?"

He stood and came over to where I sat. "I am not willing to give you up. Not now. *Not ever*. You're my mate, Angelique." He urged me to stand, then pulled me into his arms. "This will remain between us."

Wrapping my arms around him, we held each other tightly.

I leaned back to look up at him. "My decision not to kill Gilles wasn't meant to hurt you or the coven, I swear." I pressed my palm to his cheek. "I'm sorry if I've hurt you. It's the last thing I ever want to do."

"I believe you, which is why I'm willing to protect you."

"What if copies were sent to the other Elders?"

"We'll deal with that if and when the time comes."

He kissed me, this time lifting me in his arms and setting me upon the bed. Our lovemaking, full of emotion, shook me to the core. I held my sire tightly afterward, gently kissing his face as he closed his eyes.

My king.

***

I waited on baited breath for days afterward. The vampires within the coven treated me no differently than before, yet I felt myself tensing up with each sidelong glance or whisper. The constant anticipation of a public accusation caused me considerable anxiety. I did my best not to appear worried in Arsham's presence. Having brought this situation upon myself, I didn't want it to taint our bliss.

Despite everything, Arsham did his best to put me at ease. He suggested a second trip to Iceland and I readily agreed. After the miracle of watching yet another spectacular sunrise on Diamond Beach, my sire led me to his bed.

"You're not sending me into the other room this time?" I teased as he unbuttoned my blouse.

"I wanted you so badly the last time we were here, but I had to keep my vow." Cupping my breast, he added, "Now, I can enjoy you *and* the sunrise. What more could I possibly desire?"

Turning me around, he ran the flat of his hand down my spine while biting my neck. Pushing me against the edge of the bed, he positioned himself behind me. I gave in to his animal lust with pure wantonness. How could I ever tire of him?

We fell asleep wrapped in each other's arms, and flew back to London the next night feeling invigorated.

Weeks passed and nothing came of the Gilles Sauvage journal incident. If anything, it brought my sire and I closer together.

CHAPTER 18

"To the wicked, everything serves as pretext."
(Voltaire)

Arsham and I opened our eyes simultaneously only to be greeted by the sound of a blaring alarm.

"Someone has breached security," I said, already on my feet.

We dressed with haste, grabbed our weapons, and ran out into the corridor. Several other vampires wandered out of their rooms. Older vampires, like us, were armed and ready to fight. To my dismay, some of the newborns shuffled around, clueless to what was going on. Apparently, I still had work to do when it came to training them. Who sired these weaklings, anyway?

Omar must have punched in the override code because the alarm stopped screeching. He emerged from one of the control rooms and rushed to where we stood.

Rahim intercepted him. "What's going on?"

Omar glanced at us before offering a reply. "The lair may have been compromised, my lord."

Those who had overheard Omar's words gasped and began whispering.

Arsham muttered, "Impossible."

I frowned in thought. The secret entrance, which had been used by Rahim to challenge Arsham almost two years ago, had been walled up and triple barricaded. An intruder couldn't possibly have come in through there or any of the other secure hidden portals.

Omar continued in a loud voice for all to hear, "The Security Team is making a thorough sweep of the lair. In the meantime, please return to your chambers and lock your doors."

I ran up to Omar. "Tell me what you want me to do."

"The old lair needs to be checked," he replied.

I looked to Arsham, who said, "Don't go alone."

Rahim added, "I'm calling an Elders meeting in thirty minutes. Does that give you enough time for a search?"

Omar replied, "More than enough, my lord."

I selected two guards to accompany me. Thomas was one of them. Pointing to Eva, I said, "I'll need to check the lab."

Nodding, she detached herself from Micah's side. The four of us sped to the old lair. I instructed Thomas and the other vampire to search the hallway for clues.

Eva unlocked the lab and stepped aside to allow me access. "Please don't touch anything unless you have to, my lady."

"Rest assured, I won't," I said over my shoulder.

I checked everything, including the air vents. Vampires didn't breathe, but Arsham had employed human architects to create this part of the lair during Queen Victoria's reign. Naturally, they had constructed a means for oxygen to flow. The newer sections didn't have air vents since they were built by vampires. We kept the entire underground maze climate controlled and electronically ventilated in order to protect the many priceless antiques and historical paintings.

Satisfied that the lab's security had not been breached, I left Eva and joined the two males in the corridor. We scoured the entire section for clues of forced entry or anything that seemed out of place. We found nothing. I was about to lead my search team back to Omar when something caught my eye.

Following my gaze to the air vent at my feet, Thomas said, "Do you want me to go in there?"

"You're too big," I replied, already removing the fancy brass grate from the dark air tunnel. Placing my face at the mouth of the narrow opening, I deduced, "And so am I."

"What now?"

"I need you to go outside and check the grate on the opposite end. If you leave through that exit…" I stopped to point. "Then turn right, you'll come to a brick wall. Track it down to this level and report back to me at once." To the other male I said, "Go tell Omar that we've swept this section and I'm checking the vents."

"Yes, my lady."

Thomas did as he was told and returned quickly. "The grate is in its proper place but I found this stuck in the corner."

He placed a tiny piece of black fuzz into my palm. On closer inspection, I saw that it was the tip of a feather. "Good job."

"That's from the avian shifter, isn't it?"

I debated whether or not to confirm his suspicion. "I think so but don't say anything, Thomas. No need to create a panic. Continue sweeping for more clues while I report this to Arsham."

"Yes, my lady."

Arsham knew by the look on my face as I approached him that my news wouldn't be good. The Elders had congregated outside the octagonal room in anticipation of the meeting.

"Sire, a word," I said.

He excused himself and came over to where I stood. "Well?"

I showed him the bit of feather found by Thomas. "I think the avian shifter may have crept into the lair last night."

His mouth and eyes hardened. "Are you sure?"

"What else could it be?"

"You said the crow was larger than normal…"

"Yes but it could fit in that vent. I've instructed that the outside grate be sealed."

"We'll get it done tonight. I can't believe this oversight went unnoticed for so many years."

I glanced at Rahim, who watched us with curious eyes, then said, "We've never had an avian shifter threat in London."

Andrei exhaled a frustrated breath. "Are we meeting or aren't we?"

"We're waiting for Mayu," Jazmin snapped, crossing her arms in irritation.

Andrei crossed his arms too. "All this fuss. It's probably nothing more than a blown circuit."

Arsham glared at Andrei and said in a deceptively cool tone, "My vampires are following protocol. Safety of the coven is my utmost concern and, as an Elder, it should be yours too."

Andrei clicked his tongue in irritation at the reprimand. "Will someone fetch Mayu?"

Rahim frowned. "That's enough, Andrei."

Jazmin edged closer to her sire and whispered, "It's not like her to be late."

I put my lips to Arsham's ear. "I don't recall seeing Mayu earlier. Do you?"

"Go check her room. Be discreet."

I ran to do Arsham's bidding, only to find Mayu's room empty. I returned and shook my head slightly in response to his expectant look.

Joining the other Elders, I said, "Could she have gone hunting last night and simply strayed too far?"

"She rarely hunts outside of London," Jazmin replied.

"Maybe she slipped out before the alarm," Valerio said.

Micah shook his head. "The alarm was already going off at sunset, which meant that someone tripped it during the day while we were asleep. There's no way she could have been awake before then."

Arsham moved to open the door to the octagonal room. "We can wait for Mayu inside. Come."

I tracked his steps and we both froze at the sight of a plain cardboard box in the center of the marble floor.

"Don't move, sire," I said, pushing him behind me.

Grabbing my arm, he said, "Wait."

Rahim placed a firm hand on his brother's shoulder. "Let the duchess do her job."

I closed in on the foreign object with the stealth of a cat. The flaps of the box were loosely closed, allowing me to kick one of them open with the tip of my boot.

"Holy shit," I whispered when I glimpsed what lay inside. I met Arsham's eyes. "Get the Elders in here and lock the door behind them."

"What's in the box?" Andrei demanded.

I shook my head slightly, signaling for him to say no more as I waited for everyone to file into the room. The moment Arsham locked the door, I reached into the box, grabbed a fistful of black hair, and held up Mayu's severed head.

***

Needless to say, Mayu's gruesome execution came as a shock to the entire coven. The fact that a shifter found its way into our lair and had the audacity to slay an Elder provoked concern and fear amid my brethren. Rahim seemed the most upset of all, for Mayu had been his daughter.

"This is a second warning," Jazmin said, teary eyed from the loss of her sister.

"Why didn't they kill the sires?" Micah wondered aloud. "Or one of us, for that matter?"

Omar replied, "Who says they didn't try?"

"Are you serious?"

"Maybe Mayu is the only one who didn't lock her door or perhaps she stayed out too late. Something must have made her an easy target."

"Mayu didn't take unnecessary risks and always erred on the side of caution," Jazmin pointed out.

"This makes no sense," Rahim murmured.

Everyone with the exception of Andrei turned to look at me and Omar. We were on the only two Elders on the Security Team and they wanted answers.

I offered, "We're going to continue searching for clues."

Omar added, "We need to take precautionary measures, such as automatic locks and a curfew."

"A curfew?" Andrei repeated in a sour tone. "Is that really necessary? We're not children."

Omar glanced at the sires, then said, "Every vampire will adhere to a curfew starting immediately. Hunting will be done in pairs for obvious reasons."

Arsham said, "I think that's wise. What say you, brother?"

Rahim nodded. "I agree."

Jazmin looked to Rahim and said, "We need to implement the new law soon. The next time they may kill you, sire."

"I refuse to comply," Andrei said defiantly. "Caving in to silly human emotion. We are vampires! Damned by God and destined for Hell. Embrace what you are, sister."

Jazmin eyed her brother coldly. "Pity it wasn't your head in the box."

200

***

Mayu's headless corpse was later found hidden beneath her bed. Omar and I concluded that the shifter had squeezed through the vent in the form of a crow, shifted into human mode, killed the Elder, and then shifted back into a crow for its daring escape. As despicable as the deed was, I couldn't help but be impressed by the enemy's ingenuity—not to mention courage. Sneaking into a vampire coven alone took a certain amount of foolhardiness too.

Someone must have given the avian shifter a map of the lair, otherwise how would he have found Mayu's chamber? Who would do such a thing? Damien? Katya? One of their spies lurking among us? A sinister thought immediately followed: did one of the Elders help the shifter to kill Mayu?

Andrei?

I saw them fighting once and glimpsed fear in Mayu's eyes. Dozens of questions flooded my mind.

For the remainder of that week, the Security Team worked hard and made sure that the lair was impenetrable to the outside world. Arsham demanded that I remain close to his side. I sensed his fear for my safety and was touched by his concern.

One night, after we had made love, I said, "I've been debating whether or not to tell you something."

"Speak freely, my angel."

"I don't have any evidence for what I'm about to say, which is why I've kept it to myself."

Arsham leaned up on his elbow and regarded me seriously. "I trust your gut instinct more than my own."

"I think Andrei is collaborating with Katya."

"Hmm. Omar has already implied the same thing."

"I'm relieved that I'm not alone in my suspicion. Shortly before Mayu's death, I saw her and Andrei bickering after an Elder meeting. Her eyes reflected fear. Arsham…"

When I trailed off, he prompted, "Go on."

"I think Andrei is somehow connected to Mayu's death."

He regarded me with a clouded expression. "Those words cannot be uttered outside of this room. One of my Elders, my

201

mate, accusing one of Rahim's Elders of such treachery could spark war within the coven."

"I've confided in no one else but you."

"Good," he said, laying on his back again.

We both stared up at the ceiling thoughtfully.

He said, "Between you and me, I think you're right. I've been watching Andrei for months and Omar's spies are doing the same. Hopefully, they'll provide us with the evidence needed to make an official accusation."

"A wise course of action, my love."

Clasping my hand, he kissed my wrist. "It gladdens my heart when you call me your love."

I shifted my body so that my fingertips could trace circles on his hard chest. "My love, my love, my love…"

He smiled. "I want to take you out."

"Where?"

"Somewhere posh and expensive. Let's go have some fun."

I hesitated. "Would that be wise? Given that the lair is practically on lockdown, maybe we should wait a bit."

"You and Omar have already secured the lair. I'm tired of everyone moping about the place, and I need to hunt." Taking hold of my chin, he added, "Put on something sexy."

"As you wish."

On my way to my chamber, I apprised Omar that Arsham and I were going out. He suggested that Thomas and two other bodyguards accompany us.

"Stay low, be careful," Omar advised.

I selected a Giorgio Armani black mini dress that showed off my splendid tattoo. Shrugging into a leather jacket, I checked my reflection in the mirror. Satisfied, I returned to my sire's chamber.

Dressed to kill, Arsham looked amazing in a black shirt and gun metal tapered pants. His eyes roamed over me. Placing a muscular arm on either side of me, he pinned me to the wall, leaning his body against mine.

"Perhaps we shouldn't go out after all," he purred into my ear, hardening against my inner thigh.

"You had me a moment ago," I reminded him, surprised and pleased by his insatiable lust.

"I want you again."

Rather than offer a verbal reply, I dipped my hand into the front of his pants and quirked an eyebrow at him. Growling, he spun me toward the wall and slipped his hand between my legs. I moaned with pleasure as his deft fingers caressed me. Panting with desire, he took me urgently, biting the side of my neck as he did so.

Afterward, he whispered, "I can't get enough of you…"

I turned around and held him in my arms. "The feeling is mutual, my love. Let's hunt, shall we?"

We exited the lair with the bodyguards in tow, then piled into a black Mercedes sedan. Arsham selected an elegant nightclub in Chelsea. We drew the gazes of many as we entered the VIP lounge. Arsham sat down on the plush red sofa and I nestled beside him, relishing the weight of his arm around my shoulders. It felt good to dress like a lady in designer clothing and be in such a prestigious location—a refreshing change from the dive bars and seedy neighborhoods I had been compelled to frequent with Damien.

The bodyguards sat on chairs off to the side to allot us some privacy. A glamorous server came over to our table at once with a bottle of the "special vintage" Arsham usually purchased by the case. He had agreements with several club owners all over London. For a considerable fee, they would serve him his own wine no questions asked. Humans who were willing to do the latter were worth their weight in gold to vampires. After filling our goblets with blood wine, the server left our table.

A hush fell over the crowd when the lights were dimmed, then a golden spotlight popped in the center of the stage. We had a perfect view from where we sat. A Parisian jazz singer emerged from behind the curtains in a vintage yellow chiffon gown from the sixties. She dazzled the audience with her melodic voice. The range of sounds she emitted from her throat sounded ethereal. I clapped my hands in delight at the performance's conclusion.

Arsham watched me with mild amusement.

Slightly embarrassed, I said, "The singer was fabulous, wasn't she?"

"Your love for life and appreciation for beauty is something I have always admired about you."

"You possess the same trait, sire."

"Not nearly as much as you. It's one of the reasons I've always kept you close."

I glanced over to Thomas and his two companions who neither drank nor appeared to be enjoying themselves. Good. That meant they were doing their jobs. No distractions.

We listened to some modern mixes by a talented DJ and watched as humans moved on the dance floor. Thomas caught my eye and nodded, letting me know that the area had been scanned and was clean. Arsham and I eventually joined the dancers, momentarily casting our worries and stress aside. We hunted cautiously, going from one human to another in order to satisfy our thirst without killing any of them. Once we had consumed a satisfying quantity of blood, he expressed his desire to return to the lair.

"I want to respect Omar's curfew," Arsham said.

"Me too," I agreed, since I knew he believed in leading by example.

Arsham remained a few paces behind me, discreetly pressing a folded hundred pound note into the manicured hand of our pretty server. Two bodyguards stuck to his side while Thomas tracked my steps.

I ventured ahead of him to the car idling at the curb. Two vampires swooped down, grabbed each of my arms, and lifted me into the night. Thomas cried out to his companions as he flew after us. A loud caw pierced the night as a big crow attacked Thomas. I glimpsed Arsham running out of the club but my captors rounded a corner and blocked me from his view. Katya and Damien possessed considerable strength and speed, so my struggles were useless. They took me to a secluded park where the petite mulatta placed the blade of her katana to my throat. Her left arm was in a sling due to the bullet wound in her shoulder caused by my gun.

I took in my surroundings as she glared at me. Eerie shadows cast by spindly trees framed the stretch of grass on which I stood. The unnatural crow that had chased Thomas fluttered around us and morphed into human form. The avian shifter was huge.

"Here's your chance at revenge. Cut off her head and send it to Arsham," he whispered to the slayer in Portuguese.

"It's tempting but no," she said.

"That bitch shot you, Xoana. She could have killed you."

"Don't listen to him, Xoana. Arsham will make sure that you die a painful death if you cause me any harm," I warned in their language. I looked at the big Afro-Brazilian and added, "My sire is already furious that you invaded our lair and killed an Elder, so think carefully of your next move."

Surprised at my fluency in their native tongue, Xoana said, "See that, Corvo? You pissed off the vampires."

Damien intervened. "We need her alive."

"Do we, my darling?" Katya purred.

"We want Arsham to change the law not start a war," he reminded her with a pointed look.

"And yet you killed Mayu," I snapped.

"My sister was an uppity little bitch," Katya shot back.

"That's no excuse to kill an Elder," I countered.

"Damien, do you really believe that Arsham would miss the duchess? I hear he was quite the Casanova once upon a time." Eyeing me with disdain, Katya added in an amused tone, "He'll be cheating on her soon enough. I mean, with all those cute newbies eagerly hoping to fulfill his every whim, what male can remain loyal? By the way, Damien is sorry for disrupting your honeymoon."

My eyes slid to Damien. "*You* sent those photocopies."

He shrugged. "Didn't you like my wedding gift?"

"He forgave me, you know."

Katya interjected, "How disappointing."

"He's changed," I said, ignoring her comment.

Damien eyed me in an odd manner.

I continued, "Use me as a bargaining chip."

Katya laughed. "My, my, you really do have visions of grandeur." Her eyes swept over my form fitting Armani dress and designer shoes. "You have good taste, I'll give you that."

"Arsham and Rahim have already discussed changing the sacred law," I said, rising above her taunts. "We had an emergency Elder meeting the night your shifter friend over here killed Mayu. Everything you want is already in the process of being implemented."

"You're lying," Katya snapped.

Damien frowned at his lover and shook his head slightly. To me, he demanded, "Is it written in the Codex as a new law?"

"Changing the Codex is not something that is done overnight," I reminded them.

"Bullshit. They could make the announcement tomorrow." I conceded to his point by inclining my head, prompting him to add, "Let's take her with us and send a message to Arsham. Change the law—"

"Or the duchess dies," Katya said, finishing his sentence. "Imagine Arsham's face when he receives a box containing her head. No plain cardboard this time. Let's make it interesting. Do you have a preference of color, Angelique? A pink box, perhaps? Or blue to match your eyes?"

Throughout this exchange, the Brazilian shifter and the slayer studied me in curious silence. I met their eyes and stared them down to the point of them lowering their heads.

"We need to talk about our next step," Damien said. "Obviously not here."

"Let's go to my place," Katya suggested.

"Are you sure?"

"Totally. It's safe. No one knows that I own it."

I was transported to a modern apartment in Soho. Ironically, her place was only a few streets over from Damien's old flat. Jeanne was already there with two of her London slayer friends. Both were strapping young lads who eyed me with a mixture of contempt and lust.

Katya shoved me toward the sofa. "Sit down and keep your

mouth shut."

I did as I was told without preamble. I noticed that Jeanne limped slightly. It was no doubt a result from being stabbed in the thigh. Four slayers and an avian shifter stared at me while the two vampires retreated to another room in order to discuss in private what they wished to do with me.

One of the slayers nudged Jeanne and whispered, "Is she the one who killed Jake?"

Jeanne nodded as she whipped out her new phone.

"Nice phone," I commented slyly.

She glared at me. "You stole my other one."

"Actually, my brother did."

"Whatever."

"I bet you're proud of yourself."

"Shut up, Angelique."

I continued, unfazed. "Abducting me may get you what you want. Good plan."

Jeanne frowned. "That depends on your sire, doesn't it?"

"Not only him. Rahim too. Otherwise, the coven will be split. The outcome could lead to war. Hasn't your brother been keeping you posted on what's going on?"

"Vampires killing each other spares us the trouble," said the ungainly slayer who stood beside her.

My eyes bore into his, causing him to avert his gaze out of primordial fear.

Xoana took a step toward me and I pinned her with an icy stare. "You killed one of my warriors. His name was Francis and he possessed courage and honor. His younger brother, Thomas, is devastated."

"That is the nature of my existence," she replied in heavily accented English with no trace of regret in her tone.

"If I can change the *nature of my existence* and not kill my prey, why can't you change yours?" I reasoned.

"Because not all vampires think as you do—or Katya and Damien."

Corvo came to stand beside her and I said, "I had only heard legends. I didn't think shifters like him existed."

"They are extremely rare," she said.

Jeanne rudely intercepted our conversation. "Xoana, you really shouldn't be talking to her."

Xoana pressed her lips together and said nothing more.

I turned my head and caught the male slayers staring at my legs, which were on full display thanks to the shortness of my dress. I slowly crossed my legs in a provocative manner, which made them practically salivate. Jeanne scowled at only one of the boys, instantly signaling to me that she liked him.

"Is that your boyfriend, Jeanne?" I inquired.

Her eyes flashed. "Shut up!"

Ignoring her temper tantrum, I smiled at the young men. "What are your names?"

"Ignore her," Jeanne said to them.

I raised an eyebrow. "Really, Jeanne. Diplomacy, civility, and strategy are traits you should learn if you wish to navigate successfully in the world."

"If you don't stop, I'm going to get Damien."

I smiled coldly. "I'm not your enemy. Remember, I want the exact same thing that you do. Damien, too, for that matter. Don't you get it? We're on the same team."

"My name is Nigel," said Jeanne's love interest.

"Nice to meet you. And your friend's name?"

"This here is Hugh," Nigel said, eying me warily. "Are you going to feed on us?"

"Are you offering?" I asked before revealing my fangs.

Damien exited the bedroom and took in the scene. "Already cheating on Arsham?"

"There's only one cheater in this room," I replied without missing a beat.

Someone pounded on the door.

"It's after two in the morning! Keep it down in there or I'll call the police! I've already reported you to the administration. These apartments aren't to be used as tourist rentals. It's in your contract. You should read it sometime!"

The elderly woman's warning poured in from the opposite side of the door, making Jeanne roll her eyes. "That's the second time Ms. Doris came up here. Should I talk to her?"

Katya eyed the door with disgust. "That old bitch has been getting on my nerves a lot lately."

"Ignore her," Damien advised before handing Jeanne a note. "Get this into Arsham's hands ASAP."

I was about to snatch the note out of Jeanne's hand when Katya shoved me back toward the sofa. "Where do you think you're going?"

Rather than fight, I prudently sat down. There was no way I could take all of them on at once. I looked at Damien and inquired, "How many spies do you have in the London lair?"

Katya took it upon herself to reply. "Enough."

Frustrated, I watched Jeanne and the boys as they exited the flat. There was nothing I could do to prevent them from delivering that communication.

Damien turned toward me, eyes twinkling. "Things are about to get interesting."

CHAPTER 19

"People kill for love. They die for love."
(Helen Fisher)

The Elders whispered among themselves, extrapolating various theories on why Angelique had been captured. Occasionally, their eyes fell upon Arsham's empty throne. When he finally entered the octagonal room, they fell silent.

Grim-faced, he held up a sheet of paper. "This is a letter from Damien Sauvage stating that he and Katya have abducted your queen."

Rahim stood from his throne and extended his hand. "Let me see that. Who gave this to you?"

Arsham handed him the note. "It was slipped under the door of the control room. Omar found it an hour ago. I am taking this as a serious threat."

"They are explicit in their demand," Rahim said, his eyes skimming over the words. "Change the sacred law or the duchess dies."

"We have discussed this matter before," Andrei said. "We have not agreed in unison."

"Well, brother, we are forced to discuss it again," Jazmin said. "We *must* implement the law."

"We cannot allow our prey to live," Andrei countered, throwing up his hands in frustration. "I'm not the only vampire who feels this way, either. Hundreds of others do too. Our actions and decisions should be aimed at benefitting the coven, not catering to the enemy's demands."

Jazmin said, "They will kill Angelique as easily as they killed our beloved sister."

Andrei shrugged. "If that's the price that must be paid..."

She frowned at him. "How can you be so cruel? So stupid?"

Arsham glared at the contentious male. "If they kill my

mate, I shall declare war on the London slayers. How will that benefit the coven?"

Andrei scowled. "We don't have to declare war. We can fight them."

Arsham stood from the throne, ready to challenge the impertinent Elder in a fight to the death.

Rahim intervened. "Calm yourselves. Don't you see? This is exactly what Damien and Katya want from us. *Division*. It will make us easier to conquer."

Jazmin stood and addressed the sires. "My lords, I beseech you. Change the law and retrieve our queen. I'm tired of hunting in fear of being decapitated by slayers. Put an end to this madness once and for all before someone else gets hurt."

Micah, Valerio, and Omar nodded in agreement.

"Ha! They would kill us just the same," Andrei countered.

Hearing this, Arsham motioned to Omar and the two of them stormed out of the meeting.

The moment they were in the corridor, Omar said, "Sire, what do you want me to do?"

"Not here."

They walked in silence to Arsham's chamber.

Once inside, Arsham said, "What I'd like to do is kill Andrei for being such a belligerent, disrespectful—" He stopped himself. "Do you think they've…"

Arsham couldn't bring himself to finish the sentence, for the thought of Angelique suffering the same fate as Mayu was simply too painful to imagine.

"I do not," Omar assured him.

"Any news on where they're holding her?"

"I'm waiting to hear back from the scouts." Omar's hand flew to his earpiece. "Wait…I've just received confirmation that Jeanne Sauvage has been seen heading toward Soho. They're tracking her. Hopefully, she'll lead us to Damien and Katya."

Arsham began pacing. "I want every available member of the Security Team on this. We need to hurry."

"What are you planning?"

"Her rescue, of course."

"We're planning her rescue, sire."

Arsham placed his hand on Omar's shoulder. "No. I'm going there alone."

"I cannot allow that."

"But you will."

"It's too dangerous, sire."

"All the more reason why you need to let me go alone. I command it."

"Sire—"

"Stand down, Omar."

Omar lowered his gaze. "As you wish."

"You must find the address. *Fast.*" Arsham paused in thought. "What about Andrei?"

"We haven't found anything conclusive but I'm following a lead. There's a pair of newborns who are always whispering in Andrei's ear. Don't worry, we'll find the evidence you need."

"Good. Go now. I need to think."

Omar left Arsham alone with his troublesome thoughts. The vampire prince paced the room like a caged animal. A knock on the door made him pause. "Enter."

Jazmin quietly slid into the room and surveyed the rich furnishings with discretion. "Forgive the intrusion, my lord."

Arsham waved his hand and indicated a chair.

She shook her head. "No, thank you. I only came by to offer you my support. I'm sorry they took Angelique. If there is anything I can do, please let me know."

"I appreciate your concern."

"There's something else I wanted to discuss with you, my lord. It's about my brother, Andrei. You see, he has many supporters in the coven who believe as he does. Fortunately, Mayu and I have succeeded in converting several of our brethren to our way of thinking—both here and in Russia."

"Well done."

"I'm sure more will come around. Unfortunately, we don't have the luxury of time." She wrung her hands nervously. "Andrei has been working against us from the beginning, my lord. Mayu had been helping me convert vampires behind his back. He began persecuting her after she spoke in favor of the new feeding method in the meeting. Mayu died shortly afterward."

Arsham's eyes narrowed. "What exactly are you saying?"

"I think Andrei is connected to my sister's death."

He hid his surprise with a mask of neutrality. "You should be saying these things to Rahim, not me."

"I wanted to tell you first because I know you'd believe me. I also figured you had already arrived at a similar conclusion and had taken the necessary steps to confirm your suspicion."

"Assuming you're correct, what then?"

"I can go to my sire with evidence. We can even go together, if you wish."

"Rahim would believe you, regardless."

"The reason I have been at his side for so many years as his most trusted Elder is because I take nothing for granted. I will go to Rahim when I have solid proof to back up my accusation. This is why he trusts me implicitly."

"Very well. I will apprise you when the time is right."

She inclined her head. "Thank you, my lord."

She turned to go but Arsham said, "Wait…You were once famous for your psychic abilities."

"Correct."

He hesitated. "Are you able to…?"

"Come with me, my lord."

Arsham followed Jazmin to her chamber. His eyes took in the various colors and textures, the exotic works of art and lavish tapestries. Judging by the Elder's taste, he concluded that she must be an interesting female. Angelique had mentioned her fondness of Jazmin on more than one occasion.

Angelique…

"Sit, my lord," she offered before filling a chalice with blood wine. "Would you like a drink?"

Arsham politely declined.

Jazmin set the wine atop a table and eyed the ancient vampire to determine which method of divination to employ on his behalf. Extracting a velvet pouch from a drawer, she concentrated on Angelique. After taking a seat across from him, she cast the ancient stones, which were scratched and faded from centuries of use.

"Tell me everything you see," he said.

She nodded, then closed her eyes before passing her hands over the stones. Some felt hot, others cold. Some vibrated beneath her hand, others hummed in her ears. The stones had always spoken to her, regardless of good or bad news.

At length, the Elder opened her eyes. The far-off look in her amber gaze implied that she saw otherworldly things that no one else could see. Several seconds passed.

Arsham prompted, "Well?"

Jazmin met his anxious gaze. "She lives."

***

Jeanne took pleasure in shoving me inside of a crammed space and locking the door. Sunrise was less than a half hour away. I looked around my tiny prison. Shelves lined one wall and there was a state of the art washing machine and dryer pushed against the opposite wall. I also noticed an ironing board hanging on a rack along with an iron. I was in a laundry room.

I sighed. "Great."

At least they weren't tossing me outside to crisp in the sunshine and disintegrate into a pile of ash. The lock on my side of the door prompted me to turn it in order to prevent anyone from accidentally barging in during the day. I noticed a strip of light peeking through the bottom of the door. Quickly, I searched the cabinets and found some cleaning cloths. I shoved the fabric into the space between the door and the floor, then slid down the wall into a sitting position. Closing my eyes, I surrendered to the sleep of the undead while thinking of my beloved Arsham.

I awoke the next night and listened with keen interest to the chatter taking place in the apartment. Hopefully, they would reveal something pertinent that I could later use against them. Suddenly, someone pounded on the door.

"Open up, Angelique!"

I unlocked the door and Katya burst into the laundry room

214

with a frown. "Come on."

She led me into the living room where Damien and Jeanne stood staring at me. Nigel and Hugh weren't there, but I spied Corvo and Xoana drinking Cokes on the outside patio.

Damien tossed an H&M bag in my direction. "I got you some clothes. Shower is through there."

Katya frowned. "She's wearing clothes."

"You can't expect her to hang out in that fancy dress and high heels, do you?"

Katya's eyes were glued to my dress. "I'm keeping that Armani dress. It's vintage."

At least the bathroom was spacious and modern. I removed my clothing and showered, then peeked into the plastic shopping bag. Slim jeans, acrylic sweater, sneakers, a sports bra and a pair of panties. Everything was black so there had been no effort required on Damien's part to match any of the cheap garments. I hung the Armani dress on a hook behind the bathroom door, then put on the jeans and sports bra.

Someone knocked and I said, "Come in."

Damien poked his head through the door. "You're taking a long time. Is everything—"

He froze at the sight of my tattoo. I grabbed the shirt and pulled it over my head without offering any explanation.

He asked, "When did you get that?"

"Recently," I replied while slipping my feet into the sneakers. "Thanks for the clean clothes."

I exited the bathroom with Damien at my heels. Katya watched me like a hawk.

Smirking, she said, "That's a nice humble look."

You would know. Rather than voice the petty thought aloud, I pretended to ignore the spiteful Elder.

Narrowing his eyes at me, Damien said, "I know that look. Whatever you're planning in that head of yours—"

"I'm not planning anything," I said, cutting him off. "I told you, Arsham and I are on your side. Several Elders and vampires too. It's only a matter of time…"

"Not soon enough," Katya said, crossing her arms.

"What's your problem? Do you *want* to start a war?"

"Don't be ridiculous," she snapped with a glance at Damien.

I confronted her head on. "I've told you repeatedly that Arsham, Rahim, and several Elders—including myself—feed in a humane manner. We want to see the law implemented as much as you do, yet you're carrying on as if this weren't the case. What's your real end goal here? Power? Rule the coven?"

"How dare you?!"

The fact that she became instantly defensive confirmed my suspicion that there was much more at stake than altering the Codex.

Damien intervened in order to diffuse the potentially violent situation. "Let's cool it. The London coven will respond to the letter I sent them. We need to be patient. If nothing happens soon, then we'll rethink our strategy."

I regarded him levelly. "That would be the prudent thing to do but your hotheaded girlfriend here seems to want all-out war. Maybe you should start thinking with your head instead of your dick, Damien."

The Elder snarled at my impertinence, baring her fangs. I went into defense mode, ready to fight. Damien intervened by standing between us. "Back off, both of you."

Katya glared at me, then said to Damien, "I'm cool. We'll wait and stick to the plan."

Damien looked at me. "You need to start showing a little respect, okay?"

"Respect for whom? You? Her?" I glanced at Jeanne and added, "Or this useless twit?"

Katya cursed under her breath before pointing at sofa. "Sit down and stay the hell out of my face."

"Let me go," I shot back.

Damien grabbed hold of my arm and marched me to the sofa as Katya stormed into her bedroom.

Someone banged on the door.

"I'm getting sick and tired of the noise up here! Don't you people ever sleep?"

Damien went over to the door. "Sorry."

"Not all of us have the luxury of sleeping all day. I'll report your drug den to the coppers!"

Katya emerged from the bedroom and made a beeline to the door. Her face reflected deadly intention.

Damien placed himself between the old woman and Katya. "No drugs in here. Sorry for the noise, we'll be quiet."

"I'm going to kill that old bitch," Katya said after he had closed the door.

Damien grabbed the London Times from the kitchen counter and handed it to me. "Here. It's all I've got."

I didn't find it the least bit surprising that Katya didn't have books. "Thanks," I said, accepting the newspaper.

He went into the bedroom, pulling Katya inside with him.

Hugh and Nigel arrived at the flat an hour later. They barely acknowledged me before going into the other room with Jeanne. Feigning interest in an article, I overheard their whispered plans for creating an army of undead slayers. Their ultimate goal was to challenge the London coven by bringing war to their door. Although this information sickened me, I kept my expression deadpan while turning the page of the newspaper. My mind raced with ways in which to escape in order to alert my sire and brethren.

Damien left the flat to go hunting, leaving Katya to watch over me. I didn't bother looking up from the newspaper when she sat down beside me.

Crossing her legs, she said, "You have no idea what kind of male your sire is, do you?"

I said nothing, prompting her to rip the newspaper from my hands. Still refusing to look at her, I said, "You know nothing about Arsham. Or me, for that matter."

She raised her hand to strike and I grabbed her wrist. My other hand curled around her jugular. I was so fast that she flinched. "Touch me again and I'll kill you."

The cold steel of Xoana's katana scraped against my nape. "Let go of Katya."

Corvo appeared over the slayer's shoulder and said in English, "Damien said to be cool."

I released my grip. To Katya's credit, she backed off.

Xoana lowered the weapon. "Better."

Katya shot me a dirty look, then went off to join Jeanne and the slayers, leaving me alone with the Brazilians. I debated making a run for it but Xoana, guessing my thoughts, shook her head in warning.

"Don't do it," she said.

Corvo frowned at me and crossed his arms. *"Be cool."*

"Okay, fine. I'll be cool like Damien said. Tell me, how many avian shifters are there in South America?" I asked in Portuguese, opting to glean information rather than fight them.

"Less than fifty, I think," Corvo replied.

"They are rare," Xoana added.

"Rarer than feline shifters, that's for sure." Glancing over my shoulder, I inquired, "Did Katya and Damien go all the way to Brazil to find you?"

"Yes," she replied.

Wanting to keep them engaged, I inquired, "What do you two think of London?"

Xoana shrugged. "It's nice. Very old."

"Cold," Corvo corrected.

I offered a tentative smile, which they hesitantly returned. "London has lots of history and, yes, it can get quite chilly. Especially in winter."

"You are French," Xoana said.

"That's right."

"Did you kill humans in the beginning?"

I nodded. "You know how we are when we're first created."

"Monsters." Catching herself, she added, "Sorry."

"No, you're right. Newly transformed Vampires are savage beasts initially, but that doesn't mean we have to continue on that path once the bloodlust settles. We are intelligent creatures. We possess the power to change, to evolve and survive."

Xoana glanced around then whispered nervously, "I don't want to kill you."

I held her dark gaze. "That makes two of us."

Katya emerged from the room, putting an abrupt end to our

218

conversation. Xoana and Corvo retreated to the far end of the flat as Katya took a seat at the dining table.

Damien returned a couple of minutes later and, seeing the sour look on his lover's face, inquired, "What's up?"

Katya replied, "Your ex tried to kill me."

His eyes slid my way. "Go, I'll take care of this."

Katya left the flat and he said, "Is it true?"

I looked at him levelly. "She raised her hand to me."

He sighed in frustration. "I'm sorry for all of this."

"Are you?"

"Yes, and...I never meant to hurt you."

"Like you said, you did me a favor."

"That tattoo on your back...We know your brothers sport the black scorpion as a symbol of loyalty to Arsham."

"That's correct. Did your spies tell you that?"

"Yes," he replied sheepishly.

"They forgot to tell you that my tattoo is different from that of my brothers. It represents more than loyalty. Mine is a symbol of love, devotion, trust...I am Arsham's official mate. Harming him is the same as harming me."

He looked at me long and hard. "Is that a threat?"

"It's a promise that you and your girlfriend should take very seriously."

Damien said nothing more, opting instead to retreat to the bedroom. Katya also refused to speak with me after she returned to the flat, which suited me fine. Bored out of my mind, I read the entire newspaper and even did the crossword puzzle.

CHAPTER 20

"I should like to lie at your feet and die in your arms."
(Voltaire)

I cursed inwardly when Katya locked me inside the laundry room for the second time. My captors were doing a good job of maintaining constant surveillance. Shoving the cleaning rags along the door's lower edge to block out the daylight, I concluded that my only hope for freedom was to reason with Damien. Unfortunately, that wouldn't be easy.

Arsham was no doubt worried about me and Omar was out scouring the streets. If my plan with Damien failed, I would have no choice but to wait this out. I awoke the next evening and stood by the door to await my release. Mentally rehearsing what I would say to my ex-lover, I smoothed the wrinkles out of my cheap clothing.

Jeanne unlocked the door and I stepped out of my makeshift prison. My eyes settled on Xoana and Corvo eating pizza at the dining table. They acknowledged me with a fleeting glance as I sank into the sofa. Jeanne tossed a dirty look my way before joining them. I watched as she bit into a slice of pizza then wiped the strands of melted cheese from her chin.

Damien and Katya emerged from the bedroom.

Katya said, "The duchess looks like shit."

Damien studied my overly pale face. "When was the last time you fed, Angelique?"

Katya looked at her lover in exasperation. "What does that matter? We can't let her go hunting alone."

Damien opened the refrigerator and pulled out a bag of blood. We used donor banks as a last resort, and I cringed in disgust as he poured the garnet liquid into a glass.

Katya read my expression. "Beggars can't be choosers."

I accepted the glass with a grateful nod before placing it to my lips and forcing down its contents. Cold blood was simply too disgusting for words.

Katya watched me in amusement. "I'm going hunting for some nice fresh hot blood. Are you coming, babe?"

Damien shook his head. "One of us should stay with her."

"We talked about this last night, remember?"

"Katya, please."

"Jeanne, Xoana, and Corvo are here."

"None of them are a match for a vampire like Angelique. Trust me. One vampire needs to be here at all times."

Katya eyed him steadily before tossing a glance in my direction. I kept my gaze lowered in the face of her obvious jealousy.

The angry neighbor banged on the door again.

"This isn't a hotel! What do you people do all night? Don't you ever sleep?"

Katya snarled in rage as she gripped the door handle.

Damien's eyes widened. "Babe, don't!"

She threw open the door and yanked the old woman into the apartment with such force that she stumbled toward the island in the kitchen.

Gripping the counter top, she glanced around the flat with terrified eyes. "I'm going to call the—"

Katya broke the old woman's neck before she could finish the sentence.

Snap!

The lifeless human dropped to the floor with a dull thud. My eyes slid to Damien, who gaped at Katya in shock.

"What the fuck are you doing?" he demanded angrily.

Katya shrugged, unrepentant. "She's been a pain in my ass for days. Now she won't bother us anymore."

I glanced at Jeanne and the Brazilians, who stared at the dead old woman with stunned faces.

"This is wrong...this is so wrong," Damien said.

"Don't be a hypocrite. You had no qualms about killing the doctor," Katya shot back.

My head whipped round to face him. *"You* killed Caleb

221

Morgan?"

Katya smirked at me. "I killed the loudmouth woman but Damien *insisted* on destroying the vampirologist. Didn't even flinch when he did it, either."

"How could you?" I whispered.

"The man was a creep," he said in an attempt to defend himself. "Besides, his death is on *your* head. Had you not befriended Caleb Morgan, he would be alive today."

"I can't believe you're going to try to pin this on me," I said.

Katya snapped her fingers then kicked the corpse. "Get rid of this. I'm out of here."

Damien watched his lover leave the apartment before dragging the corpse into the other room. I went to the sofa and sat down, deep in thought. I had once loved this male, this hypocrite who now tried to figure out a way to hide the body of an innocent human who had been killed in such a thoughtless and wasteful manner.

Jeanne began texting with someone, most likely Nigel judging by the look on her smitten face.

Damien exited the room and regarded his sister and the Brazilians. "I don't need to remind you that what has taken place here is not to be mentioned."

They nodded in unison.

"I'm going out," Jeanne announced.

Damien frowned. "Now?"

"Nigel is waiting for me at the pub on the corner. I won't be long, I promise."

"Go," he said.

She shrugged into a jacket and exited the flat.

Damien's gaze shifted to the half-empty glass in my hand. "You should finish it. No one is letting you out of here to feed."

When I said nothing, he came over and placed his hand on my shoulder.

"Don't touch me." I stood and went over to the sink. "I've had enough, thanks."

"I'm sorry you had to witness that," he offered lamely.

"Why did you kill Caleb?"

"Jake, Jeanne, Katya and I were hoping to take down Arsham in Edinburgh. We expected him to arrive with a couple of guards, not a small army. The moment we realized that we were significantly outnumbered, we fled the apartment...I wasn't expecting you to be there."

"Come on, Damien. You knew I'd go."

"Maybe, yeah," he admitted while averting his eyes. "I didn't think things would turn out the way they did."

I went back to the sofa and he occupied the seat beside mine. He continued, "I'm sorry."

"Let me go back to the lair."

"I can't."

"You mean you *won't*."

"Don't be difficult."

"How can you allow yourself to be controlled by Katya? You of all people, who constantly preached moral virtue."

"Contrary to what you may believe, she's not a villain."

"To think that you only fed on derelicts...Now you're hiding bodies of innocent people. You've changed, Damien."

"You don't know what you're talking about."

"No? A few months with Katya was all it took for you to be okay with killing my human friend."

"It's not like that...I've already explained what happened."

Fighting with him would solve nothing. What I needed was information. "I'm curious about something. What does she say about her brother, Andrei?"

"She never mentions him."

Interesting. "How many spies does she have in our lair?"

"Enough."

I gripped his arm and he looked down at my hand. "Listen to me, Katya has a plan that she's keeping from you."

"You're wrong."

I glanced over my shoulder to make sure no one was eavesdropping. "That shady bitch isn't who you think she is. Watch your back or else you may go down with her."

He shook my hand off. "She would never do that to me."

"I've offered you a friendly warning. It's up to you to heed my advice."

Damien ran his hand through his hair, his gray eyes troubled. An uncomfortable silence stretched between us. A moment later, he reached for the TV remote control and turned on the news. We watched the world's events in silence. Earthquake in India, school shooting in the US, and a tsunami in Indonesia...

"Only bad news," he murmured. When I didn't say anything, he added, "Do you think the world will end one day?"

I glanced at him. "Humans are doing a wonderful job of destroying their planet."

"Maybe aliens will save us."

"Aliens?"

"No one believes in our existence either."

The door swung open and Katya looked from me to Damien. "What's going on here?"

"Nothing," Damien replied.

Katya walked over to the sofa. "Your turn. I'll keep watch."

He shook his head. "I'm fine."

Her eyes slid in my direction. "Afraid that I can't handle the duchess?"

"I'm not thirsty. I overfed last night," he replied, reaching for Katya's hand as he stood.

I avoided looking at either of them as they shared a kiss. Leaving me under the watchful eyes of Xoana and Corvo, they retired into the bedroom and made no attempt to hide the sounds of their lovemaking. The frigid old blood that I had consumed earlier failed to provide me with the strength and vitality I derived from living blood. In addition to the Brazilians being fast, there were two well-fed vampires in the next room. For these reasons, I resisted the urge to make a run for the door.

Jeanne eventually stumbled into the flat and I could smell the alcohol on her breath from where I sat. She had been gone much longer than an hour. Damien would be pissed off. Getting drunk on the job proved that she wasn't ready to be a slayer.

"Where's my brother?" she slurred.

Katya's erotic moan answered her question.

Jeanne smirked and shuffled to the guest bedroom. I heard

her snoring five minutes later.

At length, Damien and Katya emerged from the bedroom to relieve Xoana and Corvo so that they could get some rest. I watched as my captors retreated to the far end of the room to talk about me. Turning my face away, I pretended to study a horrendous work of post-modern art dominating the wall leading from the kitchen to the bathroom.

One of Jeanne's loud snores attracted Damien's attention. Frowning, he went to the door of the guest bedroom.

"She's drunk," Katya said.

"Yeah. Stupid kid," he said.

I risked a glance at him and saw that he was livid. He tossed his sister a dirty look before taking a seat near Katya at the dining table.

Loud caws startled us. Corvo morphed into a crow and flew to the kitchen counter. Damien unsheathed his katana as Katya ran into her bedroom to fetch a sword. The ancient weapon bore scratches and nicks, which made me nervous. How well did she know how to use that thing?

Startled out of sleep, Xoana jumped to her feet and unsheathed her weapon. "Vampire."

Jeanne exited her bedroom with disheveled hair and bloodshot eyes. "What's all the noise about?"

"Get your weapon," Damien said.

"Shit! Do you want me to call Hugh and Nigel?" she asked, fumbling with her cell phone.

"There's no time."

The collective anxiety made the air in the room crackle with tension. Everyone stood tense and ready, waiting for the door to fly open at any second. I wondered which of our warriors had come to save me. Perhaps it was Omar himself. To everyone's surprise, someone politely knocked. Damien and Katya exchanged puzzled glances, whereas my stomach sank.

At the second knock, Katya demanded, "Who is it?"

"Prince Arsham of Persia, second son of King Amir, co-sire to the London lair."

I bolted from the sofa and placed myself between my captors

and the door. "Step back, sire. Everyone here is armed."

"Stand down, Angelique. I have come in peace to negotiate your release. I am alone and unarmed."

"Leave now!" I cried.

"I said stand down."

Katya and Damien pried me away from the door and placed me between Jeanne and Xoana. Their blades were at my throat to discourage Arsham from doing anything foolish.

Corvo shifted back into human form and carefully opened the door. Arsham stood in the doorway, calm and self-assured. His glittering dark eyes, full of wisdom, accurately assessed the situation before stepping into the flat. He stared everyone down, compelling them to retreat slightly from his presence. His regality and power were indeed impressive to behold.

"I'm here to negotiate the release of my mate," Arsham said softly, his tone one of unchallenged authority.

"Stop killing humans, scumbag," Jeanne blurted.

My sire refused to acknowledge the human girl, which only made her visibly upset.

"Quiet, Jeanne," Damien warned.

Arsham's eyes slid to Corvo. "I have never seen an avian shifter. How intriguing."

When Corvo asked Xoana for a translation, Arsham repeated his words in perfect Portuguese. The shifter only nodded slightly in response.

Arsham's gaze focused on Katya. "I will negotiate with *you*, for you are an Elder. Are my terms acceptable?"

Katya nodded.

Arsham glanced at me. "Before we come to any resolution, you must unhand my queen."

They let go of me, but stood poised and ready should the need arise for their blades.

Katya said, "You know what we want."

"I do. Rahim already made the announcement to the coven." Arsham's eyes narrowed ever so slightly at the beautiful blonde vampire. "But you already know this thanks to your spies, yet you continue to hold the duchess here as hostage. Why?"

Damien shot Katya a look of surprise. "Wait, an official announcement was made? Why didn't you tell me?"

"I had to hear it from him," she replied.

Damien didn't appear convinced.

Arsham spread out his hands. "You've now heard it from my own lips. I assume my queen and I can now return to our lair in peace."

Katya appeared stricken. "How do we know you're telling the truth?"

"I'm here and I've come in peace, which means I've given in to your terms. What more proof do you require?" With a look in my direction, he added, "Have they mistreated you in any way, my love?"

I shook my head. His eyes roamed over my cheap outfit with blatant disdain but he prudently kept his opinion to himself.

"What about Damien?" Katya demanded.

"I have decided that his life will be spared. After all, he is my son," Arsham replied.

Damien laughed derisively. "I don't believe you, Arsham."

Arsham regarded my ex-lover as one would a pesky fly. "Come back with me to the lair. See for yourself that what I'm telling you is true." Turning to Katya, he added, "As for you, Rahim and I have discussed the matter at length. Your sire is ready to forgive you and so am I. You'll be required to issue a public apology to both covens, but we've negotiated your reinstatement with the Elders. Everyone agrees." When she hesitated, he graciously held out his hand. "Come."

Rather than accept the offer, Katya shook her head.

Damien studied his lover with a confused expression. "Isn't this what you wanted? What we've been working toward?"

"Be quiet," she snapped.

Damien frowned. "What are you doing? Go with him."

"You know nothing of Rahim or the Russian coven," she said, her eyes glued to Arsham's face. "I'll never return to groveling at my sire's feet."

"No one is requiring you to grovel," Arsham assured her.

Damien added, "Will she be put on trial?"

227

Arsham shook his head in response to the question.

Taking hold of Katya's arm, Damien said, "Sounds like a fair deal to me. I say we take it. We've done what we've set out to do with no casualties except for Jake."

"Don't forget Francis and Mayu," I reminded him. "Oh, and your poor neighbor whose corpse is decaying in your bedroom."

Damien's face appeared remorseful whereas Katya's did not. Tightening her grip on the hilt of her sword, she glared at Arsham. My sire and I exchanged knowing glances. This would not end well.

Katya said, "*All* Elders have to agree on a law before it can be written into the Codex and I know Andrei is against it."

Eying her levelly, Arsham said, "You are correct. You'll be happy to know that your brother and his supporters have been tried for treason. They were deliberately resisting us."

"Wait, why would they do that?" Damien demanded, looking from Katya to Arsham in confusion.

Arsham finally acknowledged Damien with a direct look. "Isn't it obvious, you fool? Andrei has been aiding his sister in her attempt to create an undead army of slayers." To Katya, he added, "When we tortured your brother with UV light and silver blades, he confessed to everything."

Katya blanched. *"You did what?"*

Arsham smiled coldly. "Don't worry. Andrei is no longer suffering. His head was severed from his body by Rahim's own hand. As for his supporters, which are also your supporters, they were shot with silver bullets and allowed to disintegrate into ash beneath UV light."

Katya's eyes filled with tears of rage. "You're lying…"

Arsham extracted a photograph from his pocket and held it out to her. The image depicted the mutilated and headless body of Andrei. Katya's face contorted into a mask of pure rage. Seeing the lethal intention in her eyes, I moved fast—too fast for the mortals in the room to discern my actions. Jeanne didn't realize that I had unarmed her until she hit the floor.

Damien's head turned toward his sister. "What the fu—"

I didn't think twice when Katya took a step toward Arsham. The cold steel sliced through the bones and tendons of her neck with startling ease.

Damien's eyes bulged in horror. "No!"

Katya's head slid slowly from the remaining stump of neck, creating a wet gurgling sound before tumbling to the floor with a dull thud and rolling toward the kitchen.

Damien gripped my hand and attempted to pry the katana from my grasp. Meanwhile, Arsham plucked the weapon from the decapitated Elder's lifeless hand. All of this happened before Katya's body hit the floor.

Jeanne pushed Xoana toward me. "What are you waiting for? Kill her!"

The Brazilian slayer lifted her katana and I shoved her so hard that she stumbled across the room. Jeanne cried out like a comic book hero before swinging her weapon at me. The sound of steel swooshing through the air made me duck in order to avoid Katya's fate. Arsham lunged forward and the deadly sharp blade cut through Jeanne's neck as if it were a stick of butter.

Damien watched in horror as his sister's mouth fell open in a silent scream. The world's last human Sauvage dropped to the floor, her head rolling off to the side with eyes staring at the ceiling. A pool of fresh, hot human blood spread throughout the floor, making me salivate with thirst.

"One Sauvage down, one to go," Arsham said coolly.

Seething with unbridled fury, Damien grabbed a fistful of my hair and yanked me backward. He tried to wrestle the weapon from my hand but failed, so he body slammed me. The hard impact caused me to lose my grip on the katana. He snatched the weapon in time to block one of Arsham's mighty blows. Blades clashed above my head.

Weaponless, I scurried away from Damien and Arsham and focused on Xoana and Corvo. They clung to the back wall, trying to watch the fight. The vampires moved too quickly for their mortal eyes to follow.

Standing before them, I warned, "Stay out of this."

"You killed Katya," Xoana accused.

"And he killed Jeanne," Corvo added, pointing at Arsham.

"Both my sire and I fought in self-defense," I shot back.

Unconvinced, Xoana lunged at me with her katana. I ducked, then moved to the opposite side of the dining table. Taking hold of a chair, I broke one of the legs diagonally against the table's surface to create a sharp stake. I thrust my makeshift weapon at the slayer when she attacked me a second time.

Corvo shifted into a crow and pecked at me in order to help his partner. He managed to rip a chunk of my cheek with his sharp beak.

"Stop it," I hissed, waving him away from me while side-stepping the sharp blade of Xoana's katana.

The crow came at me again and I rammed the stake through one of his wings. The large black bird fluttered to the floor and screeched in pain. Torn between fighting me and helping her partner, Xoana hesitated.

I held out my hand. "Give me your weapon. We can end this right now."

Her eyes darted to Corvo. "If I don't?"

"You and the shifter will die here today. That's a promise."

She thought about it. "How will we return to Brazil?"

"I'll provide you with more than enough money to get you home. You have my word."

The crow continued screeching, compelling her to nod her head in agreement to my suggestion. "We have a deal."

I pointed to the balcony. "There's a fire escape. Go!"

Xoana dropped the katana, picked up the crow, and fled the scene. I snatched the weapon and ran up to Damien.

Placing the blade at his throat, I said, "Stop."

Feeling the threat of the cold steel against his skin, Damien backed away from Arsham. The katana was still in his hand.

My sire growled and lunged forward, prompting me to pull Damien out of harm's way. "Don't kill him, sire."

"Give me one good reason not to send this Sauvage scum straight to Hell," Arsham retorted.

"He's your son," I reminded him.

Arsham snarled at my words.

I continued, "Clearly, Katya deceived him. All Damien ever wanted was for vampires to stop killing humans. I can vouch for him on that account."

Arsham pinned me with a disbelieving look. "What are you suggesting, Angelique? That I forgive and forget what's taken place here and accept him back into our lair like the biblical prodigal son?"

I hesitated. "Technically, he has the right to be an Elder."

Arsham bristled. "Don't be absurd!"

Damien echoed our sire's sentiment by adding, "I want nothing to do with your unholy coven!" His gaze fell upon Jeanne's headless body. "My sister was all that I had left in this world and you took her away…Oh Jeanne, I'm so sorry…"

I said quietly, "Damien—"

"Shut the fuck up, you traitorous bitch!"

I recoiled from his hatred.

Looking at Arsham, Damien added, "And *you*, you're nothing but a selfish murdering beast. I should have slain you when I had the opportunity."

Arsham shrugged. "I merely defended myself."

"She was only a fucking kid!" Damien spat.

Arsham eyed him coldly. "All the more reason you should have discouraged her from following in your footsteps. Vampire slaying is a dangerous profession. Really, Sauvage, you should have known better. Her death is on your head."

My sire's cruel words and mocking tone served as fuel to a fire that had already been burning out of control for a long time. In a fit of rage, Damien suddenly kicked Arsham hard in the stomach. The unexpected assault caused my sire to stagger backward. It was all the experienced slayer needed to attack.

"Damien, no!" I cried.

Damien raised the katana and lunged toward Arsham, his eyes filled with murderous intention. "Die, motherfucker!"

***

Droplets fell from the bloody blade, resembling a sprinkle of tiny rubies on the floor. My eyes traced the sharp steel to the black hilt. Damien's blood ran onto my hand and I marveled at the paleness of my skin in comparison to the vibrant red.

Fuck with me and you fuck with Arsham.

Strong hands gently pried the katana from my grip and I watched as the weapon fell to the floor. Metal crashed against tile, the sound reverberating throughout the space. He took hold of my shoulders and steered me away from the carnage toward the balcony. I avoided looking down, opting instead to tilt my head back and focus my gaze upward. The faintest flush of crimson streaked the night sky.

He bit into his wrist, then gently smeared his blood into the deep wound on my face caused by Corvo. "It's a sin to mar that perfect face."

I gripped his hand and nuzzled my cheek into his palm.

"It's all right, my love," he whispered before pressing his lips to my temple.

I fixed my gaze on the waning moon. "We must take cover."

Wrapping me in a tight embrace, he whispered, "There's still time."

A wave of relief spread through me. He made me feel safe, secure. *Loved.* "Take me away from here."

Picking me up in his arms, he carried me into the night.

EPILOGUE
DIAMOND BEACH, ICELAND
ONE MONTH LATER

The rising sun caused the ice on the beach to sparkle like stars. Glorious rays of golden light pierced plummy clouds as the fiery orb that is our sun made its majestic ascent in a russet sky. This was my third sunrise since being a vampire.

"I'll never tire of this," Arsham whispered, his eyes glued to the liquid copper horizon.

"Nor I."

He glanced at me. "I'll never tire of you."

I took his hand and lifted it to my lips, kissing the blood ruby. It was him. It had always been him. It will always be him.

The automatic metal shutters blocked our view as the serum began to wear off. He turned toward me and claimed my lips in a sweet kiss before leading me to the bed. We were fast asleep in minutes.

I awoke the next night clinging to my sire. I felt his eyes burning upon my skin before I lifted my head to meet his gaze. No words were needed to express my love for him. The fact that I had slain the last Sauvage slayer on Earth served as proof of my loyalty. It also secured my rightful place in the coven forever. My deed would go down in our history books.

The Warrior Goddess.

Arsham gazed deeply into my eyes and I drowned in them. I no longer feared the eternity staring back at me from those fathomless obsidian pools. The ancient vampire god touched me with need and desire, making me rejoice.

"You belong to me, Angelique…"

Did you enjoy this novel? The author would appreciate your review on Amazon. Thank you.

Turn the page to sample the epic novel, THE WATCHERS: A Story of Undying Love.

THE WATCHERS

A STORY OF UNDYING LOVE

C. DE MELO

ISBN-13: 978-0999787823 (C. De Melo)
ISBN-10:0999787829

PART I

THE ICON

After Dark Times the Icon shall come.
She will walk the Earth as a Sage, but will only provoke rage.
Our Mark she will bear on the Tenth and Twentieth year.

—First Prophecy of the Sacred Oracle

PROLOGUE
PRESENT DAY
LISBON, PORTUGAL

Sooty clouds conceal the moon in a starless sky as a white vein of lightning illuminates an anchored caravela. The fast and mighty sea vessel bobs like a child's toy upon the angry waves of the Tagus River. The sight fills me with dread.

My beloved stands tall and proud, the fierce wind tugging at the strands of his dark hair. Deafening thunder fills our ears only moments before icy water spills from the heavens. We are surrounded by imminent danger. My tears mingle with rain as I desperately plead with him. The thought of losing this man forever pierces my heart with excruciating pain...

I cannot bear it.

I awoke with my own sharp intake of breath and, as the cobwebs of sleep dissipated, the fragile echo of a memory slipped—yet again—from my grasp.

The gloomy light of dawn filled the bedroom. My gaze is drawn to the packed suitcases by the door. Thousands of miles away, a new life awaited...

Could it save me from this madness?

CHAPTER 1
LISBON, PORTUGAL
NOVEMBER 1, 1510

"The church bells are ringing in honor of my birthday!"

"As they do every year," my mother reminded me with an indulgent smile. "Now go out and fetch some chestnuts."

I snatched a basket and ran outside with eager steps. All Saint's Day was a holy day of celebration in our kingdom. My mother had already promised to bake apple tarts, so the roasted chestnuts would be an extra treat. Unable to resist their sweet flesh, I usually ate them the moment they were extracted from the fire, inevitably burning my tongue. My mother often scolded me for my lack of patience, but today I would surprise her by waiting for them to cool. After all, as a ten-year-old, I should start displaying a certain measure of maturity.

I followed the footpath through our vegetable garden and slipped through a cluster of trees. The sun-kissed leaves were as translucent as the stained glass windows of the great cathedral. Sunbeams seeped through the branches to create a mosaic of light and shadow on the soft grass beneath my feet.

We lived on a hill just outside of Lisbon, and I could clearly see the fortress of the Castelo de São Jorge. Soldiers moved to and fro along the battlements like industrious ants. Hugging the narrow trunk of a sapling, I admired the sparkling water of the Tagus River and glimpsed the faint silhouette of a merchant spice ship heading out to sea.

A butterfly landed on a nearby branch and I became instantly lost in the intricate maze of its wings. When it flew away, I continued toward the clearing where the chestnut trees grew. I sank to the ground and began collecting the prettiest chestnuts.

The sun warmed my back, making me drowsy, so I stretched out on the grass. The sunlight's pressure against my closed eyelids evoked a riot of colors in the blackness—tiny explosions of bluish red and greenish gold in fantastic patterns. As the lazy drone of bees filled my ears, I imagined my body liquefying and seeping into the earth. I remained in this trance-like state for a long time.

I wasn't sure when the birds stopped singing, but I could no longer hear the insects or the wind. Opening my eyes, I sat up and shivered in the unnatural, disquieting silence. Clouds had gathered in the sky above, blocking the sun.

"Veronica."

Startled, I looked around.

"Veronica..."

This time, I heard my name uttered softly in my ear, causing the tiny hairs on the back of my neck to stand on end. I peeked over my shoulder and saw him standing on the opposite side of the clearing. His serene face reminded me of the Christ figure adorning the altar of our parish church. A long cloak partially hid his powerful body and his shoulder-length hair and goatee were black as pitch.

How did I hear his whisper from so far away?

I was too stunned to move or speak as he held my gaze within the leafy shadows, his yellow eyes glowing in the dimness. Suddenly, the inside of my right wrist burned as a cluster of tiny dots in the shape of a spiral broke through the delicate skin.

"Mama!" I cried.

A moment later, my mother called out, "Veronica, where are you?"

"In the clearing!"

My mother ran toward me. At the sight of my pale face, she demanded, "What is it, child? What do you see?"

"A man is hiding in the trees over there."

Yanking me to my feet, she stood in front of me. "Hello? Is there anyone there?"

Silence.

Gripping my shoulders, she shook me slightly. "Did he speak to you? Did you speak to him? What did he look like?"

I showed her the inside of my wrist. "He had eyes like a wolf, and he did *this* to me."

She recoiled at the sight of my strange mark and shoved me toward home. I bent to retrieve the basket of chestnuts, but she hastily pushed me forward, causing me to stumble through the grass. She locked the door as soon we entered the cottage and led me to our icon of the Virgin Mary.

"Kneel, child," she said, sinking to her knees and forcing me down, too. "Hail Mary, full of grace. The Lord is with thee..."

I lost count of how many times we repeated the prayer. My mouth became dry but I didn't dare risk my mother's anger by asking for water.

She stood abruptly. "Did the man speak to you?"

I nodded. "He said my name twice."

My mother paced the room and eventually paused before the Virgin Mary. As she stared at the statue, her expression went from fear to worry to anger. "Three decades of faith and devotion—I've been nothing but loyal, yet you turn your back on me!" She fixed me with a strange look, making me squirm in my seat. "Veronica comes from the Latin *Vera Iconica*, meaning True Icon. I endowed you with this holy name hoping that it would protect you from harm."

My name held special powers?

My mother's eyes slid to the Virgin Mary's sweet face and she frowned. "Why didn't you spare my precious child?"

As the ensuing silence grew, so did the tension within our cottage. The bland gaze of the Virgin Mary combined with her mocking silence caused my mother to unravel. My father had carved the wooden icon shortly before he died—it was the most treasured material possession in our home. I cried out in shock when my mother violently struck the statue and sent it flying across the room. The figure splintered against a storage chest containing our winter supply of salted cod, and we gasped in unison as its head snapped off. It rolled along the floor and came to a stop at my feet, face up. Mary's eyes glared accusingly, as though blaming me for her current predicament. Impulsively, I kicked the head into the flames. My mother screamed in protest but it was too late. Mary's serene face became blackened and distorted as the fire greedily consumed the wood and melted the paint.

My mother turned away from the hearth to collect the headless figure from the floor. She gazed at the broken neck for a moment, caressing the cerulean robe with touching gentleness before tossing what remained of our icon into the flames.

Stunned, I cried, "Mama!"

She shrugged, mumbling something about her prayers not being heard.

***

My mother remained sullen and preoccupied throughout the day. Although she baked the apple tarts as promised, I didn't feel consoled by them. I thanked her for the treats but I could only manage a few nibbles. The tart tasted like dirt to me, and bile rose in my throat every time I attempted to swallow it down. I knew that something important had happened earlier today, but I didn't know what it was, and not knowing frightened me.

Later that night I watched my mother kneel before the hearth in order to retrieve the burnt remains of the Virgin Mary. Taking a piece of charred wood from the ashes, she etched a cross over her heart. I stared at the smudged black lines upon her skin as penitent tears rolled down her cheeks. She came to me and drew a black cross on my forehead, too. Together, we begged God's forgiveness for our heinous sins.

CHAPTER 2
BOSTON, MA
NOVEMBER 1, PRESENT DAY

The United States of America...the *New World*.

The plane began its initial descent, so I leaned against the window to take in the view. I could see the Boston skyline clearly despite the cloudy New England day. Seventeen boats glided upon the surface of the liquid lead bay.

My college buddy, Josh, sent me an email offering to pick me up at the airport. We reconnected last year through Facebook after he had casually mentioned that one of his clients served as the Department Chair of Portuguese Studies at Brown University. He also informed me that a few of my art history articles had been featured in the Portuguese newspapers of New England, capturing the attention of some influential academicians. When I told Josh that the private school I worked for in Lisbon had run out of funding, he wasted no time pulling strings. Emails were exchanged, proposals were made, and I scored a research fellowship.

My breath fogged up the window, thus obscuring the view of the bay. Hopefully, this new position at Brown offered a bit more stability than my last job. At least it would look good on my CV. I was pushing thirty and didn't have time to mess around—professionally speaking.

As bravely as I tried to look ahead to the future, I knew I'd pine miserably for my European lifestyle. How could I not? Being surrounded on a daily basis by fine art and architecture, history, culture, excellent food and wine—I was spoiled.

"*Pah-dun* me," said the corpulent man beside me in a thick Bostonian accent.

It was the hundredth time he had bumped my arm during the transatlantic flight.

"No worries," I replied, inching away from his large bulk.

"Miss, please return your seat to the upright position," the flight attendant said while pacing down the narrow aisle.

I obediently complied before stuffing the latest issue of an underground graffiti magazine into the black laptop case resting across my knees. Despite my seemingly intellectual persona and academic prowess—AKA: nerd vibe—there were three secrets about me that challenged the stereotype often attributed to art historians.

My area of expertise focused on sixteenth century Western Europe, but that didn't stop me from nurturing a passion for gritty street art with social or political undercurrents—the more radical, the better.

I wasn't so vocal about my second secret since it could potentially harm both my professional and personal reputations. Not only was I completely fascinated by U.S. government conspiracies involving U.F.O. aircraft and extraterrestrials, I was an Ancient Alien Theorist. I certainly wasn't alone in my belief that aliens came to Earth thousands of years ago to share their technology with humans. Many fellow theorists were accomplished and well-respected historians who kept a low profile, while others foolishly showed their faces in dubious conferences—or even worse—the History Channel.

"Ladies and gentlemen, please make sure that your seatbelts are securely fastened. We'll be landing shortly. Thank you."

I checked my seat belt and gazed thoughtfully at the laptop case. Stored within the laptop, carefully protected with impenetrable security passcodes, existed the third and most dangerous secret in my life: my manifesto. I've been working on it for almost a decade, and harbored no regrets over the illegal means used in obtaining much of the damning evidence. Exposing the deliberate censorship of scientific data seriously endangering the public could easily destroy elitists around the globe—the type of people who would probably seek revenge. Regardless of the threat, I believed humanity had a right to know the truth.

"Sorry," said the big man beside me as he bumped me again

with his fleshy arm.

One hundred and one.

"It's okay," I assured him as Logan's tarmac loomed into view in the window.

I peeked into the cockpit to thank the pilots before deplaning, and immediately noticed that the air seemed modern, hollow. After a ten-minute wait at baggage claim, I pulled my luggage off the conveyor belt and headed for the exit. My eyes instantly picked out Josh in the crowd. A good-looking guy, despite the extra pounds and bald spot, he offered me a dazzling smile. Irish freckles and bright blue eyes only added to his charm. Josh never had a problem attracting girls in college, but he was the type who enjoyed chasing the ones who weren't interested.

"Welcome home, Veronica," he cried in a Massachusetts accent. "Oh my God, you look even better in person than on Facebook!" He crushed me to his chest in a bear hug. "It's been a while, huh?"

"Seven years…thanks for picking me up at the airport."

"Maybe I should be thanking you. It's not every day I get to leave work early to meet a beautiful woman in Boston."

"Where's Cindy?" I asked, hoping the mention of his current girlfriend would discourage any attempt at flirtation.

"Working. She couldn't get the night off. Oh—happy birthday, by the way. You look exactly the same as you did when we were in college." Lowering his voice and cocking his brow theatrically, he asked, "Did you make some kind of shady deal with the Devil?"

"Maybe," I replied, keeping my expression serious.

He chuckled. "Here, let me help you with your luggage. Hold on. That's it? Two bags?" When I nodded, he added, "You're the dream woman."

"Well, I gave a lot of stuff away to charity and shipped my books to my new address."

"That reminds me," he said while extracting a metallic green shamrock keychain from his pocket. "I picked up your keys from the landlord."

I dropped the keys in my purse. "That was nice of you."

The moment we stepped outside, I shivered. I'd forgotten how bitterly cold autumn could be in New England.

"You missed a kick-ass Halloween party last night," Josh said as he led me toward a glossy, new silver BMW sports car. "Everyone wore awesome costumes."

"Really? I love Halloween. Nice car, by the way."

"Glad you like it. I got promoted at the law firm recently, so I gave myself a little reward." He put my suitcases and laptop bag in the trunk, and we entered the vehicle. "I'm really happy you're back. You may not believe it, but I've thought of you so many times throughout the years."

Uh oh, Veronica...

I ignored his sappy comment by pretending to be keenly interested in the scenery outside the car window. "What was that, sorry?"

"Nothing," he mumbled irritably as he maneuvered the car onto the highway.

Feeling bad, I cheerfully inquired, "Hey, have you been hitting the gym? You look pretty fit."

His face lit up. "Actually, I started lifting weights a few months ago. Check it out." He removed his right hand from the steering wheel in order to flex his bicep.

Ah, male vanity. I dutifully poked his arm. "Wow."

He dove into his entire lifting regime, complete with recipes for the perfect protein shake to enhance muscle performance. Thankfully, we arrived at the pub in a short amount of time.

Josh glanced at his flashy Rolex. "Are you tired?"

"Nope. Took a nice long nap on the plane."

"Well, there it is—O'Malley's Pub. We sure had some fun times here," he said, cutting the engine after parking the car. "Ah, the awesome years at UMASS Boston."

"Juggling work and school, pulling all-nighters to cram for exams…I was tired most of the time, but I can't complain. I had lots of fun." As he opened his car door, I said, "Wait a sec—would you turn on the light, please? I'd like to freshen up a bit."

"You're gorgeous enough already."

I rolled my eyes at him as he turned on the light. I quickly applied a coat of black mascara to my lashes and some lip gloss to my lips. I finished off with a spritz of perfume.

"Such a diva," he teased.

"Let's not exaggerate."

"Okay, you revel in your femininity—is that better?"

"Actually, yes," I replied primly, tucking the makeup bag into my purse.

He pointed to the little swirl of birthmarks on the inside of my right wrist. "I see you still haven't gotten rid of the tat."

"How many times do I have to tell you? It's not a tattoo."

"It looks too contrived to be a random design of nature."

I traced the spiral of countless dots with my left fingertip before letting it rest on the tiny star in the hollow center. "I was born with this so I'm used to it."

We both got out of the car. The muffled sounds of a bass guitar and drums filtered through the rusty brick walls as we approached the pub's entrance. The poster on the door depicted a medieval Virgin Mary statue with golden eyes and the words "ICON: Live Tonight."

Seized by a powerful déjà-vu, I began to tremble.

Josh paused mid-step. "Hey, are you okay?"

I touched the poster. "This image..."

"Icon is the latest music sensation from Providence." Josh explained as he opened the door and urged me through it. "Come on, it's freezing out here."

The band was in the middle of a song as we headed for the bar. The music had a driving beat and the sound of the lead singer's voice brought to mind supple velvet and rich dark chocolate—all things decadent. I shook my head slightly to clear it of these bizarre thoughts.

The moment the stage came into full view, I couldn't tear my eyes from the lead singer's face. *Drop-dead gorgeous.* Tall and fit with short black hair and chiseled features, he stood out in stark contrast from the other men inside the pub.

Wow. Get a grip, Veronica.

I mentally chastised myself as I scanned the bar to see if

there was anyone I recognized. The sexy musician's presence could not be ignored, however, and he soon had my full attention once again. I wasn't the type to easily fall for a guy, so this inexplicable attraction made me feel a bit unsettled. I couldn't help admiring his sensuous mouth and the strong, elegant curve of his jaw. How would those lips feel against my skin? A sudden, powerful yearning stirred deep within me and my breath caught in my throat.

I really needed to get laid. *Soon.*

His unique golden eyes slid my way as I passed in front of him, making my heartbeat accelerate. Very cool contact lenses—did he wear other funky colors, too?

CHAPTER 3
LISBON, PORTUGAL
OCTOBER 31, 1520

I stretched lazily before getting out of bed and throwing open the shutters. The pre-dawn sky flaunted the most delicate shades of violet and rose.

My mother stirred. "Veronica?"

I detected pain in her voice. "It's early yet, Mother."

She mumbled incoherently and went back to snoring. I prepared a draught to ease her discomfort. Her health had gone from bad to worse in a matter of months.

She won't be baking any birthday treats for you tomorrow...

Every year, I relived the bizarre events that had happened on the day I became physically and mentally branded. The mysterious golden-eyed stranger never visited me again, and I often wondered why he came in the first place.

My mother had eventually fashioned a bracelet by weaving leather straps together to form a thick band. Fastening it around my right wrist, she had admonished in a severe tone, "Never remove your bracelet or reveal your mark to anyone for it would be dangerous. You bear the kiss of Satan, the mark of a witch."

My mother sat up in bed. "Veronica, you're up early."

Her ashy pallor alarmed me. "It's a fine morning," I said with forced cheerfulness. "Would you like to sit in the sunshine for a bit? I could move your chair—"

"No," she cut me off, rubbing her legs while wincing.

"I have prepared a draught for you."

"I need my ointment. Would you go into the city and fetch me some?"

"Of course." I poured the hot draught into a cup and handed it to my mother. "Here, drink this. It will ease your pain."

I donned a wool cloak, placed a few coins into the pouch at

my waist, and walked down the hill. I passed the city gates and meandered through narrow streets, pausing briefly to admire the public statues on my way to the apothecary shop. After purchasing the ointment, I went to the market where vendors shouted to potential customers. The heady aromas of cloves, black pepper, and incense blended with pungent aged cheese, salted cod, blood sausages, and overly ripe fruits and vegetables. Dogs, cats, rats, and pigeons foraged for scraps between the crowded market stalls. Traders from the East displayed exotic silks dyed in shades of lilac and amber. One merchant offered silver bud vases etched with Arab curlicues.

Our widowed neighbor called out to me from a nearby donkey cart. "Veronica!"

"Good morning, Dona Maria," I said, shading my eyes from the brilliant morning sunshine.

"We're off to see the tower, my dear. Come with us."

"The Torre de Belem?" I inquired.

When she nodded, I climbed onto the cart and nodded at the familiar man holding the reins.

"You know my nephew, Norberto," Dona Maria said. "His wife is heavy with child and craves blood sausages. Pregnant women should not be deprived, is that not so?"

Norberto nodded. "Happy wife, happy life."

The Torre de Belem, strategically positioned at the mouth of the Tagus River, stood like a proud beacon to incoming ships. Constructed of pristine white stone, it glistened like dew in the sunlight. Inspired by various Portuguese colonies, the exotic design boasted stylistic elements from India and China, including an African rhinoceros.

Dona Maria crossed herself. "What an age we live in—God be praised! What say you, Veronica?"

I shook my head in awe. "It's magnificent."

Norberto eventually turned the cart around to head back.

My mother came outside to greet us. Leaning heavily on her walking stick, she said, "I wondered what was keeping you."

"It's our fault she's late," Dona Maria explained. "We took Veronica to see the new tower."

My mother invited everyone inside for a bit of refreshing ale. As soon as Norberto and Dona Maria took their leave, she regaled me with questions. I described the Torre de Belem as vividly as I could, knowing in my heart that she would not see it anytime soon.

"I think it quite fitting," my mother commented. "Your twentieth birthday is tomorrow and the splendid tower commemorates your second decade of life."

I chuckled at her grandiose thinking. She bent over in pain and I became alarmed. "Mother, are you all right?"

"A cramp, nothing more. Time to put your old mother to bed. Did you get the ointment?"

"Yes," I said, snatching it from the basket.

"You need to marry," she declared, settling into bed. I ignored her comment as I quietly applied the odiferous, greasy concoction to her legs. "I'm *serious*, Veronica."

I inquired sweetly, "Can I make you some dandelion tea to ease your stomach pains?"

"Do not ignore me!"

I set down the ointment, placed my hands on my hips, and sighed tiredly. "Are we having this conversation again?"

"You should spend more time searching for potential spouses and less time with those books of yours."

"So this week you're blaming the books. What will you come up with next week?"

"Mind your tongue, girl. You need to start behaving like the other young women in our parish. You never see them with their noses in books."

"Would you prefer an empty-headed ninny for a daughter instead of one that is dutiful, responsible, and possesses a bit of curious intellect?"

"That's not what I meant and you know it. What good is intelligence if you can't use it to find a husband?"

I sat down. "Whom would you have me marry?"

"There are plenty of eligible young men—like Tiago."

I crossed my arms. "The big buffoon with the axe?"

"He's a lumberjack. That's almost as good as a carpenter."

"Father was a carpenter," I corrected.

"Tiago could build you a house."

I imagined a lopsided house with sloping floors and shook my head. "He's far too oafish for my taste. Besides, I cannot tolerate his meddlesome sister."

"Sara can be difficult," she reluctantly agreed.

I scoffed at her. "Difficult? You're being too kind. Who else is on your marriage list?"

"Francisco."

I raised an eyebrow. "The little man who had me carry a basket of vegetables uphill to his mother's house because it was too heavy for him to do it himself? *That* Francisco?"

"He makes a decent living as an accountant in the city center." She paused with a twinkle in her eye and added matter-of-factly, "He knows how to read and write."

"I know how to read and write *and* I'm capable of physical labor. I won't marry a weakling who can be easily bullied; I would be tempted to boss him around. Next?"

"Well, I suppose that leaves Diego."

I placed my head in my hands. "He's deaf and mute."

"You are far too picky, Veronica. You do realize that you're on the brink of being called an old maid." I shrugged indifferently, which only served to further irritate my mother. "Every girl of marriageable age in our parish is already wed— except you."

"None of them seem to be living blissfully."

"Marriage is not easy, I'll give you that, but it's a blessing."

I went to the table and began chopping carrots. "Are there any turnips left? Perhaps I should gather some kale to make us a nice soup."

"This conversation is not over!" I stared at my mother as her eyes glistened with unshed tears. "Oh, Veronica, I won't be here much longer."

"You *will* get better," I said, trying to sound convincing.

"I desperately wanted to see you married and settled before..." She stopped abruptly, her face red with discomfort and—*something else.*

I became instantly suspicious when she refused to meet my eyes. "Before…?"

"Dear God, it's inevitable." I stared at her expectantly until she finally confessed, "He'll for you come tomorrow."

The golden-eyed stranger.

My heart raced uncontrollably. "How do you know? Did you have another dream?" She nodded, which made me angry. "Why didn't you tell me? Why all this ridiculous secrecy?"

"I believed if you got married and started a family he would leave you alone. Perhaps find someone else to curse. Too late for that now. He'll mark you again." My mother heaved a shuddering sigh, then sobbed. "In the dream, he warned me not to impede you from your destiny."

I paced around the room. "This explains so much. I feel as if I'm meant for something important in life; something more than being a wife and mother."

Eying me warily, she said, "You openly reject your God-given duty to wed and procreate?"

"I'm not afraid of my destiny. Actually, I must confess that I've been eagerly awaiting his return."

"What?!"

"I want to know why he came to me ten years ago." Holding up my wrist, I added, "Why do I bear this mark? What does it mean? I need answers."

"Are you mad? He's not human—he's an evil abomination of nature."

"Not being human doesn't make him evil," I reasoned. "Angels aren't human."

My mother banged her fist against the wall in frustration. "This creature is no angel. This is why I was against your father teaching you to read. It's made you a daft spinster."

"I'm sorry for being such a disappointment to you."

Despite the regret in her eyes, she remained silent.

I continued, "When he comes tomorrow, I'll face him as bravely as I can to find answers to my questions."

"You stupid, stubborn girl! He may be the Devil himself, for all we know."

"But we don't know. Who is he? What is he? How will we know if we're too afraid to ask?"

"No sane, God-fearing person speaks to a demon."

"What if he's not a demon but something else? Something beyond our limited understanding?" I paused, recalling my father's words before he died. "Remember: we are Portuguese. Father used to say that the world's greatest explorers were spawned from our bloodlines. Insatiably curious men who possess no fear are bravely sailing to places that our ancestors only dreamed of seeing. Surely, these noble traits—so common in men—can be present in women? Even in myself, perhaps?"

"Your words are clever, daughter, but extremely foolish. You're dealing with a being who is possibly far more powerful than all of our great men combined."

"Which is exactly why I wish to learn the purpose of his existence, and why he has chosen me."

My mother's lips clamped down to form a hard line and she shook her head in staunch disapproval.

The silence stretched between us until I picked up an empty basket and went to the door. "I'm going out into the garden. I'll be back shortly."

"We need more firewood," she said, not meeting my eyes.

CHAPTER 4
BOSTON, MA
NOVEMBER 1, PRESENT DAY

"Happy birthday, dear Veronica, happy birthday to you!"

My former classmates applauded, cueing me to blow out the twenty-seven candles glowing atop a chocolate cake. A wise-ass in the crowd called out for a fire extinguisher. *Masshole.*

Slices of cake were passed around while I tried to reconnect with my former classmates. Most of the women were stay-at-home moms, and it soon became painfully evident that we had little in common. The pub became stuffy as more Icon fans arrived. I wriggled my arm out of one coat sleeve before Josh helped me with the other.

"Wow." He looked me up and down. "Nice outfit."

"Thanks."

The wine red mini sheath complimented my black tights and Italian leather boots.

"You're looking pretty hot. I may have to fight somebody."

I took my seat. "Very funny."

He winked at me then turned around to talk to someone. I enjoyed my drink while listening to the conversations taking place around me. As the alcohol blurred the edges of my mind, I recalled my last psychotherapy session with Dr. Sousa. The intense memories, powerful déjà-vu, and recurring dreams that I had been experiencing on a regular basis began exactly one year ago today. Despite my psychologist's expertise and high credentials, I still had no idea what had triggered these manifestations, let alone their meaning.

"Another drink?" Josh asked, breaking my reverie.

He rested against the bar, placing his face close to mine. Icon finished their last set and, the minute the band vacated the stage, pre-recorded music poured from the speakers.

"Bartender, can we get another gin and tonic here?" Josh shouted over the noise. "Hey, are you having fun?" I nodded as he handed me the drink. "Better go easy on those, hon, you might take advantage of me when you're drunk."

The girl sitting beside me overheard his comment and rolled her eyes. Seeing this, Josh said something cocky to her and I'm pretty sure she retorted in like manner, but I only half-listened. The lead singer of Icon sauntered toward me with a feline stealth that made me squirm in my seat—in a good way. I was astonished by my sexual response to him. Wearing a snug black T-shirt and slim black pants that highlighted every asset of his magnificent body, he stopped directly in front of me. I noticed that his left bicep sported an intricate black ink tattoo. The medieval coat of arms flaunted the letter "V" surrounded by traditional Manuelino embellishments—nautical ropes, shells, and even a tiny armillary sphere. I almost gasped aloud in pure art historian delight.

It suddenly dawned on me that everyone around the bar had grown silent and still, especially the women. Without breaking eye contact, he reached for my right hand and turned it over. A tiny smile touched his lips when he caught sight of my strange birthmark. He ran his thumb gently over the delicate skin of my inner wrist, causing the mark to tingle. The simple, yet incredibly intimate, act sent a jolt of electricity throughout my entire body. Meeting my eyes once more, he turned my hand over and brought my knuckles to his lips. The gallant gesture took me off guard because it felt both natural and familiar.

"Happy birthday, Veronica," he said softly.

The way his tongue lingered on my name both thrilled and disturbed me. His strange accent triggered déjà-vu. He knew me—I was sure of it—but I had no recollection of him. My brain quickly went through a mental file. Had we shared a college class together? Did we meet at a party?

A giggling couple leaned against the bar to order drinks, thus placing their bodies between me and the golden-eyed Adonis. Before I had the chance to ask him anything, the ever-growing crowd of people swallowed him up.

"Well, *that* was weird," Josh said in a surly tone dripping with male envy. "Who does that? Walk up to a girl and kiss her hand like he's a knight in some medieval role-playing game. And what's with those strange yellow contacts? He may be a talented musician but he's a total freak."

"You're just jealous," said the girl who had had gotten sassy with Josh a few minutes earlier.

The two began to argue again so I slid off the stool. "I need to use the ladies room. Josh, would you please hold my seat and watch my drink?"

"Sure, the bathroom is—"

"I remember," I said over my shoulder.

I practically ran to the ladies room, scanning the crowd in search of my mystery man but he was nowhere in sight. I pulled out my phone and began dialing Dr. Sousa's number. "Yeah, right," I said aloud, hanging up immediately.

I couldn't tell him of yet another strange déjà-vu episode that led nowhere. Besides, Dr. Sousa had already washed his hands of me, so to speak. He had put me in contact with one of the best Past Life Regression therapists in New England and had already set up the first appointment for me.

I went into the ladies room and splashed some cold water on my cheeks. The mirror above the sink reflected an unusual brightness in my mossy green eyes and my fair skin flaunted a pink flush. Who wouldn't be in a state of heightened awareness after such a sexy encounter? I ran a hand through my long hair and took a deep breath before grabbing a paper towel to dry my hands. A blonde woman almost plowed into me as I exited the ladies room.

"Sorry," she offered. "Hey Ronnie!"

"It's Veronica," I corrected as politely as I could.

"Oops, I forgot." She cocked her head to the side. "Don't you remember me?"

I took in the fake blue contacts, overly bleached hair, heavy makeup, breast implants, and micro-mini denim skirt. How did I know this blonde bombshell? Then it hit me—the sorority girl who sat beside me in English Literature during my junior year of college. Cool girl, but not the brightest crayon in the box.

I smiled. "Long time no see, Stephanie."

"I knew you'd remember me. Go UMASS Alumni," she shrieked like a cheerleader. "Welcome home and happy birthday. How was Portugal?"

"Great."

"Did you live in *Lisboa*?" she asked, making an attempt to pronounce the city correctly.

"Yes, and nice pronunciation."

"Cool. I would love to visit Europe someday. I hear the guys are really cute. Is that true?"

I smiled at Josh when I saw him waving at me from the bar. Stephanie followed my gaze and smiled, too. "A lot of European men sport trendy haircuts and dress to impress," I replied with a shrug.

"Oh, I know. They're so ahead in fashion over there. Speaking of which, you look great." She took in my outfit with the appraising eye of a shopaholic. "I like your hair, too. It brings out your eye color. Is that reddish brown natural or from a box?"

"Thanks—oh, it's natural. You look good, too." I refrained from commenting on her overly processed hair. "Hey, I need to get back to Josh and my drink. Great seeing you."

"You, too!"

I took my seat at the bar and Josh said, "I saw you chatting with Slutty Steph. What words of wisdom did she impart?"

"She wished me a happy birthday. Why do you call her 'Slutty Steph'?"

Josh answered my question with a long look and a raised eyebrow. He took a sip of his beer and said, "She lives in Providence, you know."

"Maybe I'll see her around." I followed his example and took a sip of my watered-down gin and tonic. "Hey, after this drink I think I should call it a night. Would you give me a ride home? I know it's a long drive from Boston to Providence, but I'll pay for the gas and you can crash on the couch. The apartment did come furnished as advertised, right?"

"Yes, but there's no need for me to crash on your couch. I'm in Providence now."

This news surprised me. "You don't live in Boston anymore?"

"Nope. My firm opened an office in Providence for the convenience of our clients who live there, and that new branch is being headed by yours truly. They offered me the transfer as a promotion and it came with a decent raise. As much as I love my new car, commuting is a pain in the ass."

"I don't blame you. Boston traffic is atrocious."

"Anyway, I was saving the best surprise for last."

"What surprise?"

"We're neighbors!" Seeing my blank expression, he added, "My office is in College Hill. Your new apartment is upstairs from mine. Why do you think the people at Brown suggested that specific place to you?" When I shrugged, he said, "Because I suggested it to them, silly rabbit!"

"Oh."

"Seriously, it's the perfect location."

Being so close to Josh on a daily basis could lead to problems. I liked him a lot, but his constant flirting and attempts to date me in college grew so tiresome that we stopped hanging out for a few months until he agreed to knock it off. Maybe things would be different now that he had Cindy in his life.

He looked smug. "You're going to fall in love with the apartment, I just know it."

"I'm sure I will," I replied with forced enthusiasm.

Do you want to keep reading? THE WATCHERS is available on Amazon. Thank you.